WEDNESDAY

E. L. TODD

Fallen Publishing

Wednesday

Editing Services provided by Final-Edits.com

CHAPTER ONE

Deep Into The Night

Francesca

The sheets were warm and the bed was soft. It was late into the night, an unearthly hour that no one should be awake to experience. I was pulled away from my dreams by the distraction of gentle embraces. A rugged mouth was placing kisses all over my body, starting from my stomach and heading down to my thighs.

"Mmm..." I wanted to stay asleep but I wanted the erotic touches to continue.

My legs parted gently and soft lips moved further up my thigh.

My back arched and my body tensed. The dream was the best I've ever had. I never wanted to wake up.

Hawke's lips pressed against my folds and kissed me gently. His tongue moved around my clitoris before he sucked it, igniting all the nerves in my body.

It felt amazing.

Wednesday

He kissed me harder, chasing away the smoke that surrounded my dreams. It was a dense fog that slowly cleared until the dream disappeared entirely. A blinding orgasm took me, bringing me back to reality with a violent jolt.

"Hawke…" My fingers dug into his hair as I enjoyed the climax. It made me feel alive like I never had before. Everything was on fire, from my fingers to my toes.

When the high passed, I slowly drifted down to earth, my eyes opening and taking in the dark ceiling of my bedroom. The light didn't enter through the windows so I knew the sun hadn't risen yet. When I looked down, I saw Hawke's face between my legs.

Wordlessly, he crawled up my body until he was directly on top of me. He looked down at my naked body, his wet lips gleaming in the distant light.

"What time is it?"

He gave me an intense look like he hadn't heard a word I said. Then he moved between my parted thighs and pressed his hard cock inside me. He stretched me the moment he entered, moving through my slick.

My head returned to the pillow, and I enjoyed every move and sensation.

"It doesn't matter what time it is." He rocked into me slowly, the sweat collecting on his chest. One hand fisted my strands. As he looked deep into my eyes, his hips thrust over and over. "Time has no power over either one of us."

***

At 5:30 a.m., I showered and got ready for work. Hawke didn't have to be at the office until nine but he usually got up anyway. When I went into the kitchen for breakfast, he already had my plate ready.

It was two scrambled eggs with a side of toast. And there was a mug of coffee with just a little cream and sugar next to it. His plate was already wiped clean but his coffee was only half way finished. He read The New York Times as he sat there.

I took my seat and ate quietly, glancing at him every few minutes. We didn't talk as much as we used to because words were unnecessary. We could communicate on a completely different level, something that no one else could understand.

He turned the page and kept reading, the sun starting to rise in the distance.

Sitting together like this made me think about our future. Would we do this every day for the rest of our lives? Would we be old and gray one day and wonder where all the time went? If that day ever came, I knew I would be content.

He folded the paper when he was finished and occupied himself with staring at me. He sipped his coffee while he kept his eyes trained on me, taking in my hair and work t-shirt. "What are you thinking about?"

He couldn't read my mind. "I hope we'll stay this way forever."

He set his coffee on the coaster then snaked his hand to mine. His dry fingers rubbed across mine, feeling my knuckles. The devotion in his eyes held the promise I didn't

3

need to hear. We lost two years of our lives but that didn't matter anymore. Now we were right where we belonged. "We will."

***

We stood outside the gate and waited for Marie and Axel to exit the plane.

"They're going to be so depressed when they see us." Hawke stood beside me with his arm around my waist. He towered over me with his height, making me feel smaller than I already was.

"Why? What did we do to them?"

"Nothing. But now they're back to reality."

"I'm sure they're sick of each other by now."

He looked down at me, his blue eyes twinkling in a special way. "I wouldn't be sick of you."

"That's different. I'm pretty cool."

He rubbed his nose against mine. "And you wouldn't be sick of me."

"That's because you're really hot."

He smiled slightly, but his eyes expressed his delight even more. "True."

Marie and Axel walked off the terminal, looking noticeably tan. They still had their leis around their necks like they weren't quite ready to say goodbye to paradise.

I waved from the crowd so they would spot us. "Welcome home."

"Hey." Marie stiffened in surprise then ran directly into my arms. She hugged me tightly and rocked me from side-to-side. "I'm so happy to see you. You already did so much for the wedding, and now you're here to surprise us?"

"We thought you could use some help with your luggage." It was no secret Marie packed her entire wardrobe on every trip. "And we missed you."

"Awe. We missed you too."

"No, we didn't." Axel walked up to Hawke then gave him a high-five. "I can honestly say I didn't think about either one of you during our trip."

"It's okay." Hawke restrained his chuckle. "I didn't think about you either."

Axel patted him on the back. "That's why we're friends. Always honest."

Marie released me and backed away. "Well, I missed you guys."

"No, you didn't." Axel gave her an offended look. "I kept you entertained the entire time."

"And I was," she said. "But I'll always miss my best friend—no matter who I'm with."

Axel shook his head in disappointment. "I gave her some of my best moves. I even read a few Cosmo magazines."

Hawke raised an eyebrow. "Really? Cosmo?"

"Yeah," Axel said. "They have some pretty interesting stuff in there."

My brother was from a whole different planet. "How was Bora Bora?"

"Awesome," Marie said. "Those bungalows over the water were so cool. There were manta rays everywhere and we even saw a few sea turtles."

"How cool," I said. "Take lots of pictures?"

"Too many," Marie said. "Believe me, you're going to be bored when I show them all to you."

Axel moved his arm around her waist. "Wife, I'm jet-lagged. Let's head home."

"Yeah, I'm pretty tired too," Marie said. "You guys should come over tomorrow."

"Sure thing," I said. "Let's get your luggage and give you a lift."

"You guys don't have to do that," Marie said as she waved it off.

"We insist." Hawke took my hand and walked with me to the baggage claim. "Technically, the wedding is still going until you get to your doorstep. Frankie and I are just completing our duties."

Axel walked with his arm hooked around Marie. "Maybe we should have a wedding every weekend so we have these two at our beck and call."

Hawke turned to Axel. "Be careful. When our day comes, you two will be the maid of honor and best man...so I suggest you be nice."

A smile immediately formed on my lips. It was difficult for me to give this relationship another chance in the beginning, but now, I didn't have any regrets. Hawke and I were exactly where we should be, and I wasn't afraid he would take off again.

This was our happily ever after.

CHAPTER TWO

A Trip Down Memory Lane
Francesca

Marie and I got a drink after work. I changed into a dress when I left the bakery so I wouldn't be caked with sugar and flour. Some of it was in my hair but nothing would get that out besides a shower.

"Tell me everything about the honeymoon." We both had apple martinis placed in front of us, each with an umbrella.

"Girl, I've never been to any place nearly as nice. Hawke gave us an excellent recommendation."

"Wow. I've never even been on a vacation before."

"Ever?" she asked incredulously. "I guess that makes sense because Axel hasn't really either."

"It just wasn't common in our childhood."

"Well, this place would give you a heart attack. The food was amazing, the service was impeccable, and the location was glorious. It was such a bitch to get there but it was worth it."

Wednesday

"The flight was long?"

"Twelve hours," she said. "And then we had to take another plane from Tahiti to Bora Bora. I didn't get much sleep on the plane so I was jet-lagged the first day."

"But you probably forgot about all of that when you got there."

"Instantly." She snapped her fingers.

It was hard to believe Axel almost ran out on the wedding. If Hawke hadn't found him, the outcome may have been very different. "I'm glad you guys worked everything out. When he talked to you before the wedding, I had no idea what he was going to say."

She took a long drink like she needed the alcohol to kick in. "I was terrified too. I had no idea what he was going to say either. But when he told me, I honestly didn't care. Those first few months of our relationship are just an indistinct blur. Axel is nothing like that anymore."

"He's really not."

"He's already such a great husband. He always carries my bags and looks after me... It's really sweet."

It was hard to imagine my brother being sweet. Most of our interactions were just us butting heads. "He really loves you, Marie."

"I know he does." She couldn't hide the joy on her face. Her features lit up like the Manhattan skyline. "I'm very lucky."

"When are the babies coming?" I smiled because I knew that would make her squirm.

"Uh, no. Not right now." She shook her head dramatically. "I already have to take care of Axel. That's enough work as it is."

"You guys would have cute kids together."

"And you'll be the number one babysitter."

Babysitting wasn't an interest of mine, but I would love to spend time with my niece or nephew. "Let's cross that bridge when we get there."

She finished her cosmo then waved down the bartender for another. "How are things with you and Hawke? You seem happy."

"Really happy." The two years we were apart were unbearable. I managed to hold my head high and keep moving forward, but it wasn't that easy. Now that we were together again, it made me realize just how empty my life was without him. Now I felt whole, like nothing was missing.

Marie smiled. "I wonder when he'll propose."

"I don't know about that. It's still too soon." But being his wife would be a dream come true. We were already committed to each other in an unbreakable way. Married or not married, we were destined to be together in one way or another, even if it was just as friends. I couldn't escape him, and he couldn't escape me.

"Time isn't an accurate measurement of most things. When you know, you know." She sipped her drink then played with the umbrella.

If Hawke asked, I wouldn't say no. But I didn't think he would ask—not yet.

Wednesday

"Why don't you guys move in together? Axel and I did that, and we don't have any regrets."

"We'll see where it goes." I wasn't in a hurry to change anything. I was very happy with the way things were.

"Anything new with you? With work?"

My life was pretty uneventful at the moment. "Not really. You're the one with the interesting lifestyle at the moment."

"Yeah, it was magical." She smiled as she remembered the big day. "I'm sad it's over."

"You have Axel every day for the rest of your life. It's not really over."

That cheered her up. "You're right. I landed the perfect man."

"I wouldn't go that far..." Marie was blind to Axel's faults, whereas I saw them crystal clear.

"Hey, Frankie." A familiar voice sounded in my ear, and I recognized it even though I hadn't heard it in a while.

"Hey, Kyle." After our last conversation, I didn't expect to see him again. It'd been several months since we stopped talking. When he stopped texting me and stopping by the shop, I assumed he'd finally moved on—which was a good thing.

He looked the same as he used to. His hair was a little longer than it used to be, but that was the only difference. His arms and shoulders were still powerful, and he had a boy's charm in a man's body. "I saw you across the room and wanted to stop by and say hi." He turned to Marie. "Congratulations on your wedding."

"Oh, thank you." Marie immediately smiled at the compliment. She liked Kyle the first time she met him.

Kyle turned back to me, a beer in his hand. "So, how's it going?" The vibrant sense of life he used to possess was absent. It reminded me of a match that wouldn't light no matter how many times you scraped it.

"Good. You?"

"Couldn't be better." He said it with fake enthusiasm and took a drink.

Marie grabbed her phone and looked at the time. "Gosh darn, I'm late for my hair appointment." She grabbed her purse and left the table. "I'll catch up with you later, Frankie."

That was just an excuse and I knew it. "A hair appointment?"

"Yep." She walked out of earshot and disappeared out the door.

Kyle stood at the table with the beer still in his hand. "Sorry. I didn't mean to chase your friend away."

"You didn't." She would get an earful about it later.

He glanced at the seat Marie had just vacated. "Can I join you?"

I immediately thought of Hawke and how pissed he would be if he spotted us together. But then I remembered why I was with Kyle in the first place. "Of course." I hadn't thought about Kyle much since Hawke and I got back together. When I did, I was always hoping he'd moved on and found a great girl. But judging the hollowness of his eyes, that hadn't happened yet. "What's new with you?"

Wednesday

"You remember that trial I told you about?"

"Yeah."

"It's still going." He sighed before he took another drink. "The defendant has a damn good lawyer and he's searching for every loophole possible. But I'm not letting him get away with it. I won't settle for anything less than life in prison."

I would never forget about how passionate he was about his cases. He didn't take cases very often, choosing to play golf or spend time at home, but when he did, he was a behemoth in the courtroom. "I'm sure you'll win, Kyle."

"Losing isn't an option at this point." He grabbed the umbrella from my drink and stuck it in his beer. "Why don't beers have these umbrellas? They'd be a lot more fun that way."

"Because men wouldn't order them."

"I don't know about that. I sure would."

Just like old times, he made me smile. "Seeing anyone?" Please say yes.

"There's this girl I've been seeing for a while, but I'm going to break it off."

"Why?"

"I'm just not feeling it with her." He didn't make eye contact as he spoke. "She's too clingy. Makes me uncomfortable."

"I'm sure it's just because she's into you."

"She's pretty and everything, but I don't really think about her when I'm not with her." He shrugged then took another drink. "I never cared about having a relationship before I met you. But now that I know what it's like, I really want one—a real one." He looked up and met my gaze. "I guess I'm a one-woman kind of guy now. Never expected it."

"Maybe you've matured over the past year."

"Maybe. But the more dates I go on, the more I dislike dating altogether. So much talking..."

I chuckled. "We tend to do that. Why don't you try Tinder?"

"Every time I use that, I just hook up with people."

"eHarmony?"

"Nah. I'm not doing that." He surveyed the bar before he turned back to me. "So...you and Hawke are still an item?" The hope in his eyes was unmistakable.

"Yeah. And it's going to stay that way." He kept forcing me to hurt him, and I absolutely hated it. I missed Kyle because he'd become a good friend. Sometimes, I wished we could still hang out and catch a ballgame. But I knew that wasn't possible—for his sake.

"Well, I'm happy for you." Despite his sadness, he seemed sincere. "I hope I find something like that—someday."

"You will." There wasn't a doubt in my mind. Kyle was the perfect guy. I even judged myself for leaving him in the first place.

"Got any cute friends to hook me up with?"

"None that are single."

He sighed. "The good ones are always taken."

"Yeah, it seems that way."

13

Wednesday

He clanked his beer, which was nearly empty, against mine. "Well, I should head out. I've had too many already."

"I can walk you home."

He finished his beer then chuckled. "I'm alright, Frankie. But thanks."

CHAPTER THREE

It's Just Business

Hawke

Samantha spoke through the intercom. "Mr. Taylor, I have Olivia from Thick Whiskey on the line."

I immediately rubbed my temple at the mention of her name. She was a snooty brat that inherited her father's company. The rest of her team was a pleasure, but she was a bit of a nightmare. "Thank you, Samantha." I grabbed the phone and hit the flashing button.

Without saying a word to indicate I was on the line, Olivia spoke first. "Hawke."

I spun a pen in my hand, the one that held my financial logo along the side. "Hello, Olivia. Hope you're well."

"I'm very well. Actually, I have new business for you."

Olivia allowed me to invest her money in life insurance companies, and I ended up making her a ton of extra money she didn't even need. "You know me. I love new business."

Wednesday
"Great. Let's meet in the Bahamas. I love it there."

Olivia and I had a business relationship. Together, we made a lot of money. But we also had a personal relationship as well. "My schedule is really tight right now. Can we have a meeting over the phone?"

"Busy?" A sarcastic laugh escaped her mouth like that was completely absurd.

"Yes."

"I'm a lot more adventurous when I'm at the beach with a drink in my hand."

I knew she would be pushy. She was pushy in the bedroom as well. "I'm sorry, Olivia. I'm no longer available in that regard." She was a good lay and didn't want something serious, exactly what I wanted when we were together. She and I were on and off, usually taking a trip together to screw and plan her investments. But now that couldn't happen anymore.

"No longer available? Does that mean Hawke has settled down?"

My eyes drifted to the picture frame on my desk. Marie took it years ago. Francesca and I were in the kitchen with a batch of fresh muffins. We were both taking a bite out of one with my arm around her shoulders. "Yes."

"Oh really?" She was disappointed because there was something she wanted but couldn't have—something very rare.

"Really."

"Who's the lucky girl?"

"Her name is Francesca."

"Please don't tell me she's an Italian model."

"She's not."

"How long has this been going on?"

I didn't like all the personal questions. My relationship with Francesca was my private business, and I didn't like sharing it with anyone, especially a woman I had a meaningless fling with. "If you want to do business, give me a call. If not, I'll talk to you later." I grabbed the phone and prepared to put it back on the receiver.

"Whoa, hold on."

I sighed before I returned the phone to my ear. "Yes?"

"Didn't mean to upset you, Hawke."

"So, can we schedule a meeting for next week?"

"I'd still prefer to meet in person. How about our usual place?"

This woman was unbelievable. She actually thought she could seduce me if we were alone together. "Fine by me. I'm always looking for an excuse to get away. But Francesca will be accompanying me."

Olivia's silence showed just how pleased she was by that.

"Leave the details with my secretary." I hung up before Olivia could say anything else.

***

I just stepped out of the shower when my phone lit up with a text message.

What's my grizzly up to?

Anytime I saw her name light up my screen, I smiled. *Eating a jar of honey.*

17

Wednesday

If I came by, would I be eaten too?

It's a real possibility. I leaned against the wall with a towel wrapped around my waist.

I guess I'll take the risk. The second her message lit up, there was a knock on the door.

My eyes moved to the entryway, and a slow smile spread on my lips. *Is that you?*

Maybe...

I set my phone aside before I opened the door.

Francesca's eyes immediately darted to the towel around my waist. Her eyes grazed over my hard chest, which still had a few water droplets, and then a mischievous smile spread across her lips. "I think I found the honey jar."

I pulled her inside my apartment before I shut the door behind her. "Why didn't you just knock to begin with?"

"I didn't want you to think I was weird for stopping by."

I guided her against the door, my head craned down toward her. "You can stop by whenever the hell you want."

"I can?" Her eyes glanced at my lips before they moved down to my chest.

"Yeah." I kissed the corner of her mouth, loving the way she responded to me. Even though I couldn't feel her heartbeat, I could see her slight reactions. When her lips parted, she took a quiet breath. Her eyes became hazy, like she couldn't see anything farther than an inch in front of her face. She was drowning in me, just the way I drowned in her. Without reading her mind, I could tell she craved me. She

18

wanted to lick her tongue across my chest and taste every water drop.

She eyed the towel around my waist before she grabbed it in her small fingers. Then she looked up at me, her intentions written all over her face.

The second she texted me I got hard. Whenever it came to her, I was turned on. I'd been with a lot of gorgeous woman in my time, here and back in South Carolina, but none of them had the effect Francesca did. She had an unnatural touch, a sexy charm that couldn't be compared.

She yanked on the towel until it came loose. When it thudded against the floor, she looked down at me, unashamed at her open gawking. "Grizzly is happy to see me."

"Always." My arms hooked around her waist, and I lifted her to my chest. Being with her was such a gift that I could never take for granted. She chased away the darkness when she came into my cave and brought the light. Now I was whole.

I was happy.

***

Francesca slithered out of the bed.

I snatched her and dragged her back. "Where do you think you're going, Muffin?" I returned her to my chest then brushed my lips past her hairline.

Her stomach rumbled loudly, answering my question for me.

I smiled from ear-to-ear.

"Hope you didn't hear that..."

Wednesday

"I did." I guided her to her back before I placed kisses over her flat stomach. "I need to feed my girl."

"Yes. Feed her pizza."

I avoided eating out as much as possible, unless it was a restaurant where I could order something remotely healthy. Francesca was the opposite. She ate whatever she wanted when she wanted it. She had a perfect figure no matter what she ate. I suspected every woman in the world hated her because of that. "I'll make the order."

"Yay." She kicked her feet playfully.

I chuckled. "The little things make you happy, huh?"

"No." She ran her hands up my chest to my shoulders. "The big things do, actually."

Seeing the spark in her eyes brought my dick back to life. Sometimes, I wondered if this was all a dream, one of my regular fantasies. I hadn't been happy in so long that I couldn't recognize when it was right in front of my face. So much time had been wasted without her. How did I survive for so long? "We'll order that pizza later." I moved on top of her because I wanted another round.

Instead of insisting on being fed, she wrapped her legs around my waist and gave me a gentle squeeze. Her hair was sprawled across the sheets, and her eyes were lit up like the fourth of July. Sometimes, I couldn't believe how we met. She was working behind the counter at a coffee shop, and the rest was history.

And I found my other half.

***

20

Francesca consumed half the pizza on her own. She sat at the table and inhaled her food like she was starving.

Amused, I watched her.

"What?" She grabbed another large slice from the box and dropped it onto her plate.

"Nothing."

"You're staring at me." She picked up a pepperoni and shoved it into her mouth.

"Maybe I like to stare."

She grabbed another pepperoni and threw it at me.

I shifted my body and missed it.

"I know I eat a lot but I'm hungry."

I raised an eyebrow. "I wasn't thinking that."

"Well, you shouldn't stare at a lady while she's eating."

"Even if I think she's cute?" I missed our playful banter. I could be myself around her—completely and absolutely.

"Well...in that case." She held up her slice and took an enormous bite.

I whistled quietly. "Day-yum."

She laughed before she took another bite.

I glanced at the clock and noticed the time. Whenever Francesca was with me, a weird time vortex was created, and time passed at a remarkable pace. Every time I glanced at the clock, two hours had passed but it felt like five minutes. "Can you take time off work?"

"Why?" She finished the slice and pushed the plate away.

21

Wednesday

"I have a business trip in the Bahamas, and I'd like you to come with me."

Her jaw dropped and practically hit the table. "Say what?"

I pressed my lips tightly together and tried not to laugh.

"A free trip to the Bahamas with a hunky man?" She jumped out of her chair and started to do the hula, shaking her hips like she wore a grass skirt. "Hell yeah, I'm in."

"The hula is a Hawaiian thing."

"Whatever." She kept dancing in the middle of my kitchen. "I'm going to paradise."

I decided to leave the part about Olivia out of it. She didn't need to know.

"Wait." She stopped dancing and her sadness emerged. "Are you going to be working the whole time?"

"No. I should only have one meeting. The rest of the time we can relax."

She returned to doing the hula, waving her arms around like she'd done this many times before when no one was watching. "Marie is gonna be so jealous."

"She just went to Bora Bora for her honeymoon."

"Yeah, but that was then. This is now." She fell into my lap and wrapped her arms around my neck. "Since you're taking me somewhere nice, I should do something for you."

I liked the sound of that. "You'll be working the entire time we're there."

"What? I'm not baking. The humidity would ruin all of my creations."

"You'll be working for me." The look in my eyes said everything my lips didn't.

She nuzzled against my cheek then brushed her nose against mine. "I never thought I'd be so excited to go to work."

CHAPTER FOUR

Bad News

Francesca

I just finished washing my hands when Marie walked into my kitchen. She wore a tight purple dress with black shoes, and judging the flustered look on her face, something was wrong. "I have to tell you something."

"What's up?"

"When I was talking to Axel, I mentioned we ran into Kyle the other night. He said he was going to tell Hawke because he had the right to know."

I sighed then rolled my back. "Goddammit, Marie."

"I honestly didn't think he would say anything."

"Hawke is gonna rip into me."

"I know, I know. I'm sorry." Her hair was in loose spirals, but it didn't look as pretty as it did before she ran all the way back here. She seemed genuinely distraught for blowing my secret. "It was my fault."

"It's okay." She kept all my other secrets. "Hawke just asked me to go on a trip with him so this is going to put a damper on the mood."

"I know. You guys have only been together for a few months, and now I put unnecessary strain on it."

"Don't worry about that." Breaking up was the last thing I was worried about. We would fight and butt heads often, but that didn't mean we weren't staying together forever.

"How pissed do you think he'll be?"

"I—"

"Extremely." His dark voice entered my kitchen and made us both stiffen. He walked through the hallway and emerged without either one of us noticing.

Marie cringed then glanced over her shoulder, seeing him stand there in a black suit and tie. If we didn't know him, we'd both be terrified for our lives. She shouldered her purse tighter then slowly headed for the hallway. "Ugh, I have to go. Just remembered I had to…"

Hawke kept his eyes glued to me, the insufferable rage marked across his visage. He slowly stepped farther into the room, his aim trained on me.

I smoothed out my apron but didn't give in to the fear. "We really shouldn't have this conversation at work."

"You shouldn't have been with him at all." He didn't yell, but his quiet voice was somehow more terrifying. He closed the gap between us and stood right in front of me.

"We talked for a few minutes. That was it."

Wednesday

"Why do you keep talking to him at all?" He rested his hand on the counter beside me, blocking me in so I had nowhere to run.

"Because we ran into each other. It happens. Don't tell me you don't see your bimbos from time to time."

"I do." His hand formed a fist. "But I don't have a drink with them."

I understood why Hawke was jealous. He'd seen Kyle in the flesh and knew we had a relationship. I even met his parents. It wasn't just a meaningless fling. While I didn't love him, there was something there. "Hawke, of all people in the world, you shouldn't be threatened by anything or anyone. I told Kyle you were my soul mate and the only man I would ever love. He and I spent time together and had some good times, but he always knew you were the real person I wanted. Your jealousy is unfounded, and frankly, it's ludicrous." I stepped away and removed my apron. It was covered in flour and sugar and I needed to replace it.

Hawke didn't move. His hand remained on the counter, and he stared at me with a stoic expression. His thoughts were invisible, even to me.

This would probably lead to one of those fights that stretched on for days, maybe even a week. But I refused to apologize for a crime I didn't commit. I would run into old flames for the rest of my life. I refused to be rude to them just because they were a lover in the past. "I should get back to work. I have to make a birthday cake for—"

"You're right."

Whoa, did he just say that? I grabbed a clean apron from the pile then looked at him.

He removed his hand from the counter and placed it in his pocket. Then he slowly walked to me, the hostility in his eyes now gone. "I'm sorry."

First, a free vacation, and now, a quick apology. It was going to be a good week. "It's okay."

"I already lost you once, and I don't want to go through that again. My life without you was..." He rubbed the back of his neck as he tried to find the right wording. "Agonizing. I don't want to go through that again, not when I'm so happy."

My fingertips kneaded the fabric of my apron, and my eyes softened.

"But I should never worry about losing you, not when we're forever."

My lips automatically lifted in a smile, loving the way he said those final words.

He pressed his forehead against mine and closed his eyes, feeling the resonating sound that erupted between us. Everything else faded to the background. It was lunchtime so the front of the store was packed with customers. The constant ringing of the cash register was heard in any part of the shop. But the circle that surrounded us isolated us from everything else—from the whole world.

***

I could hardly sit still in my seat. I stared out the window and rubbed my palms together anxiously, excited to get off the plane and feel the heat of paradise.

Wednesday

Hawke watched me with an amused expression. "Excited?"

"That's an understatement."

"Practiced your hula?"

"In fact, I did."

He grabbed my hand and rested it on my thigh. "I want a private show—the coconut bra and everything."

"Deal. It's the least I can do since you're bringing me along."

"You can come to all my business meetings if you want. I won't have to beat off in the shower."

My spine prickled at the imagery. The idea of Hawke pleasing himself and thinking of me was the biggest turn on in the world. When we were just friends, I used to think about it when I had a go with my vibrator. "You can still do that…"

He turned to me, the same amused expression on his face. "I will. If you do something for me."

I suspected I already knew what it was. "I'm down with that."

***

We were led to our private bungalow over the water. There were a hundred spaced out across the quiet cove. Far past the lagoon were sailboats and fishing boats. People even cruised by on jet skis.

It was better than the pictures.

"This place is amazing." The only vacation I ever went on was Disneyworld, and I was young so I don't remember it very well. This place gave the word vacation a whole new definition.

"I'm glad you like it." He moved his arm around my waist and guided me inside the bungalow. Our luggage was already sitting there, and the room was decorated with finery.

I opened the backdoor and saw the private plunge pool and the deck that led to the water below. "So sick!"

Hawke leaned against the doorway with his arms across his chest. He still wore the same amused expression that had been glued there all day. "It's a nice view."

I stuck my feet in the water of the pool and felt the coolness wash over my skin. "Have you been here before?"

"A few times."

"Now I understand why you aren't as excited."

He sat beside me and removed his shoes. "I am excited. You make me excited." He stuck his feet in the water and sat beside me, staring across the cove and to the world beyond.

"Thanks for bringing me along. It's the greatest trip I've ever been on."

He rubbed his nose against mine before he kissed the corner of my mouth. "Paradise doesn't mean much when you're alone and miserable." Love was in his eyes as he stared at me, showing me a world of hollowness before we found our way back to one another. "But now I can truly cherish it, see the beauty of it, because I'm complete."

***

Wednesday

Hawke got dressed then grabbed his satchel. "Alright. I'll probably be working for most of the day. But tomorrow, we have the whole day to do whatever you want."

"Can we go snorkeling?" I stood in my pink bikini with a towel tucked under my arm. I applied as much sunscreen as my skin would absorb so it wouldn't dry out in the sun.

"Sure." He hooked his arm around my waist and gave me a slow kiss. "What are you doing while I'm gone?"

"Hitting the pool."

He gave me a fond look before offering up another kiss. "All the guys at the poolside are going to have a hard-on because of you."

"Oh, whatever." I grabbed my beach bag and shoved my things inside. "I'll see you later."

He gave my ass a playful smack. "Alright, Muffin."

***

I spent the entire day by the pool. Other people rested under the cabanas with their pretty drinks, and a few kids were in the kiddie pool. I brought a few books to read, something I'd neglected after I opened my shop. Since then, I didn't have time to read or lounge around anymore. My life was devoted to my bakery.

While I missed Hawke, I was okay on my own. I ordered lunch at the poolside and even took a nap. Not once did I go into the water because I was too relaxed on the beach chair.

The sun started to set and I looked at the time. Hawke was still working, and I couldn't believe he'd been at it all day. How long could people talk about money? At least I would have him all day tomorrow. I really wanted to give those jet skis a whirl.

I set my book down because I couldn't read anymore. The dying light hurt my eyes, and if I kept squinting like that, I would have premature wrinkles. Just when I looked up, I noticed Hawke coming down the ramp in my direction. He left the line of cabanas and reached the main resort.

And then I saw his client.

It was a woman about his age, and she had pretty blonde hair that trailed past her breasts. It was curled at the ends and shined with a distinct softness. Her features were abnormally perfect, so I could only assume she was a model or an actress.

The first thing that came to mind was jealousy. Hawke spent the entire day with that woman, a perfect ten. I wasn't wearing any make up and my hair was tied up in a bun.

I felt hideous.

Hawke spotted me then came my way, the woman by his side. She had a snooty look to her, like she didn't like me before she even met me. "Hey, Muffin." He leaned down and gave me a kiss like he always did. "Have fun today?"

"Yeah. I chilled by the pool and drank all day. It was heaven." I looked at the woman and waited to be introduced.

"Francesca, this is Olivia." Hawke stepped away slightly so we could shake hands. "We're almost finished. We're just going to wrap up a few things at dinner."

He was still working? With her? "Okay. I'll see you later then."

Wednesday

Hawke gave me another kiss before he stepped away.

"It was nice meeting you, Olivia."

She gave me a cold look. "You too."

***

I sat on the deck of the cabana and waited for Hawke to return. Jealousy was eating me alive and I judged myself for it. Just last week, Hawke and I got into a fight over Kyle, and I told him he needed to calm down.

Now I needed to take my own advice.

It didn't matter how pretty she was or how rich she was. Hawke and I were meant to be together, and no one could take him away from me. I was worried over nothing, and I knew I needed a reality check.

After a few minutes of convincing, the jealousy finally left my body. Hawke could be with anyone he wanted, even supermodels. If I weren't enough for him, he would have left long ago.

An hour later, Hawke returned to the bungalow. "Got tired of the pool?"

"I started wondering how many kids peed in it."

He smiled slightly then removed his shoes and socks. He sat beside me on the deck and let his feet dangle in the water. He kept his back perfectly straight as he stared across the black ocean. The sun was nearly gone and the stars started to come out. The warm breeze moved through his hair, making it shift slightly.

I could stare at him forever and never grow tired of it. The distant light from the stars reflected in his blue eyes, looking like a private galaxy that I got to enjoy. His rugged features made him hard and a little intimidating, but underneath that brick and mortar was a man with a soft heart. He reminded me of myself in so many ways. "How did the investment go?"

"Good. She gave me a large amount."

I was curious to know how much money he used on transactions but I didn't ask. He probably didn't mind sharing the information, but his client might. "Have you worked with her before?"

"Many times. Her family owns Thick Whiskey."

Damn, she was stupid rich. "Good for her."

"She doesn't appreciate it. She grew up with money and doesn't understand the value of a dollar."

Sounded like every rich person I met. "At least she's investing it instead of spending it."

"I guess." He looked up at the stars and kicked his feet slightly in the water.

The fact he worked with her before was a dead giveaway to my greatest fear. More than likely, he slept with her. The idea of him being with such a beautiful woman made me sick, but I forced myself to stop thinking about it.

Hawke turned his gaze away from the sky and watched me. "Did you have a good day?"

"That's a stupid question." I forced a chuckle and hoped it sounded sincere. "I sat under a cabana while people waited on me hand and foot. Yes, it was a good day."

Hawke knew me well enough to see through my mask. He could tell I was trying to hide something, and within a few seconds, he figured out what it was. "It happened a few times but it never meant anything—to either one of us."

I looked away in embarrassment. He could read the pain on my face so easily despite how hard I tried to hide it.

"She wanted to have another fling on this trip, but I told her I was off the market. She didn't like that answer so I asked you to come along. Now she knows I'm being serious."

I looked out into the water, watching it grow darker with every passing second. "I'm bug repellent?"

He chuckled under his breath. "I guess, if you want to put it that way."

Actually, I was pretty concerned that he had to bring me along anyway. Did that mean she wouldn't give up until she got what she wanted?

His hand moved to mine. "You're the one who told me I have nothing to worry about. The same thing applies to you."

"I never said I was worried."

"Muffin, I can see it in your eyes."

The women in his life before I came along didn't matter. But the ones that came after did. They never should have been with him in the first place. He should have been mine for the past two years. They took something that didn't belong to him. Together or apart, he was always mine. "It just bothers me sometimes. I'm not worried you're going to run off with someone else, and I honestly don't blame women for wanting you. I just regret that time we lost. She got to have you when you should have been mine." The last thing I wanted was to hurt him, but I had to speak the truth.

He kept his eyes glued to me, never blinking. "I understand."

I finally looked him straight on, seeing the remorse on his face.

"I feel the same way about Kyle. Except, that was entirely my fault."

It was but I didn't gloat.

His thumb moved across my knuckles. "We're together now and that's all that matters. Nothing will keep us apart—ever again."

When he said beautiful things like that, it was impossible for me to be upset. I got lost in those dark eyes and drifted away in the form of a dream. Whenever we were together, it seemed like we were in an entirely different place, living in an alternate world where no one else could follow.

I removed my dress then slid into the water in my bikini. The water was a little cold but it felt good against my skin. Slowly, I untied the top of my bikini and let it float in the water.

Hawke's eyes were trained on me. He watched every movement, seeing my top drift across the surface.

I untied my bottoms then gathered them with the bikini top and placed them on the deck. My hair was still in a bun so I pulled it loose and let it fall around my shoulders. The ends fell into the water and immediately became soaked.

Hawke stared at me for minutes, appraising my body through the water. He watched my nipples harden from the cold. Then he slowly undressed himself, tossing aside his shirt and pants. When he pulled down his boxers, his hard cock fell out, proving he was pleased by what he saw.

He slid into the water then walked through it until he was right in front of me. The water level only reached the bottom of his chest, but for me it was almost to my chin.

He dug his wet hands into my hair before he gave me a slow kiss, the kind that wasn't meant to be lustful. It was slow and careful, treasuring my lips like it might be the last time he ever felt them. He didn't use his tongue at first. By the time he gave it to me, I was already writhing in the water. No matter how many times he made love to me, I was always desperate for more.

He gripped my ass then lifted me until my legs were around his waist. Without breaking the moment, he continued to kiss me until my back was pressed against the glass of the plunge pool.

His lips left mine and he looked me in the eye, the desire and endless love burning like a candle. "We need to be quiet."

"Okay." I wrapped my arms around his shoulders and tightened my knees around his hips, wanting him inside me.

His mouth was on mine again as he tilted my hips and inserted his cock into me. It made a slow entrance, stretching me in the best way possible. He moved until he was completely inside me. Then he remained still, my back pressed to the glass. "Sometimes, I want to stay like this forever." He sucked my bottom lip while he remained idle.

Anytime he was inside me, I was a different person. I was impatient, passionate, and aggressive. When I had him, I always wanted more. There were no words to express how I felt about this man. I told him I loved him before, but those words weren't enough to show my meaning. Nothing in the English dictionary would suffice. I'd never been with a man and felt this way, like my heart might give out because I'd given him everything. He didn't just have my heart, but my entire soul.

My hand scratched down his back, feeling the prominent muscles underneath the skin. My fingers traveled down his spine until I felt the hard curve of his ass. He had such a nice behind. I loved gripping it when we made love. "Come with me."

He pressed his face to mine and slowly thrust inside me, making the water rock against the glass in the form of waves. We normally kissed during sex but now we just stared at each other, looking into each other's eyes. He always made me crumble within minutes, and not just because he was good in bed. When he opened his heart to me like this, when I could see through his eyes and into his soul, that's when I tightened around him and felt myself explode. "Hawke..."

He watched my face light up in ecstasy while he struggled to hold on. He was purposely holding himself back, not wanting to end this too soon.

"Come on." I gripped his ass and pulled him farther into me, wanting to feel the weight of his release. He was the only man I allowed to come inside me, because he was the only one who deserved the honor.

His body tensed under my grasp and he dug his fingers into my ass as he released. His eyes held mine the entire time, and for a moment, his look glazed over, like he traveled to the same place I'd been just a moment before.

He winded down and kept himself buried inside me, my back still pressed to the glass.

I wanted to stay this way all night until the sun rose the next morning. My arms returned around his neck, and I kissed him slowly, wanting to feel our bodies rub together under the light of the moon and the stars. I wanted to do this forever, until the end of time.

CHAPTER FIVE

Sunny Day
Hawke

Leaving paradise and returning home wasn't as bad as I thought it would be. But I knew that was because Francesca was with me. It didn't matter where we were or what we were doing. As long as we were together, I was happy.

The leaves started to turn red and gold, and Central Park's typical green landscape had faded away. Before the winter months even arrived, it was clear it was going to be one hell of a winter.

"I miss the Bahamas." Francesca pouted her lips as she picked at a muffin.

"We'll go again some other time." I sat beside her at the table in the break room next to her office. On days when neither one of us had much time for lunch, we had something small from her bakery.

Wednesday

"I just can't believe such beautiful places exist. I know you see them in magazines and everything, but I just assumed they were photoshopped and everything."

I'd been there before and thought the same thing. But when she accompanied me on the trip, it had a magical feel to it. When we go on our honeymoon, I'll make sure we go somewhere really nice—not that we'll be leaving the bedroom much. "I'm glad you liked it."

"Maybe I should quit and become an investor. That way I can travel the world."

"Or you can tag along with me everywhere I go." I'd prefer that. I used to be a lone wolf, preferring solitude instead of company. But when I found Francesca, all of that changed. She was the only person I wanted to spend time with, to live my life with.

"I don't want to cramp your style."

I rolled my eyes. "I want you to cramp my style." I broke off a piece of the muffin and ate it. My will power diminished, and I had to take a bite.

She ate the last piece and sighed like she regretted it. "Do you have plans for Thanksgiving?"

I always spent the holidays alone. Sometimes, one of my regulars would be in town for business so we drank and screwed all day, both trying to fight off the loneliness and forget about the people we truly missed. "No." I was surprised Francesca asked me that. She should have figured that out on her own.

"Want to spend it with us?"

The holidays were the most difficult time of the year for me. It reminded me how alone I was. While everyone was having their perfect day with their perfect family, I was drowning myself in the biggest bottle of scotch I could find. As a child, the holidays were the worst. Dad seemed to drink more often because of the pressure, and he took it out on Mom and I. "There's nowhere else I'd rather be."

"Great. It'll be a nice Thanksgiving."

"Where will we be having it?"

"Yaya's place."

The last time I saw Yaya was at the wedding. She smiled at me from across the room, clearly happy that Francesca and I were back together. She was such a sweet lady and had always been so good to me. I felt guilty for hurting her granddaughter. "Where does she live now?"

"In a townhouse a few blocks away."

"I didn't know that." Francesca and I hadn't talked about it. We were too invested in each other to think about anyone else.

"Yeah, she really likes it. There's a small backyard so she can have a garden. I know coming to the city was a big change for her, but that was the best Axel and I could do."

"You picked it out for her?"

"Yeah. Axel and I decided to split her rent down the middle so it doesn't burden either one of us too greatly."

I never knew that either. "You and Axel pay her rent?"

"Of course," she said. "Yaya isn't going to work."

When I really thought about it, the knowledge didn't surprise me. Francesca and Axel were generous people, and they always looked after their own. After losing people they cared about, their bond only became stronger. "That's sweet of you."

"Well, she's Yaya. She raised us and took care of us. We'll always do the same for her."

It reminded me of myself. I kept depositing money into Mom's account even though she refused to use it. If she just took off, she'd have enough to live for the rest of her life.

Francesca caught the sadness in my eyes. "Have you talked to your mom lately?"

"Not since Axel's wedding." I remembered the phone call and how strange it was. She said she dropped her phone in the sink but how certain could I be?

"Is she doing well?" Francesca always tiptoed around this subject, knowing how much it pained me just to talk about it.

"I'm not sure. If she weren't doing well, she wouldn't tell me. But we had a strange conversation."

"What did she say?" Her full focus was on me.

"She called and sounded panicked, like something was wrong. I tried talking to her, but the line went dead. I assumed the worst, that she was being beaten with an iron, so I was just about to call the police. But she called back and said everything was fine, that she dropped her phone in the sink."

Francesca felt a strand of hair near her ear, something she did when she was nervous.

"To this day, I still don't know if she was telling the truth. And I have a feeling I never will."

Her hand moved to mine on the surface of the table. "I'm sorry." The sincerity in her voice pained my heart. She felt exactly what I felt at any given time. She shared the load with me, making sure I was never alone in my shadow.

"I know."

She brushed her thumb across my knuckles. Her hands were petite in comparison to mine, probably half their size. "One day, we'll have our own family. We'll be the parents we never had, and our lives will be full of laughter and love. It'll heal the scars we both carry and give us something to live for besides each other."

My fingers interlocked with hers. I wasn't ready for kids at the moment, but the idea of Francesca being pregnant and swollen with my child gave me a strong sense of joy. "You're right."

***

"How was the honeymoon?"

Axel sat across from me wearing his suit and tie. We were having lunch together at our favorite Chinese place. "Dude, I already told you when you picked me up from the airport."

"Well, Marie and Francesca were there." And he wouldn't be totally truthful if it were anyone besides just him and me.

"It was amazing. I can't describe it better than that."

"Your little confession didn't mess anything up?" Axel refused to marry Marie until he told her what he did two years prior. I didn't think it was necessary but he was adamant about it.

"No. We haven't talked about it. I really don't think Marie cares."

I knew she wouldn't.

"I was super nervous on the wedding night though." He wiped away the invisible sweat on his forehead. "So much goddamn pressure. I thought I was going to explode from the stress."

"Why? It wasn't your first time."

"I know. But I wanted it to be perfect for her." He held his chopsticks and picked at his white rice. "How much would it suck if we made love and I was a two-pump chump? Or I didn't make her come? Or it wasn't romantic enough? All the pressure is on the guy and not the girl."

"How'd it go?"

"It went well—I think."

I didn't make a joke because I knew Axel was sensitive about this.

"I lasted long enough and then we cuddled together for the rest of the night. So, I don't think I disappointed her. But sex on the honeymoon was much better. I could actually chill out."

"Did she bring any lingerie?"

"Tons." He grinned from ear to ear. "And she looked damn hot. But then again, that woman looks hot in anything."

I ate my stir-fry then checked the time. "Francesca invited me to spend Thanksgiving with you guys."

"Cool. Marie is coming too. It'll be our first year as husband and wife. Pretty cool, huh?" He wiggled his eyebrows.

I used to be jealous of what Axel had with Marie but now it didn't matter at all. What I had with Francesca was out of this world. It was something no one else could understand but us. I finally felt complete, like I knew where I belonged. "Very."

"Yaya makes the best—" He stopped then pointed his chopstick at me. "Wait, you already know. You've eaten her cooking before."

"Yeah. And I miss it."

"It won't be the same as it was in the cabin but it's still pretty nice."

"I'm sure it will be." I was just grateful I had somewhere to go this holiday. When I was alone, all I thought about was my broken family. It fell apart from substance abuse and a bad temper. My life had been robbed from me, and I could never get it back.

"But I guess as long as you're with Frankie, you don't really care." Axel didn't want me to be with his sister in the beginning but he quickly came back around. Seeing us together obviously changed his mind about the whole thing.

"True." That woman was my rock.

"I heard you guys went to the Bahamas."

"We did."

"Sounds like you're trying to copy us."

I chuckled. "No. I had to travel for work, and I thought I would take her with me. She really loved it. She said she's never seen a more beautiful place."

"She's easy to please," Axel said. "She doesn't need much."

I raised an eyebrow at the comment. "Did you just give Frankie a compliment?"

"Uh...no. I was just saying." He quickly shoved food into his mouth and didn't make eye contact with me.

"I'm gonna tell her what you said."

"Ha. Like she'd ever believe you."

"She knows I would never lie to her." I knew I had him there.

His face paled slightly. "Goddammit."

***

I knocked on her door.

"Come in."

I walked inside then set the grocery bag on the counter. "Hawke to the rescue."

"Thank you so much." She opened the bag and pulled out the flour and almond extract. "You're a life saver." She turned back to her kitchen counter where a mixing bowl sat.

"Whoa, hold on." I grabbed her by the elbow and turned her back to me. "I think I deserve a little more than a thank you."

She glared at me with her eyes but her smile said otherwise. "Demanding, aren't we?"

"Hey, I never do anything for free." I glanced at her lips.

"What do you want for your heroic act?"

"A kiss from the most beautiful woman in the world."

Instead of softening like I expected, she put her hands on her hips. "Well, Scarlett Johansson does owe me a favor..."

E. L. Todd

I pulled her into my chest and looked down at the face I constantly saw in my dreams. "That's not the woman I had in mind."

"Well, I don't know Blake Lively so you'll have to figure that one out on your own."

"Troll compared to you."

"What?" she asked incredulously. "Have you seen her?"

Actually, I had no idea who she was. "It doesn't matter. I knew you were the woman of my dreams the first time I laid eyes on you." I leaned in and kissed her lightly on the neck and shoulder. She was melting like butter at my touch, and I loved having that effect on her. She had the same effect on me, whether she realized it or not. My lips moved to hers, and I kissed her hard on the mouth, loving the jolt in my heart every time our mouths moved together.

She pulled away first but there were stars in her eyes. "Is that a sufficient thank you?"

"For now." I gently squeezed her ass then walked to the mixing bowl. "What creation are you making today?"

"Almond muffins."

"Sounds good."

"I wanted to make something new for Thanksgiving, so I thought a mix of almonds and cranberries would be the right touch."

"Good thinking."

She stirred everything in the bowl by hand then used her mixer to get it perfectly smooth.

Wednesday

I stood by and watched her the entire time, loving the way her tits shook under her shirt as she moved. Her hair was pulled back in a ponytail and it showed off all her perfect features.

She poured the batter into the cups then licked the bowl, like always. "Yum."

I fingered the batter then held it up to her, wanting to watch her suck it off my skin.

She grabbed my wrist and pulled it to her mouth. With the sexiest look I'd ever seen, she wrapped her lips around her finger then sucked the batter off.

My cock stirred.

She licked it clean before she placed the pan in the oven and set the timer.

"How long until they are done?"

"Thirty minutes."

"Perfect."

"Perfect for what?"

I grabbed her hand and pulled her into the bedroom. "You'll see."

***

Axel and I ended our basketball game then walked to the taco shop.

"I'm so out of shape." Axel sat down with his tray of food. "That wedding really took it out of me."

"You don't look any different."

"Of course," he said. "But I can't run as fast as I used to. I need to start hitting the gym again."

I went every morning and every afternoon after work. It was time-consuming and a little obsessive, but I loved the way Francesca looked at me. She stared at me like I was the hottest guy she'd ever seen. When we made love, she dug her nails into my chest in a possessive way, like every inch of my body was hers exclusively.

Which it was.

"Start it up again."

"But Thanksgiving is next week..."

"If you want to let yourself go now that you're married, that's your decision."

"Shut the hell up." He ate one of his tacos in just a few bites. "I'm not letting myself go. Are you kidding me? I have a smoking hot wife. If I don't stay in shape, someone might snatch her away."

"Give Marie a little more credit than that."

"But it's true. Some pretty boy might woo her right off her feet. I have to stay in great shape so her eyes will stay on me." He pointed his index finger at his chest. "Why do you work out like a beast every day?"

A lot of reasons.

"We both know it's to get laid."

"Not completely." I packed on a lot of muscle once I became an adult. I wanted to be an opponent my father was afraid of, and I succeeded. But I didn't expect Axel to understand that. "Why don't you start boxing with me? It's good exercise and it's not boring."

"I don't know... I don't want to mess up my hands."

I gave him a look that told him he was pathetic.

Wednesday

"What? I don't want to have arthritis when I'm forty."

I shook my head in disappointment. "You're right. Marie is going to leave you for a real man."

He kicked me under the table. "Knock it off."

It was something that actually bothered him so I let it go.

He finished his food then tossed his dirty napkins onto the tray. "So...do you think you're going to propose soon?"

I was surprised by the question but I hid my reaction. "Would you be cool with it if I did?"

He shrugged. "Like you care."

"Actually, I do." This was a little different than just going out with his sister.

"As long as you treat her right, it doesn't matter to me."

I knew he cared more than that, but he was trying to play it cool.

"So, are you?"

"I've thought about it."

"What's holding you back?"

"Nothing." Marriage didn't scare me at all. I would love it if Francesca had my last name and was by my side all the time. If we hadn't broken up years ago, that probably would have happened already. "I just don't want to rush into anything unless she's ready. I know I really hurt her, and I'm still trying to make up for that."

"It seems like she's over it."

E. L. Todd

"Yeah, I think so too. But I want to make sure. The last thing I want is for her to think I'm only asking because I'm trying to make up for what I did."

"I doubt that would cross her mind."

"I'd still rather wait a little while. When I'm ready to ask, I'll let you know."

"Cool." He rested his elbows on the table. "It's crazy to think you might be my brother-in-law someday."

"I *will* be your brother-in-law. I just don't know when."

Wednesday

CHAPTER SIX

Thanksgiving

Hawke

When I woke up that morning, a beautiful woman was beside me.

Her dark hair was sprawled across the pillow like stalks of grass. Her eyes were closed but they still emitted their natural light. The curve of her upper lip was strikingly similar to a bow, and when her lips were slightly parted, they looked absolutely kissable.

She was wrapped around me like I was another pillow on the bed. My chest was her favorite place to sleep, and she always rested her head there and listened to my heartbeat.

She was the love of my life.

That morning, we didn't wake up to an alarm clock. The sun filtered through the windows and awoke us naturally, bringing light into the apartment and chasing away the cold.

Wednesday

She released a quiet sigh, which she did every morning just before she opened her eyes.

I stared down at her and waited for the moment I'd been anxious to experience.

Her lids opened, and the vibrant beauty of her eyes immediately went straight to my heart. She was an absolute vision in the morning, well rested and satisfied from the previous night.

The morning was my favorite time of the day. Now that I woke up with Francesca, everything was different. No longer did I wake up next to someone I couldn't remember. There weren't any empty glasses of booze on my nightstand. And there weren't used condoms on the floor. All that sadness was replaced with the light Francesca brought with her.

She took me in slowly, distinguishing dreams from reality. Her eyes lingered on my face and mouth, recognizing it from the night before. Her hand slowly moved up my chest before she kissed me where my pectoral muscles met. "Grizzly."

"Muffin." My hand slid through her tangled strands.

"Happy Thanksgiving." Her voice was raspy like it usually was in the morning.

"Happy Thanksgiving."

She cuddled back into my chest and closed her eyes. "What time is it?"

I glanced at the clock on the nightstand. "Eight."

"Good." She released a happy sigh. "We have eight hours until we have to be there."

I chuckled quietly before I kissed her hairline. "Then let's go back to sleep."

***

She removed the pecan pie from the oven and set it on the counter to cool. "Wow, that smells good."

I leaned over the pie and took a whiff. "It does."

She grabbed a fork then eyed the pie, desperately wanting to try a piece.

I watched and waited, knowing her desire would never outweigh her need for perfection.

She sighed then dropped the fork. "I'll wait until dinner."

I smiled to myself. "Anything else we should bring?"

"No. We have everything covered. And Yaya will take care of everything else. She lives for this sort of thing."

I was already dressed and ready to go, but Francesca was a little behind because she spent the afternoon making her pies.

"Just let me finish my make up and hair."

She usually didn't wear make up, and I liked that. She could be beautiful without pounding on eyeliner and mascara. She was a natural beauty, having porcelain skin that was flawless even though her face was always caked with sweat and flour at work. And everything else on her face was already perfect. She didn't need to make any changes. "Why make up?"

"It's a special occasion."

"You look great without it."

"I just want to dress up a little bit."

55

Wednesday

I didn't make any more objections.

She removed her apron then glanced at the pie. "Can I trust you two alone?"

I eyed the pie and looked at her again. Then I shrugged.

"Be strong."

I'd never been a sweet tooth. That changed after Francesca walked into my life with her muffins and delicious cookies. Now treats lingered everywhere, and there was nowhere to escape. "I'll try."

She turned around and headed to the bathroom, her ass shaking the entire time she walked.

I leaned against the counter and watched her go, loving the sway of her hips and the arch in her back. She was a diamond in the rough and she didn't even realize it. Maybe that was why I was so obsessed with her.

Why everyone was obsessed with her.

***

"Happy Thanksgiving!" Axel opened the door.

Francesca stood in front of me with the two pies in her hands.

I was behind her, my hips in perfect alignment with her perky ass.

"Happy Thanksgiving." Francesca shifted the pies to one hand so she could hug him.

Axel walked around her and embraced me instead. "You're right on time."

I patted his back and tried not to laugh at the cold way he ignored his sister.

56

"Hey." She gave him a look of death. "It's Thanksgiving. You have to be nice to me."

Axel made a talking gesture with his hand and rolled his eyes.

Francesca kicked him in the shin. "Asshole."

He cringed then rubbed the injured area, groaning under his breath. "I'm definitely not hugging you now."

"Good." She marched into the house with her nose in the air. "I don't want one anyway."

"Whatever," Axel said. "My hugs are awesome. Right, Hawke?"

I shrugged. "I've had better."

"Oh whatever." He hopped on one foot into the house.

Marie emerged from the kitchen and saw Axel limping. "What happened?"

"Your best friend kicked me." He gave Francesca the stink-eye.

"Why?" Marie immediately turned on her.

"He's being a dick." She handed the pies off to Marie.

Marie accepted that explanation without further question. "Let's get these in the kitchen. Did you just make them?"

"Yeah." Francesca walked with Marie down the hallway.

Axel stood up straight and shook off the pain. "My lady should defend me."

"Why? You were being an ass."

"Dammit. Not you too."

Wednesday

We walked into the kitchen where Yaya was working endless pots on the stove and in the two ovens. "Everyone is here. Happy Thanksgiving!"

"Happy Thanksgiving, Yaya." Francesca hugged her then looked down at her apron. "That's cute."

"Thanks," she said. "Marie got it for me."

"Where's mine?" Francesca turned on her.

"You aren't my grandma," Marie said. "Why would you get one?"

"Because I work in a bakery."

"That's like saying I should give Axel money because he works with money," Marie countered.

Axel put his arm around her waist. "What's mine is yours, so keep it."

Yaya turned to me, and instead of being disappointed I was there or having mistrust in her eyes, she gave me the warmest smile I've ever seen. "So nice to see you, Hawke." She gave me a hug that contained more love than I got from either of my parents.

"It's nice to see you too, Yaya. Thank you for having me."

"Nonsense. You belong here."

Those words hit me in a strange way. I never felt like I belonged anywhere, not until I met Francesca. The truth of her statement rang loud in my ear and pierced my heart. "Thank you."

"I hope you're hungry. I made way too much food."

"I'll eat it all. Don't you worry."

She laughed then patted my stomach. "Everything should be ready in a few minutes."

"Do you need any help?"

"I got it. But thank you, dear."

***

Axel lay on the ground of the living room, his hands on his stomach. "Dude, I'll never eat again. I'm so full."

Marie rolled her eyes as she saw her husband lay on the carpet like a child. "Babe, get up."

He remained still. "Can't...move."

There was nothing Yaya's grandchildren could do to drop her smile. "Are you guys planning to have kids soon?"

"God, no." Marie realized how strongly she blurted that out so she backpedaled. "I mean, I already have a baby." She eyed Axel on the ground.

Francesca chuckled. "Marie has a point."

"I'm not a baby," Axel argued. "Babies can't be sexy."

"And you aren't sexy either," Francesca argued.

"Ha." Axel moved his hands behind his head. "Ask Marie about that."

Marie responded immediately. "Right now, you aren't."

"Whatever." Axel stared at the ceiling, his eyes closing. "You'll say otherwise when we get home."

Francesca looked at me and rolled her eyes.

It was cute when she did that so I leaned in and gave her a quick kiss.

Wednesday

That wiped the irritation off her face immediately. The glow moved into her eyes, the same one I saw when we made love.

My hand moved to her thigh, and I gave her a gentle squeeze. While I loved being with her family, I always preferred just being with her. Even when we didn't make love and we just lay together in bed, I was at peace.

Axel sat up, his hair pushed up in the back from the carpet. "Alright. What's for dessert?"

Marie shook her head. "You just said you were full."

"I am," Axel said. "I just need something sweet, you know?"

Marie rolled her eyes but that look of love was still there.

Francesca left the couch and my hand slithered back to my own thigh. "I brought pecan and pumpkin. Who wants what?"

Axel's hand shot into the air. "Both!"

Marie crossed her legs and adjusted her skirt. "None, but thank you."

"What?" Axel turned to her. "Are you crazy?"

"I'm not hungry right now." Marie was obsessed with her figure. She only ate the bare minimum and worked out like an Olympic runner, at least that's what Axel told me.

Axel gave her an irritated look before he turned to Francesca. "Bring her a slice of pecan with vanilla ice cream."

"Axel." Marie threatened him with just her voice.

"Baby, you're smoking hot." Axel said it with complete seriousness, like he wasn't placating her just to get

60

her to cooperate. "You make all the other girls look like shit—except Yaya."

Francesca put her hand on her hip and glared at him.

"You can have a damn piece of pie on Thanksgiving." He turned to Francesca and snapped his fingers at her. "Now fetch it."

I didn't have a sibling so I didn't know if this relationship was normal, but I had a feeling it wasn't.

Francesca kicked his arm as she walked by. "Coming right up."

Axel rolled over and groaned. "Ugh."

Yaya scooted closer to me and grabbed my hand. "I'm so glad you're here, Hawke."

She always made me feel welcome with a few simple words and a smile. "Me too." A necklace of pristine pearls was around her throat, and she wore a cheetah print jacket.

"How are things at work?"

"Good. I had a business meeting a few weeks ago and I took Francesca along."

"She told me. She said it was the most beautiful place she'd ever seen."

I smiled at the memory, loving the fact I did something to make Francesca happy. "We had a good time."

"I'm so glad you two found your way back to one another. Francesca took the break up hard, but after she got back on her feet, she was strong. She pushed on and went through all the motions but she was never truly happy. I could see it in her eyes."

Wednesday

I knew she wasn't telling me this to make me feel bad. She had good intentions. "I was miserable too."

"Now that you two have each other, don't ever let go. Life has so much more meaning when you have someone special to share it with."

I learned that the moment I fell in love with Francesca. Suddenly, the world was a beautiful place. There were so many things I wanted to do and experience—with her. Just the sound of a bird or the feel of raindrops was a cherished experience. "I know what you mean."

CHAPTER SEVEN

The Boxer

Francesca

I was mixing the ingredients for the custard frosting when Laura walked in. "Yaya is here."

"She is? Thanks." I set my spatula on a paper towel and covered the bowl so it wouldn't be exposed to all the flour in the air. I headed to the front, and the closer I got, the louder it became. Voices echoed in the bakery, and the cash register rang nonstop.

Yaya was sitting at a table in the corner, her half sandwich and half salad in front of her. I noticed she didn't have a dessert so I grabbed a few cookies before I joined her at the table. "Hey, Yaya."

"Hey, sweetheart." Her eyes lit up like always when she saw me. "Having a good day at work?"

"Absolutely." I leaned over the table so we could hear each other better. It was always so loud in that place. "I just need to invest in a pair of headphones."

She chuckled. "Is it loud in the back too?"

"Not really. Thankfully."

She ate her sandwich and took a bite of her pickle. "Are you working on anything new?"

"I'm making a wedding cake for two bowling champions. Their cake has a bunch of pins on top with bowling balls. It's actually really cute."

"Awe. That is cute."

"I just have to figure out how to make the bowling balls. I would use sugar but I'm afraid they're too big and might collapse."

"You'll figure it out, sweetie. You're so smart."

I smiled. "Thanks, Yaya." She was always my personal cheerleader.

"Things seem to be going well with Hawke." She moved on to her salad.

"Yeah." I released a sigh from my lungs, feeling lighter than a cloud. "It's perfect."

Yaya smiled at the happiness in my voice. "He's a good man."

"He is." Even if he didn't always believe it himself.

"And really handsome."

I chuckled. "That too."

"He adores you. I can tell every time he looks at you."

Sometimes when I wasn't looking at him, I could feel his gaze on me. There were times when we didn't speak, just had a conversation with our eyes. I could feel his thoughts with a single stare. Now I knew other people noticed it too.

"It doesn't matter how successful he is, what kind of family he comes from, or what he has to offer. The most important thing is love. And he loves you, dear."

"I know he does." I never told Yaya why we went our separate ways. The one time she asked, I didn't give an answer. Thankfully, she didn't hold anything against Hawke after he left. She accepted him with open arms, the way she accepted everyone.

"You guys are going to get married someday. I can tell."

"I know." There was no one else I'd ever want to be with. Kyle was a good friend and would have made an excellent partner, but with Hawke, it was different. It was true and powerful.

I eyed the clock on the wall and knew I'd let my frosting sit for too long. "I'm sorry, Yaya. I have to go."

"It's okay, dear. I know you have to work."

"I'll see you later." I gave her a kiss before I headed back to the counter.

"Frankie." An older man wearing a beige jacket and a baseball cap gently grabbed my arm. He held a cup of hot coffee in his free hand.

He was a regular customer. I recognized his face. "Hello, sir. What can I do for you?"

"That woman you were talking to..." He nodded to the back where Yaya sat. "Is that your grandmother?"

"Yeah, she is. Why?"

"Well...is there a grandpa in the picture?" He smiled in hope.

Wednesday

"Actually, there's not. And she's a very nice woman."

"Ooh...I think I'm going to buy her a cup of coffee then."

I smiled. "Good luck. Hope you don't strike out."

"Back in my day, I was known as a bit of a ladies man. Met a lot of women in the military."

"You're a veteran?"

"World War II."

"Thank you for your service." I grabbed his shoulder and gave him an affectionate squeeze. "Now go sweep her off her feet."

He tipped his hat to me. "I don't need to be told twice." He slowly walked to the table where Yaya was sitting, and I watched from my place near the counter. He stopped beside her and engaged her in conversation. After a few minutes, she laughed at something he said.

And I knew Yaya made a new friend.

***

I just got off work and immediately wanted to see the man of my dreams. *I want my grizzly.*

I want my muffin.

Then can I come over?

Always.

Well, I'm going to shower before I head over.

I'm just about to hit the gym. Come by in an hour.

I knew he ran in the mornings and did boxing in the afternoons. *Where do you work out?*

A boxing facility.

Can I watch?

66

Sure. But it can get violent.

You know violence doesn't bother me.

It's called Brawl. I'll see you soon.

K. I didn't mind watching Hawke get sweaty and hot. That sounded like free porn.

***

The only thing Hawke wore was his running shorts. The endless muscles of his back and chest acted as bulletproof armor. Every time he moved, the muscles shifted and recoiled, showing his strength and power. His spine was defined by the muscles on both sides of it, protecting it from everything. The thickness of his arms would terrify any opponent, and when the veins popped with adrenaline, it turned him into a beast.

A trainer held up two boxing targets for Hawke to destroy. They were pressed to the size of pillows, and the trainer wore a helmet for extra protection. A whistle was between his lips, and the second he blew on it, Hawke charged.

He threw his entire body into the momentum, landing solid punches that drove his trainer back. Punch after punch, the sound of the mat clapped through the entire gym. Other boxers hung at the end of the ring, watching Hawke move.

He danced on his feet, never staying in one place too long. All the muscles of his body were contracting, tightening and bulging with the extra blood. Sweat formed at the nape of his neck and dripped down the valleys between the slabs of muscle.

Wednesday

He never broke his concentration, giving his entire effort completely. He pushed the trainer back with heavy blows, and alternated hands, never using the same one twice. Sometimes, he used his right hook, and other times, he threw his elbow up and forced the trainer to skid across the floor.

The trainer didn't seem phased by the aggression. Actually, he didn't seem surprised at all.

Like it was life or death, Hawke came at him again. The fury on his face was unmistakable. He wanted to kill someone—anyone.

A guy by the ring spoke to his friend. "Damn, what's he pissed about?"

The other guy shrugged. "Everything?"

I knew exactly what he was pissed about. He carried endless grief and this was the only way to release it. His anger built up deep inside him until he was about to blow. He needed this—to stay sane.

Hawke never tired even though ten minutes had passed. His entire body was covered in sweat, sleek like he just stepped out of the rain. Despite his exertion, he looked like he could go on forever.

"Enough." The trainer rested his hands and removed his gloves. "Good job, Hawke. You should consider going pro."

Hawke was out of breath. He removed his gloves slowly then tossed them on the ground. "No. I'd kill someone."

The trainer laughed like he was making a joke.

E. L. Todd

But he wasn't.

Hawke climbed through the ropes and jumped to the ground. He wiped the sweat from his forehead with the back of his forearm. He didn't make eye contact with me right away, knowing exactly what I was thinking and feeling.

I crossed my arms over my chest, understanding the kind of pain he was in. Nothing had changed since we went our separate ways. He was still suffering, unable to control his rage and let it go. The same demons still haunted him.

He massaged his wrists before he looked up at me, ready to see the disapproval on my face.

I stared back at him, giving nothing away.

He slowly approached me, rubbing his sore knuckles. As if he expected me to call him a monster, he watched me and prepared for a lecture.

My hands reached for his, and I slowly massaged the pain from his muscles. I worked each one, feeling the tension in every tendon. His hands were much larger than mine, and they actually felt heavy when I held them.

I brought his hands to my lips and kissed each knuckle, treasuring the man I loved. It didn't matter how angry he was. It didn't matter how much he'd been tortured. He was still the same person to me. "You were great."

He stared at me without blinking.

I moved in to his chest and pressed a kiss to the skin over his heart, tasting the sweat on my lips.

He took a deep breath when he felt me, like he was relieved I didn't think less of him.

"Let's go home."

Wednesday

***

Hawke immediately headed into the bathroom and started the shower. "Get in with me."

"You want me to shower with you?" I sniffed my armpit. "Do I stink?"

He wasn't in the mood for a joke. His hands gripped my shirt and pulled it over my head. Then he unclasped my bra with ease. His eyes scanned my body, taking in my small breasts and petite shoulders.

When he looked at me like that, I couldn't think about anything else but him. I melted at his feet, yearning for his touch.

He removed my jeans and panties before he undressed himself. His dick was hard like it usually was when he looked at me, but it didn't seem like he was in the mood for sex.

We both stepped under the warm water and let it drip down our bodies. My hair became soaked and stuck to the back of my neck and shoulders. I stared at his chest and watched the water follow the grooves between his muscles as it fell down.

He grabbed a handful of soap and massaged it into my skin, rubbing my hips then my shoulders. His eyes never left mine, watching every reaction I made. "I'm not any different."

I knew what he was referring to, and it had nothing to do with the shower. "No, you aren't."

His hands glided down my chest to my stomach. "I'll always be this way—fucked up."

"You aren't fucked up, Hawke. You're just angry. A lot of people are."

"I want to hurt someone." He swallowed the lump in his throat. "I box because I want to hurt someone."

"But not me."

He took a deep breath at my words. "No, never you."

My hands moved up his arms, feeling the muscle underneath. "There's only one person you want to hurt—and he's not innocent. It's okay to feel that way. I don't think less of you."

"You don't think less of me when I'm on a rampage?"

"Never." I kissed his chest.

"When my mom was in the hospital, he was there." He mentioned this the night he left me but he never went into detail about it. It was the last conversation we had before he walked out. "Something inside me snapped. I attacked him and beat the shit out of him right in the hospital. It took five security guards to pull me off of him, and when they did, he was bloody. To this day, I wish I had a little more time. I could have snapped his neck and ended his life then and there."

I knew he meant every word but that didn't scare me. He wasn't getting revenge for what happened to him. He was protecting his mom, someone weak and helpless.

"Why won't she just leave?" His eyes glazed over like he was talking to himself rather than me. "She has enough money. She could even live with me if she wanted. If there's anyone he's afraid of, it's me."

"It's out of your control. Don't beat yourself up over it."

Wednesday

"She doesn't call me when she's in trouble anymore. But I still worry that something bad is going to happen—and I won't be there to stop it."

I understood his need to protect his mom but he couldn't stop living his life because of her. "You can't help someone who doesn't want to be helped. I know this is easier said than done, but you have to let it go."

"It's not that simple."

"I know."

"I hope he dies." The unmistakable conviction was in his voice. He wasn't saying it just because he was angry. He meant every word. "I hope he falls and breaks his skull open."

I wished for the same thing. "Don't forget where you are. You're here—with me." I cupped his cheeks and looked him in the eye. "When it's just us two, no one can touch us. No one can take our happiness away."

He slowly came back to me, his eyes coming back to life. His grip on my hips loosened and his breathing returned to normal. The fury was slowly leaving his body, revealing the calm man underneath.

When the shadow passed from his eyes, I kissed him. "There's my grizzly."

His lips stretched into a slight smile before he kissed me again. "You always bring me back into the light." His hands glided up my back, feeling the small muscles under the skin.

"And I always will."

***

Hawke leaned against the headboard as I straddled his hips. He watched my every move as his chest expanded with uneven breaths.

I sat in his lap and felt his hard dick directly underneath me. The wetness from between my legs rubbed against his shaft, and I moved slightly to spread it across his dick.

A quiet moan escaped his lips and his hands moved to my thighs.

"No touching." I grabbed his wrists and returned them to the bed.

His eyes narrowed in irritation. "Why not?"

"Because."

His hands closed into fists.

I ran my fingertips up his stomach to his chest. When I reached his shoulders, I massaged them, feeling the powerful muscle that could protect me from anything. I slowly rocked my hips, grinding against his throbbing cock.

He loved it but hated it at the same time.

I wrapped my arms around his neck and pressed my chest against his. Every time I moved, my boobs moved too, the nipples dragging against his warm skin. I pressed my forehead to his and watched his lips, seeing them open in desire.

I heard his knuckles pop because he was squeezing his fists so tightly.

I gave him a languid kiss, tasting him like I had so many times. Our mouths moved slowly, taking their time.

Wednesday

While I loved everything about our physical relationship, I particularly loved kissing. It was deeply satisfying.

"Muffin..." The quiet desperation was in his voice.

"No touching."

He released a growl.

I inserted his tip into my entrance and felt the thickness stretch me. His dick throbbed slightly when it entered my wetness. A groan from his throat accompanied it. I slowly slid all the way down until I had him entirely within me.

He took a deep breath like it was the greatest sensation he'd ever known. It always felt like the first time, like we were never prepared for how good we felt together.

I let him sit inside me for a few seconds before I slowly started to ride him, my gaze fixed on his. I held on to his shoulders for balance and moved him in and out. He was the perfect size, big enough to push me to my limit but not so big it hurt.

His hands moved to my ass and gripped it tightly.

"No touching."

He sighed and removed them.

I bounced up and down, enjoying every inch of him as entered me. When his head pushed my lips apart, it was the sexiest sensation I've ever known. My tits shook with every move I made and his eyes were fixed on them.

"You're so beautiful it hurts sometimes."

I dug my nails into his chest as I moved.

"Slow down."

I grinded against him gently, taking him in with restrained slowness.

"Just like that." He put his hands behind his head and watched me.

Seeing him enjoy me made my body light on fire. Now I wanted him to touch me, to grip me and never let go.

"Muffin, let me touch you." He kept his hands behind his head as he watched me ride his cock.

I grinded into his hips, feeling my clitoris drag across his pelvic bone. I was almost at my threshold, about to come around his hard dick.

Without waiting for permission, he gripped my ass and rocked me with him. His fingers rested in the crevice between my cheeks, trailing to the back of my entrance. His lips found mine, and he kissed me hard on the mouth, digging his other hand into my hair. "Together."

I was already there, just seconds from exploding. "I'm gonna come."

He moved me harder with him, still kissing me. His body tensed under me and his breathing went haywire.

I dug my nails deep into his chest as I felt my body convulse. Everything felt so good. Moans escaped my lips and my eyes glazed over. I looked into his face and saw him reach the same ecstasy that I did, falling into a whirlwind of emotions. We released together and rode the high until it slowly dissipated.

I remained on top of him, loving the feel of him inside me even though he was semi-hard. I could feel the weight of his seed, and that was a turn-on in itself. Hawke stared at me, still catching his breath.

Whenever we were together like this, it felt like no one else existed. It was he and I—against the world.

"Thank you for giving me this." He pressed his forehead to mine, his hands gripping my waist.

I knew what he was referring to.

"For giving me you."

CHAPTER EIGHT

Daydreams

Hawke

I was supposed to be reading the stock reports that just came in, but instead, I was twirling a pen between my fingers while thinking of something else entirely. Now, I struggled to focus my thoughts on work because I had something much more meaningful in my life.

I'd never been this happy.

Somehow, it was better than before. Our hearts connected and fell back in place exactly where they had been before. Francesca was the only person I could be myself around—completely. I could say anything and she would understand it, not take it in the wrong way like most people would.

Every day, my reality was a dream. People found love every single day, but most people didn't have what I had. They didn't have the person who shared the other half of their soul. They didn't have that one special person the universe created just for them.

Wednesday

Only I did.

Years ago, I would have said destiny and soul mates were the stupidest thing I ever heard of. It was some sissy bullshit chicks made up so they would have some romance in their lives. But when Francesca came into my life, I couldn't deny the truth. The evidence was right in front of my face, and one day, I couldn't ignore it anymore.

It was the truth.

Tim, one of the investors in my office, walked through my open door. "We're headed to the strip club tonight. You in?"

I had a good relationship with my employees. Since their salary was based off their hard work, they had no one to blame but themselves if their checks were insufficient. That allowed them to think of me as a friend instead of just their boss. "No, thanks. Have a good time." The strip club was one of my usual stops when I went out with the guys. It was one of those experiences that made you feel like shit, but for whatever reason, you couldn't stop doing it. But now I had absolutely no interest in it. The only woman I wanted to see strip down to her panties happened to be the woman I shared my bed with every night.

"Maybe next time."

Maybe never. "Sure."

He walked out of my office and let me return to daydreaming about The Muffin Girl.

***

She called me after work. "I want to see you."

"Then come over." She always waited for an invitation, never showing up on her own. I never understood why. I wanted her to come and go as she pleased. There was no reason to give me a heads up when she was coming. It's not like I did anything I shouldn't be doing.

"Okay. I'll be there soon."

After I hung up, I grabbed my extra key and placed it on the floor in front of the door. When ten minutes had passed, I heard her footsteps outside. She stopped but didn't knock, probably because she saw the key on the floor.

"This is what I want you to do." I kept the door locked so she couldn't come inside. "Pick up the key and open the door."

"Why?"

"Just do it."

She stuck the key in the door and got it unlocked. "What was the point of that?" She opened the door and walked inside. "Did you change your locks or something?"

"No. That is your key now."

"What?" She eyed it in her hand.

"Muffin, just come over whenever you want. You don't need to ask if it's okay."

"But...this is a big step."

It was? If anything, I expected her to be disappointed I hadn't already proposed by now. "No, it's not." I snaked her keys out of her purse and placed the new key on the ring. "Just come by whenever you want. I want you to feel comfortable here."

Wednesday

She eyed the keys in my hand then smiled. "Maybe I'll come by just as you get out of the shower..."

"Perv."

"What?" she asked innocently. "I'm just being honest."

"I like your honesty." I pulled her to my chest and kissed her forehead. The second her body was against mine, I was on cloud nine. All the weight on my shoulders disappeared.

She examined her keys again. "I'd give you mine but I left my spare at home."

"You don't have to give it to me."

"I know. But maybe you'll walk in on me when I'm in the shower." She looked up at me, and that cute smile I loved was there.

"That sounds nice."

"Now who's a perv?"

I kissed the corner of her mouth and felt myself slip away. Whenever I was with her, I was in a different universe. Time and space had no hold on either one of us. We existed alone, two souls attached with an ethereal glow.

***

The empty pizza box sat on the corner of the bed, a few crumbs inside. Francesca finished the last piece then wiped her fingers. I didn't like eating in bed but Francesca made me reckless.

"Guess what?" Her knees were pressed to her chest and she was naked. Her hair fell down her chest, hiding her tits from view. While her skin was exposed, all the good stuff was hidden. Somehow, it was sexier than her being completely on display.

"What?" Sometimes, I didn't listen to a word she said. I just watched her lips move. Everything she said was important, but sometimes I fell under her spell. Her beauty captured me, making me paralyzed.

"Some guy hit on Yaya last week."

"A guy?"

"Yeah, a guy her age."

"Really?" I'd never heard of Yaya dating. Actually, the thought never crossed my mind. "What happened?"

"I don't know. I haven't asked her yet."

"I figured you would pester her to death."

"I'm playing it cool." She scrunched her toes, showing her purple nail polish. "Yaya was never up in my business when I was growing up, so I'm not going to be nosey."

"It wouldn't be nosey. You're just curious."

She shrugged. "She's a grown woman. If she has something she wants to share, she knows I'm always eager to listen."

Francesca never told me what happened to her grandfather. Since she never mentioned him, I assumed she didn't know him very well. Maybe he passed away before she was born. "What happened to your grandfather, if you don't mind me asking?"

"Papu?"

I tried not to smile. "What's Papu?"

"It's grandfather in Greek."

"That's cute."

Wednesday

"I didn't know him very well. He was gone when I was just a baby."

"I'm sorry." She'd lost so many people it was hard to believe. "What happened?"

"Cancer." She scrunched her toes again and stared at her nails. "You never talk about extended family. Do you have any?"

I shook my head. "My dad never talked about his family. My mom had a sister but she died a long time ago. And I never knew any of my grandparents."

"Both of our circles are small. We'll need to repopulate."

Fatherhood wasn't exactly my calling but it didn't sound so bad with her. I'd love to hold her hand as we took our kids to the park. The responsibility would be stressful, but I was sure we could handle it. "I look forward to knocking you up."

She gave me a playful kick. "Is that all you care about?"

"Sometimes." I looked at her long, slender legs. "Like right now." I grabbed her by the ankle and gave her a hard tug. She laughed then dropped to her back, her legs in my lap.

"You're such a caveman, I swear."

I crawled on top of her then pinned her hands above her head. "You say that like it's a bad thing."

"I suppose it's not." Her eyes sparkled like a green Christmas ornament. There was so much life deep inside, and when I looked hard enough, I saw her thoughts. I saw the future she pictured for us. Her hair was sprawled across the comforter and her lips were slightly parted, like she was desperately waiting for me to kiss her.

I kept her waiting, teasing her. "I thought about you every day when we were apart." That wasn't a stupid, romantic line. That was nothing but the truth. It didn't matter how many women I slept with, I never forgot about the girl I actually loved. Sometimes, when I got coffee in the morning, I thought of her in The Grind. Sometimes, I thought I spotted her on the street but it turned out to be some random brunette. And she was always in my dreams, my sacred place.

Her eyes grew serious, seeing the sincerity deep within me. "As did I."

I wrapped her legs around my waist and dug one hand into her hair. I'd fallen so hard for this woman. She had me wrapped around her finger, a puppeteer to my entire body. She could control me absolutely—and she didn't even realize it. "I'm lucky you never stopped loving me." After what I did, I couldn't have blamed her if her heart moved on.

She ran her hands up my chest until she cupped my face. "And I'll never stop loving you."

***

Axel and I went out to a bar that night. Marie had her friends over so Axel had to find something to do outside the apartment.

"What are you getting Marie for Christmas?"

Wednesday

He drank half his beer but didn't pick it up again. "I found this jacket from Nordstrom I think she'll like. It's gray. That color always brings out her eyes."

I nodded. "That's nice."

"And I'm trying to write her a poem."

I was about to take a drink of my beer when I stopped. "What?"

"You know, a poem." He spun his coaster in his fingertips. "Some kind of love song."

"You don't strike me as the poetic type."

"Yeah, I'm realizing that. I've been trying to write it for a month. That shit is hard."

"What made you decide to do this?"

He shrugged. "I got her some nice things to open on Christmas, but I wanted to make her something, you know? Marie likes stuff like that. It's our first Christmas since we've been married, and I want it to be special."

Since the gesture was sweet, I didn't tease him about it. "Maybe you should do something else?"

"Like what?"

"Something you're good at."

"Dude, I'm not good at anything. You know that."

That wasn't true but I wasn't going to waste my time arguing it. "What about your wedding vows?"

"What about them?"

"What if you wrote them out in your handwriting? Something like that."

"Hmm...that's not a bad idea." He rubbed his chin as he remained deep in thought. "And I can do that."

"That shouldn't be too hard."

"No, it won't." He gave me a playful smack on the forearm. "Thanks, man. I've spent so much time getting nowhere with that poem."

"Maybe next year."

He laughed. "It'll take me a whole year to write it."

"So, you didn't get anywhere with it?"

"I got a few lines but it wasn't that great." He took a drink of his beer then eyed the TV in the corner.

"Can I see it?"

"It's really bad…and I'm not just saying that."

"We're always our worst critic."

He pulled out his wallet then unfolded a yellow piece of paper. He tossed it at me. "There you go."

I opened it and began to read.

Marie, your ass is off the hook,

Better than any book.

Your heart is big.

But your tits are bigger.

I tried to keep a straight face as I finished it. It wasn't the worst thing I ever read but it wasn't the best either. I folded it back up and handed it to him. "Stick with the marriage vows."

He shoved it into his pocket. "It's hard, okay? Not a lot of things rhyme."

I couldn't wait to tell Francesca about his little poem.

"What are you getting Francesca?"

"Not sure yet."

Wednesday

"She's so hard to shop for." He ran his fingers through his hair like he was anxious just thinking about it. "I got her a recipe book one year and she threw it at me."

"Well, she doesn't need a recipe book."

"I was just trying to do something nice and she was a total brat about it. So...good luck."

Francesca didn't care about materialistic things. If I got her a new phone or some Beats headphones, she would never use them. Designer clothes and shoes weren't her thing either. The only luxurious thing she seemed to enjoy was our vacation. But I couldn't give her that.

"You want to use my poem?" He pulled it out of his pocket again.

I tried not to laugh. "I'm good, Axel."

CHAPTER NINE

Christmas Eve

Hawke

The Muffin Girl closed at four since it was Christmas Eve, but I knew it would be insanely packed the entire day. I didn't work because there was nothing to do during the holidays. No one was working because they were spending time with their families or traveling. Most of the guys took an extended two-week vacation.

I stayed home and waited for her, knowing she would come over the second she could. It was difficult to be apart no matter how short the time period was. When I said goodbye to her in the morning, it was always painful. And when she walked through the door, it felt like an eternity since I'd last seen her.

The lock turned and the front door opened. "Baby, I'm home."

It took her a while to get used to her key but she finally got the hang of it. "I've been watching the door for the past hour."

Wednesday

She was still in her work clothes. Flour and sugar was caked on her black t-shirt, and her hair was in a braid. She set a pie on the counter. "I thought we could indulge tonight."

Being in a relationship had its drawbacks. For instance, I ate a lot more because I was always with someone. But I had to keep myself in check otherwise my eight pack would disappear. "Christmas is early."

She immediately pulled off her shirt and tossed it aside so she wouldn't get flour all over my apartment. Then she removed her jeans and stood in her bra and panties.

I whistled loudly. "I've been a good boy this year."

"You have." She headed toward me then jumped into my arms.

I gripped her ass then kissed her hard on the mouth, feeling higher than a cloud. "Want to take a shower?"

"With you? Or without you?"

"Always with me."

"Then, yes, I would."

***

We ate the pie right out of the box, forks in our hands.

"Damn, this is good."

"We make the best Dutch apple pie. I know that's a little cocky but whatever." She dug in and scooped out enormous chunks.

"It's not cocky when it's true." I only took a few bites because I'd never cared for sweets. "Are we going over to Yaya's tomorrow?"

"Yep. And I got her the cutest purse. It's pink and it's Guess."

"That's nice of you."

"I think she'll like it. Pink looks good on her."

"What did you get Axel?"

She ate another bite before she set down her fork. "He loves the Yankees so I got him and Marie tickets."

"He'll love that."

"What did you get him?"

"A basketball."

She chuckled. "Actually, he'll love that."

"What did you get Marie?"

"Well, since she's married now, I got her a cooking set with her new last name engraved into the dishes."

It didn't surprise me how thoughtful she was. "That's perfect."

"Well, Marie liked to cook but she wasn't very good at it. Maybe now she'd be more excited to practice."

The Christmas tree was in the corner by the window, and the lights flickered. She and I decorated it just like the last time we spent Christmas together. Now that she was mine, the experience was different. It was one of the greatest moments of my life, actually being happy during Christmas time.

My gift for her was under the tree, and I knew she brought mine over the other day. I was relieved when she only got me one present because I did the same for her. Neither one of us cared about the number of gifts we exchanged.

Any gift I got her would never compare to the one she'd already given me. Her journal was a sacred possession, and I still read it when we were apart so I could feel close to her. It kept me company on the loneliest nights of my life.

"Should we exchange gifts with everyone else?" I'd prefer it if it was just the two of us, but we could do whatever she wanted.

"How about we do it tonight—at midnight?"

"That sounds perfect."

She closed up the box and left the forks inside. Neither one of us were hygienic with our food because we shared everything. "I can't believe I ate half this pie."

"I can. I watched you do it."

"Don't remind me."

I tickled her side. "You're lucky you eat everything in sight but remain so tiny."

"I'm not tiny. I've got an ass and a tummy. Marie is tiny."

"She's too skinny." I grabbed her hip and pulled her into my lap. "You're just perfect."

"You'd say that even if I weren't."

"In my eyes, you'll always be, so you never have to worry about that." I kissed her bare shoulder and squeezed her against me. Her ass was in my crotch, and I loved the way it felt.

"So, what should we do while we wait until midnight?"

"How about we make love in front of the fire?"

"Ooh...that's romantic."

I lifted her in my arms and carried her into the living room where my fireplace sat. I hadn't used it in years but I knew it worked. I set her down on the ground then turned on the gas.

"Now, all we need is a bear rug."

I got the fire going then turned back to her. "You have your grizzly for that."

***

We lay naked together on the floor and watched the clock strike midnight.

"Merry Christmas." She dug her fingers into my hair before she kissed me.

Our lips touched lightly, sending chills down my spine even though we spent the whole evening making love. "Merry Christmas."

"There's no one else I'd rather spend it with."

"Me neither." I placed kisses down her body, kissing her shoulder and then her flat stomach.

"So, are you ready to open presents?" Her eyes beamed with excitement, and I knew it was because she was anxious to give me her gift, not the other way around.

"Yeah."

She walked to the tree and fetched the two gifts. Then she set them on the ground beside us. My gift was in a small jewelry box, and hers was much bigger. I didn't have a clue what she got me.

"Who wants to go first?"

I grabbed the small box and handed it to her. "You go." I spent a lot of time on her gift, and I knew she would love it.

She didn't hesitate and ripped the wrapping open. When she uncovered the dark wood of the box, she popped it open. Inside was a platinum necklace with a locket in the shape of a heart.

She lifted it from the box and examined it. On the front was an engraving in small cursive writing. *We Are Forever*. Her eyes watered as she read it. She sniffed loudly then blinked the tears away. She hadn't even opened it yet.

Her small fingers found the groove and she popped it open. Inside was a small picture of us. It was taken in South Carolina. I remembered the day perfectly. Francesca just made a new muffin creation, and once they were out of the oven, we got into a small food fight. I snapped a picture of us together on my phone but never showed her. We were just friends at the time, but even then, I knew what she meant to me.

"Hawke..." Tears poured down her cheeks as she held it in her palm.

The sight brought warmth to my heart. Making her happy was a selfish act because it brought me so much joy. She didn't care about money or jewels. All she cared about was the love underneath. "I'm glad you like it."

"Like it? I love it." She closed the locket then gripped it in her small fingers. "It's absolutely perfect."

It took me a while to hunt down the perfect necklace for her. I wanted something nice, something that wouldn't rust for the rest of her life. I ended up going to Tiffany's for it, but she didn't need to know that.

She put the necklace on then felt it dangle around her throat. It fell right above her chest, the perfect location. "Thank you so much." She moved into my arms and hugged me tightly, the tears from her eyes soaking into my shoulder. "You're so sweet."

"Merry Christmas."

"Merry Christmas."

I continued to hold her, feeling happier than I'd ever been in my life. I'd lost so much and experienced so much sadness, but when Francesca loved me, I forgot about all that baggage entirely. She breathed new life into me.

When she pulled away, her eyes were dry. "Now open mine." She handed the box over.

I examined it before I ripped the wrapping off. Underneath was a simple cardboard box without any clues to what was inside. I broke through the tape and pulled out a blanket.

At first, I didn't understand what she was giving to me. While I appreciated anything she wanted me to have, I didn't understand why she would give me a blanket. When I turned it over, I recognized the fabric. The blanket was constructed of different pieces of fabric, combined together in a collage.

"My old t-shirts..."

"I had a lot of them when you left. I still kept them. It was too hard to throw them away. I thought I would make this, so we can cherish those memories every day."

I gripped it in my fingertips as I stared at her. "You made this?"

She nodded.

"You know how to sew?"

Wednesday

"It took me a while to figure it out, but I eventually did. Do you like it?" Hesitation was in her eyes, like she wasn't sure how I felt about it.

"Muffin, I don't even know what to say… I can't believe you kept them."

"I could never throw away anything of yours—no matter what."

Both of us decided to exchange gifts from our past. The irony wasn't lost on me. I feared we'd never be able to recover from what happened, but somehow we had. And not only that—we were stronger.

I dropped the blanket onto my lap before I looked her in the eye. The fire glowed dimly in the hearth and the Christmas ornaments reflected in her eyes. It was absolutely silent with the exception of the crackling flames. My heart thumped with too much blood but I felt oddly calm at the same time. She and I had something so special it couldn't be described in words. It was supernatural and unbelievable. I had the love of a woman that wouldn't just last till the rest of my days, but beyond that.

I pulled her into my lap then wrapped the blanket around her naked body, enveloping her inside it. The locket hung from her throat, shining brightly in the light of the flames. Even though she was naked and on top of me, I wasn't aroused. I felt something a lot deeper than that. The words that left my mouth were ones I hardly ever said. They simply weren't necessary for the two of us. "I love you." My arms hooked around her waist, and I rested my face against her chest, right where her locket was located.

She wrapped her arms around my neck and rested her head on mine. "I love you too."

Wednesday

CHAPTER TEN

Christmas Day
Francesca

While Hawke and I wanted to see my family for the holidays, we really wanted to continue lying in front of the fire, making love endlessly to the sound of the flames. The blanket would be wrapped around us, enveloping us in warmth.

We walked through the door with pies in our hands and greeted everyone. Axel and Marie were both wearing ugly Christmas sweaters, keeping up a tradition I don't recall starting.

Marie gave me a hard hug. "I'm so glad I have an excuse to spend the holidays with you."

"Me too."

"An excuse?" Axel asked. "Marrying a hunky man is an excuse?"

Marie rolled her eyes then took the pie from my hand. "Yaya is in the kitchen…and she's not alone."

"Say what?" I blurted. "That veteran guy is here?"

"How'd you know?"

"They met at the bakery."

"Yeah, he's here. And he seems really nice."

"Awesome." Yaya deserved a companion that made her happy.

Hawke hugged Axel. "What's with the sweater?"

"What do you mean?"

"It's just...interesting." Hawke stared at the white unicorn on his shirt and the elves surrounding it.

"It's supposed to be ugly," Axel said. "That's the point."

Hawke hadn't attended many Christmas parties in his time so he was clueless to the tradition.

"Nevermind." Axel brushed it off.

I walked into the kitchen and greeted Yaya. "Merry Christmas."

She threw her arms up in excitement. "Merry Christmas, sweetheart." She kissed my cheek before she hugged me. "So happy you guys are here."

"Me too, Yaya." When I pulled away, I spotted the man from the bakery. He wasn't wearing his ball cap this time, and surprisingly, he had a full head of hair. He had the same smile on his lips that I'd seen before, and his enthusiasm reminded me of Yaya's innate spirit. "Merry Christmas."

"Merry Christmas." He hugged me like we'd known each other forever. "Yaya invited me to spend the holidays with you. My kids are on the west coast, and I'm too tired to fly."

"Understandable. I'm Francesca, by the way."

He waved my comment away. "I know who you are. The Muffin Girl."

I smiled.

"I'm Joe. It's a pleasure to formerly meet you."

"You too." I pulled Hawke to my side. "This is Hawke, my—" Saying boyfriend felt oddly out of place. He didn't feel like a boyfriend. He was something much deeper than that. But I couldn't find the right word. "Hawke."

"It's nice to meet you, sir." Hawke shook his hand. "You better treat Yaya right. You got two guys to deal with."

Axel cracked his knuckles loudly.

"Oh, stop." Yaya slapped Axel on the wrist.

"I've got no reason to be scared," Joe said. "So continue your threats all you want."

"Good answer," Hawke said.

"If everyone is done making threats, dinner is ready." Yaya removed her apron and set it on the counter.

Joe walked to her side. "You need help setting the table, dear?"

"Sure. Can you carry the turkey?"

"Sure thing."

I smiled while watching their interaction, seeing how well they worked together. "Don't chase him off," I whispered to Hawke and Axel. "I really like him."

"I like him too," Marie said. "They're so cute together."

***

We exchanged gifts after dinner. I made Yaya a custom blanket with pictures of Axel and me from our childhood. She was moved to tears, like she usually was.

Wednesday

Marie loved the handwritten letter Axel made of his wedding vows. Marie got me a picture frame of the two of us on her wedding day. Overall, it was truly a great Christmas.

"What did you get Hawke?" Marie asked.

I was a little embarrassed to say it out loud. "I made him a blanket."

"A blanket?" Axel blurted. "Sorry, Hawke."

"I made it out of his old t-shirts…" I swallowed the lump in my throat as the awkwardness set in the air.

"And I loved it." Hawke stuffed the ripped wrapping paper into a garbage bag.

"What did he get you?" Marie asked.

I pointed to the locket at my throat. "It has a picture of us inside."

"Awe," Marie said. "That's so cute."

"That is cute," Axel said in agreement.

"What's the writing on the front?" Yaya squinted her eyes as she tried to get a look.

I didn't want to say that part out loud. People would probably think it's cheesy and over-the-top.

Hawke answered before I did. "We are forever." He didn't seem the least bit embarrassed by the words he had engraved, even in front of his best friend.

"Awe…" Marie's eyes watered and she quickly fanned them.

Axel's happiness died away. "What the hell, Hawke?"

"What?" Hawke asked.

"I gave her a really great gift and you had to stomp all over it with your damn locket." He grabbed a ball of old wrapping paper and chucked it at Hawke.

"No." Marie grabbed his wrist. "I loved it, Axel. I'm just happy my best friend is happy." She kissed him on the cheek and hugged him tightly.

Axel visibly melted the second Marie paid attention to him, like always. He breathed a noticeable sigh and rested his head on hers, like there was no place on earth he'd rather be than in her arms.

***

A blizzard hit Manhattan and shut down most modes of transportation. Snow piled on the streets and the sidewalks, and schools were closed. I loved the winter snow, but I hated being cold. Unfortunately, they went hand in hand.

The alarm went off at five. and I slowly moved out of the warm bed, immediately feeling the cold air against my naked body.

Hawke stirred the moment I left his arms. "What are you doing?" His hair was messy from rolling around the night before, and his eyes were heavy with sleep.

"I've got to work." I crawled over the bed and placed a kiss on his chest. "I'll see you when I get home." I moved back to the floor then pulled on the shirt he tossed aside the night before.

"You're going to work?" He sat up and ran his hand through his hair. "Muffin, there's a blizzard outside." His voice was raspy from sleeping all night.

Wednesday

"Yeah, but the show must go on." I grabbed my work clothes from my bag and began to change.

"You aren't going to work." Now his voice was clear, and the anger shined through like the sun on a cloudy day.

I turned around, feeling my skin prickle with irritation. I didn't respond well to commands. Anyone who tried bossing me around always wasted their time. "Yes, I am."

"Do you understand how dangerous it is out there right now? The subway is closed."

"Good thing I'm not taking the subway." I pulled on my jeans and black t-shirt.

"Goddammit, Frankie." He kicked the blankets off and stood at his full height. Naked and chiseled from stone, he was a powerhouse of muscle. "Now isn't the time to be stubborn. If schools are closed and the subway isn't operating, do you think there will be many customers?"

"There will always be customers. What do you think people are going to do on a snow day? Sit around and eat muffins."

"Then let your workers take care of it. You stay here."

"I have stuff I need to do." I pulled my hair into a ponytail then grabbed my jacket.

"If you think you're walking out of here, you're in for a surprise." He approached me with tense shoulders, the threat in his eyes.

If this were any other time, I'd crawl on top of him and ride him until I was satisfied. But right now, I was too irritated for that. "I'll be fine. I can take care of myself."

"Against a storm? The wind is thirty miles per hour. Unless you have superpowers, I don't think you can beat it."

"The shop is only two blocks away. I'll be fine."

He took a deep breath like he was trying to calm himself down. Then he slammed his fist hard into his chest, releasing his pent up frustration.

"Was that supposed to scare me?"

"It should."

I zipped up my jacket then pulled up my hood. "I'll see you later." I turned away and left the bedroom.

"I don't think so." He grabbed me by the wrist and dragged me back. "I'm not letting this happen. It's not safe. My office isn't even open and money never sleeps."

I twisted from his grasp. "Because you can work from your computers. I can't make a birthday cake here."

"Actually, you can."

I was tired of arguing so I walked away.

"How can I stop this from happening?" He followed me all the way to the front door.

"You can't." I turned around and tried to appear as menacing as possible despite my short stature. "You need to learn that if this is going to last forever, you'll never be able to boss me around or make decisions for me. While I take your thoughts into consideration, I'll do whatever the hell I want." I unlocked the door.

"Whoa, hold on." He pushed the door shut with his palm. "Let me get dressed."

"Why?"

"If you're still going to go, then let me walk you."

Wednesday

"Are you insane?" He was going to walk through the snow and back just to make sure I got there okay? "Hawke, I'll be fine."

"How will I know that? Your cell phone won't work so how will I be able to check? What if you don't make it to the store? How will I find you?"

Damn, he was a drama queen.

"I'm not stopping you from going. Therefore, I'm not breaking any rules."

I narrowed my eyes.

"You could spare me the trip if you just stayed home."

"Hawke, I have to work."

He sighed then walked into the bedroom. "Then give me a minute to change."

***

The weather conditions really were terrible. Snow constantly blew in the hard wind and the sidewalk was slippery and wet. Hawke held my hand and guided me forward, making sure I didn't slip or drown in a pile of snow. We didn't speak because we couldn't be heard anyway.

Now I was dreading the walk back to the apartment.

Despite my expensive winter coat, I was still freezing. There was no one else on the streets because of the weather, but then again, I couldn't see more than a few feet in front of me. Everything was a blanket of white.

It would normally take me two minutes to cross one block, but today, it took nearly ten minutes. Thankfully, I wore gloves. Otherwise, my fingers would have frozen off.

I kept walking when I bumped into something solid. I was off balance for a moment, unsure what I hit. Hawke's hold on me stopped me from falling. Then out of nowhere, a blade was held in my line of vision.

"Your purse." He grabbed the strap from my shoulder and tried to yank it off.

I was being robbed and threatened at the same time. I should've let him take my bag, but I was pissed some asshole was taking advantage of a girl trying to get through the snow. "Go to hell." I threw my palm up and hit him right in the nose. He stumbled back, my purse still clutched in his hands.

Hawke shoved me out of the way then cornered our assailant. He kicked the knife out of his grasp then punched him hard in the face. "You picked the wrong person to fuck with." He ripped the purse out of his freezing hands then kicked him hard in the side. It was clear he wasn't done because he pulled his fist back.

"Hawke, that's enough." I grabbed his arm and pulled him away.

"I don't think so." He twisted from my grasp and chased after the mugger.

"Hawke. Stop."

He slowly lowered his hand and looked at me.

"He's homeless in a blizzard. I don't need to say more than that." I grabbed his hand and pulled him with me.

He walked beside me with the same glare on his face.

I knew I would get an earful for this later.

We reached the bakery and welcomed the warmth of the place. It was quiet inside, the polar opposite of the outside. Not many customers were there, but people still showed up.

Hawke pulled back his hood then ran his fingers through his hair. "I'll pick you up at three."

"You don't need to come get me."

He gave me the darkest glare I've ever seen. "Trust me on this. You better be here at three." He dared me to defy him, to say the wrong thing to make him snap.

"Fine."

"Thank you." He didn't seem at all grateful, just irritated. Without saying goodbye, he turned on his heel and returned to the storm. In just a few seconds, he disappeared into the canvas of snow.

***

Hawke walked inside right at three.

I knew it would be World War III when we got home. The threat was clear in his eyes. He was beyond pissed at me, even though ten hours had come and gone. I grabbed my purse and met him at the entrance.

He didn't say a word to me.

"I'm ready."

He pulled up my hood then walked out.

It was a little easier to walk back since the wind was moving with us. The snow was thick in the air, not the cute snowflake kind. The weather was so intense even a polar bear wouldn't last.

There were no muggers this time, and we returned to his apartment without any complications. The second we entered the building, the warmth greeted us. I removed my gloves and pulled down my hood before we even entered his apartment.

Once we were inside, he threw off his gloves and jacket, unable to wear them for a moment longer.

It was nice to be home after the long day I had. It was still fairly busy despite the insane weather. Customers had nothing else to do but sit around and drink coffee.

Hawke stared me down like a bomb about to explode. "What?"

"What?" His eyes narrowed to slits. "Are you serious right now?"

"We got there and back just fine. Chill."

"Chill? Don't fucking tell me to chill."

Here we go. "Don't cuss at me."

"Don't piss me off."

"Look, I had to work today. You didn't have to walk me."

"If I didn't walk you, that mugger would have had you."

"Had me? In case you don't remember, I punched him in the nose. I can handle myself."

"It could have gone much differently."

"But it didn't." It was always the worst case scenario with him.

"I admire you for being so strong and brave all the time. I really do. But sometimes your courage is borderline stupid. You can't defeat everything, especially Mother Nature."

"It was two blocks. Two." I held up two fingers.

Wednesday

"I don't care if it was next door. You aren't immortal, Frankie."

"Stop calling me that." I hated it when he referred to me that way. It was insulting.

"It's your name, right?"

"You know that's not my name." He only called me muffin, nothing else.

"Well, you aren't my girl right now so I don't know what else to call you."

I threw my glove at him. "Don't talk like that."

"Then don't act like that." His eyes burned with fire.

"You know what?" I picked up the glove from the ground and put it on. "I'm going home."

He released a loud laugh. It sounded terrifying. "You're funny, Frankie."

"I'm serious."

"I'm not letting you walk out that door. You can wait until the storm passes. After that, do whatever the hell you want. I don't give a damn."

"You don't tell me what to do."

"Actually, I do." He placed his body in between the door and me. "Last time I checked, you were mine. Instead of seeing my requests as commands, see them for what they really are. I'm a man madly in love with this girl, and all I want to do is protect her, not control her. I've never told you what to wear, what to do, or who you can hang out with. The only time I ask for anything, it's for your safety. You need to learn to respect me and knock off his childish behavior. Despite your stubbornness, I love you. I love you so damn much. What do I have to do to make that clear?" He stepped closer to me, forcing me to back up. His arms hung at his sides but his stance was still threatening. "Grow. Up. Frankie." He walked around me, his shoulder sliding past mine, and entered the bathroom. A moment later, the shower started to run.

I breathed a deep sigh before I removed my coat and sweater. I was so determined to keep my independence that I forgot I already committed to sharing my life with someone else. I couldn't have both—all the time. I didn't have to do what he said, but I should be more sensitive to the things he asked for. He was right when he said he didn't ask for much. If I wore a skimpy dress when I went out with Marie, he never made a comment about it. If he saw me talking to a handsome guy at the bakery, he never got jealous. He never looked through my phone when I was in another room. He was the perfect man—nearly all the time.

I removed my clothes before I walked into the bathroom. He was washing his hair as he stood under the warm water. Even through the distorted glass, I could see the details of his perfect physique.

I got into the shower then closed the door behind me.

He kept his back to me, ignoring me.

I came behind him then rested my forehead against his back. "I'm sorry."

He rinsed the shampoo from his hair then stood still. "For what?"

"Being...stubborn."

Wednesday

He turned around and faced me, the aggression absent from his eyes. "I'm sorry I called you Frankie."

"It's okay." I gave him a small smile, silently asking if we were okay. "I know you mean well. I shouldn't get so worked up over it."

"You're independent and I get that. It's hard to let someone else take care of you."

At least he understood it. "We're okay?"

"No matter how pissed I am, we're always okay." His arms moved around my body and brought me close to his chest. Soap dripped from his body to mine. One hand rested on the small of my back, spanning the entire area with just his palm. "You're my world. You'll always be my world."

"Thanks for putting up with me. I know I'm a lot to handle."

"You're a lot of woman." He pressed his forehead to mine. "And I'm man enough to handle it."

CHAPTER ELEVEN

Ready

Hawke

On Christmas day, Francesca introduced me as Hawke. She didn't specify what I was to Joe, what our relationship was, or what we meant to each other. It didn't bother me because I understood. Boyfriend wasn't the right word to describe me at all. I was a lot more than that. Just saying my name was better than a meaningless label.

And that's when everything changed.

I didn't want to be her boyfriend anymore. What we had was light-years beyond amateur love. The gifts we exchanged were evidence enough. I didn't need more time to figure out how I felt. My bachelor days were long gone, and I never wanted to revisit them.

I wanted to marry her.

***

"Dude, why are we here?" Axel tightened Marie's jacket around her body to keep her warm from the cold.

When he didn't think it was enough, he wrapped her in his own jacket.

"Babe, I'm fine." She pushed it off her shoulders.

"No. I don't want you to get sick." He wrapped her up and placed his arms around her.

I would never get over how attentive Axel was. When he was a bachelor, he didn't give a damn about anyone but himself and his cock. "I want you guys to help me with something."

"What?" Marie asked.

I turned to the jewelry store we stood in front of. "Help me pick out a ring."

Marie's jaw dropped and she let out a scream that made the other pedestrians swerve out of her way.

Axel was just as surprised. "Holy mother fucking shit."

Marie jumped up and down. "She's going to be so happy. Oh my god."

"Wow." Axel forgot about the cold and rubbed his temple. "This is huge."

"I should have done it a long time ago." Like, on our first date.

"You want us to help?" Axel asked.

"I think I know what I want to get her. I just want you to be there." I pictured the ring Francesca would wear every day for the rest of her life. I didn't know much about rings because I never put any thought into it before.

"Then let's do it!" Marie headed into the jewelry shop first.

Axel chuckled. "Déjà vu."

***

"This one is gorgeous!" Marie pointed into the glass box. A large diamond sat on a platinum ring.

"That's flashy," Axel said. "What about this one?" He pointed to a princess cut with diamonds in the band.

I didn't see her wearing either one of those. "I think I'm going to custom design it."

"That's perfect!" Marie clapped her hands in excitement.

Axel looked threatened. "I didn't customize your ring but it's still nice."

"It's very nice, Axel." She kissed his cheek to stroke his ego.

He relaxed slightly.

I met with the designer and we took a seat in her office.

"So, what did you have in mind?" She placed an iPad in front of me and held a stylus in her fingertips. "We can literally do anything you want."

"Well, I want it to be different than anything she's ever seen." It had to be unique. That was a criteria of mine.

"Of course. Why don't you swipe through some of the examples to get an idea?" She handed over the stylus.

I slowly began to piece together everything I wanted, picking the platinum metal and designing the band. I created three segmented bands that stretched across the top and molded together so it had an earthly feel to it. I placed the engraving inside the band then admired my handiwork.

It was the ring.

I pushed the iPad back to her. "This is it. Size five."

Axel stared at it with a confused expression. "Are you on a budget or something?"

"Why?" I narrowed my eyes, unsure why he asked that.

"Well...there are no diamonds." He pointed at the picture. "Unless you just forgot."

"I'm not putting diamonds on it." I didn't see Francesca wearing that. She'd want to wear her ring to work but if it contained an enormous rock, she wouldn't feel comfortable. What was the point of having a ring if she couldn't wear it every day?

"Why not?" Axel asked. "If it doesn't have a diamond, she's not going to like it."

"No," Marie said. "It's perfect for her. I can see her wearing this."

"Oh..." Axel gave up and fell quiet.

"I want her to have something no one else has ever seen," I said. "And this suits her."

The designer gave me a smile. "The ring will take six weeks to be created. And you'll have to pay up front—no refunds."

"That's fine." I pulled out my card and handed it over.

"This is so exciting," Marie said. "In six weeks, Francesca is going to be your fiancée."

Six weeks was a long time. I'd have to be patient. "I can't wait."

"Then she won't be my problem anymore," Axel said. "She'll be all yours."

"She was never your problem." Francesca took care of herself from the very beginning. She didn't need anyone else—and that included me.

"How are you going to propose?" Marie asked.

I knew a long time ago. "On our first Christmas together, she gave me her journal. It was something really personal and beautiful. I started my own journal years ago, so I was going to give that to her—with the ring inside."

Wednesday

CHAPTER TWELVE

Winter Wonderland

Hawke

The blizzard moved on and the snow started to melt. People returned to their busy lives, waiting for spring to arrive. I went back to work and met a few more clients. Six week was a long time to wait, but it wasn't that long in the span of our lifetime. I could be patient.

When I came home from work, Francesca was already there. She let herself in and made herself at home.

I loved coming home to her. "Hey, Muffin. How was work?"

"Good. I hired a few more employees. Maybe that will speed up customer service."

I grabbed a beer from the fridge. "Maybe you should get a bigger place." It was the first thing I thought when I walked into the crowd at lunchtime.

"Too much work."

"Or open a second location."

"Definitely too much work."

Wednesday

I sat on the couch beside her and gave her a kiss. "Too bad there's not two of you."

She grinned. "You would love that, wouldn't you?"

"I don't know... I can hardly handle one of you as it is."

"Have you ever had a threesome before?"

I tried not to flinch at the question. She didn't usually ask me about my prior sex life. When we got back together, she was haunted by the women I'd slept with. If she asked me about it now, she must be fine with it. "Yes."

She grabbed my beer and took a drink.

"Why do you ask?"

"Just curious."

I took the beer back and took a long drink. "What do you want to do tonight?"

She leaned back into the couch and put her feet up on the coffee table. "Would you judge me if I said I wanted to stay home and do nothing?"

"No."

"Because that's all I ever want to do now. I never want to go out."

"I feel the same way."

She leaned into my side. "We're an old married couple."

"What's wrong with that?"

"We're boring."

"If people saw us in action, they wouldn't think we're boring." I kissed the top of her head.

"I used to make fun of Marie when she and Axel got serious. Now I'm doing the same thing."

"I like staying home with you every night. Honestly, there's no one else I'd rather be with."

She hugged and squeezed me like a stuffed animal. "Me too."

***

She pushed me on the bed then pulled my boxers to my ankles.

I propped myself on my elbows and watched her kneel on the floor. She was just in her bra and panties, and I knew what was coming next.

She grabbed a cup of ice water and took a drink, playing with an ice cube in her mouth.

My dick automatically hardened because it knew what was about to happen. I loved being buried deep inside her, but being inside her mouth was just as good. She gave awesome head, the best I ever had. I wanted to come just thinking about it.

She kept the ice cube in one cheek and set the glass on the ground beside her.

An ice cube blowjob. She's never given me one of those before.

She started at my balls and licked the sensitive skin. The coldness of her tongue immediately made my cock twitch. It gave me a rush of arousal that was practically blinding.

She slowly made her way up my shaft until she reached my tip. When she was there, she rubbed the ice cube across the tender skin. The ice cube was smaller than it was a few minutes ago but it still felt good. Then she took me all the way into her mouth, the ice cube sliding by as she moved her tongue around.

It was awesome.

She massaged my balls with her fingers and continued to move my dick in and out of her mouth. She made slow strokes, somehow heightening the experience through her restraint. The ice cube continued to melt but her mouth was as cold as a freezer.

I dug one hand into her hair then thrust from underneath, feeling my balls ache with the urge to release. She looked so beautiful when my dick was in her mouth. The view made me want to come just as much as the feeling. I wanted to last longer but I couldn't. Her mouth felt too incredible.

I gripped the back of her neck then released with a groan, filling her throat with my seed. It was a long orgasm, the kind that made me high for a few minutes.

Francesca sucked everything off before she pulled her mouth away. Then she licked her lips.

Fuck, she was sexy.

She took another drink of the water before she stood up.

I was satisfied but I wanted to keep going. With her, foreplay was just as good as the sex. I grabbed her by the wrist and pulled her to the bed. "Now it's my turn." I took a drink and got an ice cube in my mouth. Then I went down on her, giving her the same pleasure she just gave me.

***

Francesca went out with Marie that night so I stayed home. There was a fashion show for the magazine Marie worked at, and Axel wasn't interested in sitting through that—not that I blamed him.

The apartment was unusually quiet. It hadn't been like this in a long time. Francesca was usually there, filling the air with the smell of her baked goods. Sometimes, she was singing in the shower. And other times, she was doing a load of laundry. She pretty much lived there without her stuff.

I loved this apartment but knew we needed an upgrade. It was perfect for the two of us, but there would be additions to our family eventually. We needed a backyard, something with scenery. I'd probably have to commute to work from the suburbs.

Never thought I'd live in the suburbs.

I sat on the couch and drank a beer while I watched the game. Knowing Marie and Francesca, they would be out until three in the morning. Those two hit the town hard. When I saw them together at Marie's bachelorette party, things were pretty crazy.

My phone rang with a number I didn't recognize, but the area code was from South Carolina. It was ten o' clock at night so I had no idea who would need to get ahold of me at this hour. I answered anyway. "Hawke Taylor."

The voice on the line spoke professionally. "Mr. Taylor? Mr. Theodore Taylor?"

Wednesday

I hated my first name. Absolutely loathed it. My cheerful nature deflated like a popped balloon. If anything could set me on edge, it was that. "Speaking."

"This is Dr. Tiberius, from South Carolina Medical Center."

The TV faded into the background, and I couldn't hear a word of it. The images blurred together, and I wasn't even sure what I was looking at. All sense of time and gravity left me. I started to drift. "Please tell me she's okay." I've gotten this phone call before. I knew the drill.

"I'm sorry, sir. We did everything we could, but we lost her."

What?

Lost her?

I released the bottle in my hand and felt it roll across the couch. The beer spilled everywhere, forming a puddle on the floor. The smell of beer came into my nose and burned my nostrils. "I don't understand…"

"She lost a lot of blood and went into cardiac arrest. We tried to stabilize her, but there was nothing we could do. I'm sorry for your loss, Mr. Taylor."

I slowly rose to my feet, feeling weak. "She's dead?"

My mom is dead?

"I'm sorry, Mr. Taylor." Dr. Tiberius repeated himself because he didn't know what else to say. "I know this is hard."

I gripped the phone and felt my hands shake. Anger washed over me like it never had before. Bloodlust blurred my vision. All I could think about was snapping his neck then stripping his limbs for sport. I wanted to roll his body into a ditch and feed the crows.

"The EMTs said she fell down the stairs and collided with a cabinet. It toppled on top of her and—"

"No. Her husband beat her to death."

Dr. Tiberius fell silent.

"She was murdered."

"I'm sorry, sir. That's what the EMTs told me."

I gripped the phone so tightly it almost shattered. "I'll be right there."

***

I burst through the door and searched for her room. "I'm looking for Carol Taylor. What room is she in?"

A doctor standing behind the counter with his chart looked up at me. He gave me a sad look before he set his chart down. "Mr. Taylor?"

I knew who he was. "Where is she?"

"The coroner is about to take her to the morgue."

"I want to see her." There was nothing I could do for her. I was too late. I left her all alone and didn't protect her like I should have. I should be in her place right now, lying on a metal table with a sheet draped over my body.

"I don't think that's a good idea."

"She's my mother." I wanted to hurt this man even though he hadn't done anything wrong. I wanted to hurt everyone.

"I'm sorry. You can see her after they process her in the morgue. It's the protocol."

Wednesday

I stepped back so I wouldn't grab him by the neck. "I need to speak to the police."

"They were here a few minutes ago. You might be able to catch them. Room 113."

Without saying thank you, I headed to her room, the place where she died. Blood pounded in my ears and my body screamed in mortal agony. This was a day I feared would come to pass. It was here and I couldn't turn back time. I couldn't change what happened. I couldn't bring her back to life.

Two police officers were still there, finishing their report.

"I'm Hawke Taylor, Carol's son." I didn't want to bother with the introductions but it wouldn't get me anywhere if I didn't.

"We're so sorry for your loss, son." Officer Bradley shook my hand. "We're just finishing up."

"She didn't fall. Her husband beat her to death." There was no way two police officers didn't see the signs. They should have taken one look at her and knew what happened.

The other officer stared at me blankly. "That's a strong accusation."

"My father is a violent drunk. He used to beat the shit out of me when I was young. He's done the same thing to my mother. I'm telling you, it wasn't an accident. You need to arrest him."

Officer Cunningham flipped through his chart. "According to our records, she's had a lot of falls in the past."

"Abuse."

E. L. Todd

"We can certainly look into it," Officer Bradley said. "But we were on the scene when the EMTs arrived. It was pretty clear it was an accident. Your father was in tears."

Because he was a fucking psychopath. "I'm telling you, that's what happened."

"Were you there?" Officer Bradley asked.

"No...but I know that's what happened."

"If this happened in the past, why wasn't it ever reported?" Officer Cunningham asked.

I knew right then I would never get any help from the police. All they cared about was sticking to the protocol, not listening to the actual facts. It made their lives easier just to file their reports and move on, not opening up the case again. "Because my mom was scared. I tried convincing her to leave but she never would. Now she's dead." I felt my heart drop as I said the words out loud. "Dead."

***

I stood in front of the counter then pointed to a pistol in the case. "That one."

The guy pulled it out and handed it over. "She's a beauty. Not ideal for hunting, but it's always good to have a backup."

I would be hunting—but not for animals. "I'll take it."

"Great. I'll put it on hold for you." He returned the gun to the case then opened a drawer.

Put it on hold for me?

He placed a piece of paper in front of me. "Complete this background check and it's all yours."

Background check? "How long will this take?"

125

Wednesday

"Five business days."

I didn't have that kind of time. "Come on, guy. I'm a normal dude."

"I'm sorry, son. It's the law."

I forked out extra money. "This is yours if you just look the other way."

He stared at it like he was intrigued. But then he grabbed a piece of paper and wrote a name down. "Private sellers don't have to do background checks. Give this guy a call." He shoved the paper toward me and left the cash on the table.

***

I paid for the pistol and shoved it into the back of my jeans. I was going to blow my father's brains out, and I had absolutely no reservations about doing it. He deserved to die a painful death. Actually, a quick blow to the head was too good for him.

I headed to the house and noticed his truck wasn't outside. The house was dark and quiet. No lights were on. I stopped at the house to investigate anyway, wondering if he was hiding out.

I used the loose window from the back to get inside. Once I was there, I saw the house looked exactly the same as it always had. Except, there were pieces of furniture missing. The coffee table was gone and one of the dining chairs was missing.

I knew what happened to them.

I explored the house and found the dresser that supposedly fell on my mother. When I got to it, I stopped, knowing this was the location where her life began to ebb away. I stared at the hardwood floor and felt my jaw clench in rage.

I explored the house further and searched for the piece of shit that was my father. Every room was empty, and the guest room had all the broken pieces of furniture my dad tried to hide from the police. It was safe to say he wasn't there.

But when he came back, I would deal with him.

***

My phone had been off for a while. I didn't want to talk to anybody. Right now, all I cared about was killing the fiend that took my mother's life away. If I spoke to anyone, they might try to stop me.

I didn't even want to speak to Francesca.

I stayed in a hotel a few miles from the house. This place was my hometown, but it didn't feel like home. Now it was a ghost town, a place I never really knew. I'd spent so much time trying to get out of this place that I didn't realize I should have stayed behind.

I didn't try hard enough to save my mother. All I had to do was drag her out of the house when my father was at work and throw her in the back of my truck. I could have taken her somewhere safe. We could have started over. And when he came after her, I could have protected her.

But I didn't do that.

I let her die.

***

Wednesday

I turned on my phone to make a call. The second it was powered on, it rang with Francesca's name on the screen. She must have been calling nonstop in the hope I would turn on my phone at the right moment.

I sighed in irritation, not wanting to listen to her at the moment. I just wanted her to go away. "Yeah?"

"Hawke?" The panic in her voice rattled my ears. "Where did you go? I came to your apartment and you were gone. I've been so worried about you. I'm so glad you're okay."

"Okay?" I released a maniacal laugh. "I'm not okay. I'll never be okay."

She paused, the fear transferring over the line. "What's wrong?"

"What's wrong?" I laughed again, not sounding at all like myself. "I'll tell you what's wrong. My mom is dead. She was beaten to death. That's what's wrong."

Another stretch of silence. "Oh my god…"

"That pathetic excuse for a man killed her. And I let it happen."

"Hawke…"

"Now that I've gotten you up to speed, I have to go." My thumb moved for the END button.

"Wait, wait. Are you in South Carolina?"

"Where else would I be?" She did nothing to deserve my hatred, but I couldn't control it. My entire world was upside down, and I couldn't distinguish friend from foe. All I felt was numb. I knew this day would come, and despite that foresight, I still hadn't prevented it.

"Where are you, exactly?"

"Don't come down here. I just want to be alone."

"Hawke, please."

"Are you deaf?"

Francesca didn't flinch at my hostile behavior. Normally, she would scream back but this time she let me get away with it. "Save me some time and tell me. Otherwise, I'm going to waste time and resources looking for you."

"Good luck with that." I hung up then made the call I wanted to make in the first place.

Wednesday

CHAPTER THIRTEEN

On The Line
Francesca

I banged my fists on the door as hard as I could. "Axel! Open up!" I tried calling them but both of their phones were on silent while they slept. "Come on." I threw my fists harder, bruising them in the process.

Axel opened the door in just his sweatpants. "Shit, what the hell?" His hair was messy and his eyes still contained the distant memory of sleep. "Do you have any idea what time it is?"

"Emergency." I was slightly out of breath from throwing my body against their front door. "Hawke."

"What?" His attitude completely changed when he heard what I said. "What happened?"

"His mother died." I breathed through the stitch in my side until the cramp went away. "His father killed her." I still couldn't believe it happened. Hawke feared this day would come, and unfortunately, he was right. "He took off yesterday, and I haven't been able to find him. But I finally got ahold of him and he's in South Carolina."

"Oh shit." He crossed his arms over his chest, disbelief on his face.

"He's out of his mind. When I talked to him on the phone, it was like I was talking to a completely different person. He's…I don't even know."

"Poor guy."

"I'm worried about him. We all need to see him, talk him off the ledge."

"The ledge of what?"

"From murdering his father." I shouldn't say it out loud but it was the truth. I wouldn't put it past Hawke to do something like that. When his temper flared up, he was more hostile than a nuclear bomb. He lacked self-control.

"Let us get dressed and we'll go." He stepped back inside his apartment.

"Please hurry."

***

"Do you know where he is?" Marie asked from the front seat.

"He wouldn't tell me." He'd completely shut me out. Now I was just an annoying stranger to him.

"Let's think," Axel said. "Where would he be?"

"He might be at the hospital," Marie said. "That's where his mother passed away."

"But that was twenty-four hours ago," I argued. "They've moved her body since then."

"Do you know where his dad lives?" Axel asked.

"No…" He never told me.

"Well, he has to sleep somewhere, right?" Marie asked. "He's probably staying at a hotel somewhere."

"And it's probably near the hospital." Axel slammed his hand on the wheel, thinking back to when we all lived in the area. "And there's only one hotel in that location. He must be at the Marriott."

"God, I hope you're right." I had a feeling it wouldn't be that easy.

"Let's get his room number from the front desk," Axel said. "We'll go from there."

***

To our luck, he had checked into the hotel. Once we knew what room he was in, we ran down the hallway until we found it. My heart was pounding so hard I could barely contain it. It was about to explode and pop out of my chest at any moment.

I knocked on the door lightly, hoping he would assume it was room service or something.

No response.

"Knock again," Axel whispered.

I rapped my knuckles against the door but didn't hear a sound from inside.

"He must not be here." I wanted to grip my skull and scream.

"What's he doing at five in the morning?" Marie asked.

I didn't want to think about it.

***

Wednesday

We waited outside his room for him to return.

"Try calling him again." Axel sat on the ground with Marie across his lap. She was sleeping.

"I did. His phone is off." I paced in front of the door. I hadn't slept in forty-eight hours but the need for rest left my body. Hawke was in serious pain and my body couldn't relax for even a second.

"Come on, Hawke..." Axel stroked Marie's hair.

I was absolutely terrified Hawke would go to jail for murder. It was gonna happen. I could feel it.

The elevator at the end of the hall beeped before the doors opened. I immediately turned and hoped I'd see Hawke step out.

And he did.

He was wearing the same clothes I saw him in the day he left. He carried himself differently, like an invisible weight sat on top of his shoulders. His eyes were downcast to the floor. He didn't look up until he was closer to the door.

When he saw me, he didn't look pleased. Somehow, he looked even angrier than he sounded on the phone a few hours earlier. The sight of my face didn't soothe him like I hoped. In fact, he looked murderous. "What did I say?" His aggression came out like a blunt axe.

He was suffering more than I could imagine, and I kept that into consideration. When I lost both of my parents around the same time, I wasn't myself either. I was pissed at my father for voluntarily leaving, and I was angry at the world. No one understood his reaction more than I did. "We love you and want to be here for you."

E. L. Todd

"Well, I don't want you here. You wasted your time." He pulled the key out of his wallet and headed to the door.

"Hawke." I placed myself between him and the door. "I understand what you're feeling—"

"Shut your goddamn mouth. You have no idea what I'm going through. Your father may have killed himself, but he didn't murder your mom. It's not the same thing." His eyes were wide like a serial killer. He wasn't himself at all.

I didn't put him in his place because it wouldn't get me anywhere. I needed to keep him calm, not escalate the fight. "Then explain it to me. I want to listen." It was hard to believe that we were madly in love and happy just a few days ago. Now that felt like another lifetime.

"I don't give a shit what you want. I want you to leave—and not come back." He shoved me aside with his massive arm so he could get to the door. The push wasn't hard but he would never do something like that if he was himself.

"Whoa, hold on." Axel rose to his feet, his patience non-existent. "She's trying to be there for you and that's how you treat her? I don't care what happened to you, Hawke. No one talks to my sister like that."

I appreciated that defense but it would just make things worse. "Axel, take Marie and meet me in the lobby."

Hawke breathed hard and stared Axel down, like he might rip his head from his shoulders.

Axel didn't move.

"Please." I understood Hawke better than he did. I could talk him off the ledge.

135

Wednesday

Axel took Marie's hand and walked away.

When they were gone, I turned back to Hawke. "It's just me." I kept my voice gentle, hoping that would coax him out of his rampage.

"Is that supposed to mean something to me?" His voice was ice-cold. "Frankie, I just want to be alone. I didn't ask you to come down here. I don't want to look at you or talk about how I feel. All I want is solitude."

Watching him brush me off so coldly stung. He should run to me, not away from me. But his emotional state put him on a completely different level. He wasn't the man I knew. "Then let me be alone with you."

He got the door open but didn't let me walk over the threshold. "Go back to where you came from." He walked inside and let the door shut behind him.

I caught it before it could close and let myself in, uninvited.

Hawke turned around and glared at me. "You want to get killed?"

"You wouldn't hurt me." I knew he was a different person at the moment but that didn't change anything. The man I loved was still in there. He wouldn't raise a hand to me no matter how upset he was. The only damage he would ever do would be from his words.

"You're sure about that?" He turned and faced me head-on. "My father and I aren't any different. We have the same name, the same appearance, and we have the same unbridled temper." He closed the gap between us and looked down at me with ferocity in his eyes. "I'll break your neck and put you in the ground. Leave before it's too late."

I took a step closer to him. "You aren't your father." I tilted my head slightly and exposed my neck to him. "I'm calling your bluff, Hawke."

"You shouldn't."

I stared down at him without blinking. "You protect people, not hurt them. And you're the greatest man I've ever known. You wouldn't hurt anyone. And you certainly wouldn't murder anyone."

"Yeah?" He reached behind his back and withdrew a pistol. "You really think so?" He waved it in front of me.

The sight of the gun made my heart race but I still wasn't scared. "Then shoot me."

He clenched his jaw and stared me down, irritated he wasn't getting his way.

I grabbed the barrel and pointed it at my chest. "That's the only way you're getting rid of me."

Like I suspected, he quickly pulled the gun away and stepped back, terrified that it was ever pointed at me to begin with. He shoved it into the back of his jeans. "Please leave." Now his voice came out calm, like he accepted defeat.

"No."

"Then be quiet." He pulled his shirt off and undressed. He put the safety on the gun and set it on the dresser.

I stood there and watched.

"I'm going to sleep. Let yourself out." He got under the covers then turned off the lamp.

Wednesday

I stood there for a few moments before I undressed and got into bed beside him. When my body hit the mattress, he turned over and faced the opposite direction, closing himself off from me all over again. I didn't kill his mother, but he was treating me like I did. "I'm so sorry about your mom, Hawke." I ran my hand up his back.

"Don't touch me."

I pulled my hand away and held it to my chest.

After a long pause, he spoke. "The police think it was an accident. She fell down the stairs and crashed into the dresser. When I corrected them, they didn't believe me. My father is off the hook—just like that."

I held on to every word and tried not to make a sound.

"She lost so much blood she went into cardiac arrest and died."

I closed my eyes as the pain washed over me.

"And that asshole walks free."

It wasn't right.

"So, I'm going to do what the justice system won't. I'll take care of it myself—and stand by and watch him die."

I knew he was upset and heartbroken. No one could blame him for that. But this wasn't the answer. "You have every right to be angry, Hawke. But killing him isn't the answer."

"Yes, it is. But I should have done it a long time ago. She might still be here."

"It's not your fault."

"It is my fault," he said coldly. "I knew this day would come, but I didn't stop it."

138

"You did everything you could—"

"It wasn't enough. I'm putting a bullet in his brain the second he shows his face. I don't care if I go to jail for the rest of my life. It's worth it."

"Hawke, you don't want to carry that on your shoulders for the rest of your life. You aren't a killer."

"Yes, I am."

"It won't change anything. It won't bring her back."

"No. But at least it'll give me a smile." He kept his back to me and never turned over. He kept the entire world between us, making sure I couldn't infect his space.

He was too far gone to be helped. I didn't know what to do. Normally, he looked me in the eye but I couldn't even get him to do that. Of all people, I could always bring him back from the brink of insanity.

But now I had no power at all.

Wednesday

E. L. Todd

CHAPTER FOURTEEN
Getting Away With Murder
Hawke

I slid out of the bed without waking Francesca. She would try to impede my plans, and I didn't have time for that. All I wanted was for her to disappear, to go back to New York and leave me in peace.

I got dressed then shoved the pistol into the back of my jeans. Hopefully, my father had returned to the house by now. He had to make an appearance eventually, especially for the funeral.

He couldn't hide forever.

I knew he was terrified of me. He knew exactly what was coming. After the way I broke his nose and jaw at the hospital, he knew I would do something far worse now.

The fact he took off amused me.

Because he was scared.

I wanted to scare him as much as possible, to give him the greatest dose of anxiety just before I killed him. For my entire life. I had to walk on eggshells around the house,

141

unsure what would set him off. My mom had to do the same, waiting on him hand and foot just to make sure he didn't turn to scotch.

Payback's a bitch, ain't it?

I grabbed my keys and headed to the door.

Francesca blocked the path, standing in her bra and underwear. The sight used to turn me on, but now I didn't feel anything. She was just an obstacle in my way, a problem I wanted to remove. "Hawke, don't do this."

"Get out of the way."

"You're angry right now, as you should be. But this isn't the answer."

"Get out of my way or I'll make you." I stepped closer to her, threatening her with my entire body.

"Then you're going to have to make me because I'm not moving." She stood her ground, hiding all the fear bottled deep inside her.

"You think he deserves to live?" Nothing would piss me off more. My mother didn't deserve to die, and he certainly didn't deserve to live. How was that fair?

"I didn't say that."

"It sounds like it."

"He'll get what's coming to him, Hawke. You don't need to pull the trigger."

"But I deserve to." I should have killed him a long time ago.

"I promise you, you'll get satisfaction the moment you take his life. But every moment after that will bring you nothing but guilt and grief. Your mother wouldn't want you to do this, Hawke."

Those were the only words she said that got to me. My mother wouldn't want me to take his life. She would still protect him out of love if she could, even if she knew he would kill her one day. I didn't call that love. I called that stupid. "I'm doing this no matter what you say. So just move out of the way."

She didn't take a single step. "Right now, you should focus on your grief. Take care of the funeral arrangements. Prepare to say goodbye. Don't waste your time on someone who isn't worth your attention."

When my mind was set, I never changed it. I was going to do this whether she liked it or not. Nothing could rob me of my revenge. I would put this guy in the ground once and for all. "Move."

"No."

"Now."

"No." She crossed her arms over her chest.

"Fine." I kneeled down and threw my body into her legs, forcing her to flip over my shoulder. I held her in the air then turned around and placed her on the bed.

She fought me the entire way. "Hawke, no." She grabbed on to me, wrapping her legs around my waist so I couldn't get away. "Don't do this. I'm not letting you do this."

I twisted from her grasp and held her down with one hand. "Knock it off."

"You knock it off." She kicked me.

143

Wednesday

I pinned both of her hands above her head. "Don't make me hurt you."

"You never would."

"Yes, I would. Don't doubt me on that." I left the bed and headed to the door.

She charged me from behind then jumped on me. "No. I'm not letting you make the biggest mistake of your life."

I headed back to the bed and pulled her off me. "The biggest mistake of my life was letting him live in the first place." I shoved her onto the bed again. "Do I have to tie you up? Because I will."

"If you leave, I'm calling the cops."

That was a bad threat to make. "Well, you better do it fast. Because I don't need much time." I pulled away and darted out of the room before she could grab me again. Nothing was going to stop me from doing this. My pistol was loaded and ready to fire.

Now I just needed a target.

***

When I pulled up to the front of the house, his truck was outside.

It's show time.

I parked right outside and didn't bother hiding my truck. If he was watching, I wanted him to know I was coming for him.

I wanted him to know his time was up.

The side gate was always unlocked so I took that route. I headed around the side of the house until I reached the back. The window was always loose, so I stuck my hand inside and unlocked the back door. Then I grabbed my gun and moved inside.

The living room was exactly the same as the last time I saw it. He probably just stopped by to grab a few things, assuming he would be in and out quick enough for me not to notice him.

I rested my gun by my side and listened to the sounds of the house. The floorboards creaked upstairs from his heavy footsteps. He was in the bedroom, probably gathering some last minute things. He intended to run and I doubted he planned on attending the funeral.

His footsteps were heard across the ceiling until they reached the stairway. Some of the floorboards creaked under his weight as he moved down. When he reached the last stair, he appeared in the entryway, a suitcase in his hand.

He was definitely taking off.

I stood absolutely still, waiting for him to notice me. He was determined to get out as fast as possible so he didn't pay attention to anything around him.

He fished his keys out of his pocket.

"Going somewhere?"

He jumped into the air and dropped his keys on the floor. They fell with a loud thud, echoing inside the small house.

I lifted my gun and waved with it.

He wasn't the scary man I remembered. He immediately recoiled in stark fear, his wide eyes giving him away. He was far more afraid of me than I ever was of him.

Wednesday

Over the past few years, his stomach had grown, extending far past his waistline from all the liquor he consumed over the years. It bulged far out, his pants barely able to fit around his waist. He still had a full head of hair, and his eyes were identical to mine. While we looked similar, I didn't notice those characteristics. I only saw a monster.

He didn't speak. His hand clutched his chest and he breathed hard, like he was about to have a panic attack. He stepped back, like the extra distant would protect him from a flying bullet.

I pointed the gun straight at his head and closed the gap between us. I rested the end of the barrel right between his eyes and gave him a genuine smile. "I've been looking forward to this for a long time."

He trembled underneath me, practically pissing his pants. For a bully, he was the biggest coward I'd ever seen.

I didn't mention Mom because there was no need to. He didn't bother denying it, knowing I would figure it out. He raised both hands in the air and started to plead for his life. "I'm sorry…"

"Did Mom say that before you killed her? Did you give her mercy?"

He continued to shake, unable to stand still.

"I won't grant mercy to someone who doesn't give it." I cocked the gun.

"Please don't." Tears bubbled in his eyes.

I would be lying if I said I didn't enjoy this.

"I…" He flinched slightly then gripped his chest. He took a deep breath but didn't seem to get enough air. Then he fell back on the floor, convulsing as if he was having a seizure.

I lowered the gun.

His eyes remained wide and open, but eventually they became lifeless. His hand still covered his heart, and he started to foam at the mouth.

He was having a heart attack.

I should have called 9-1-1 but I didn't reach for the phone. I stood over him and watched him die, seeing him suffer in his last moments of life. Francesca was right when she said I didn't have to pull the trigger. If I did, I would be a murderer. But to stand by and refuse to help him just made me negligent.

When his body finally stopped moving and his eyes glazed over from death's presence, I knew he was really gone. I kneeled down and examined him, seeing the foam drip from his mouth. I'd fantasized about this moment for so long, but I didn't feel the way I assumed I would. There was no joy or the ecstasy of sweet revenge.

I felt nothing.

***

My mind was in a daze all the way back to my hotel room. I couldn't get the picture of him out of my head, lying there like a worthless excuse for a human being. The sight of the gun made him panic and induced a heart attack.

How pathetic was that?

It was a death worthy of a coward, and was better than taking a bullet right between the eyes. Now that he was gone, I expected to feel free, like a weight had been lifted from my shoulders. But nothing had changed. I was exactly the same man.

My mom was still gone. Nothing would bring her back or give her the life she deserved. If only I did that sooner, Mom would have lived out the rest of her life. The regret was killing me inside.

When I walked into my room, I'd forgotten about Francesca. My mind was in a whirlwind of emotions.

She was sitting on the bed, and she jumped up the moment I walked inside. Instead of looking scared, she seemed relieved I returned. She didn't ask if I killed him. All she did was stare.

"Why are you still here?"

She rose from the bed, her arms across her chest.

Why wouldn't she just leave me alone? "Just go."

"Why are you pushing me away?"

"Because I want to be alone," I snapped. "I already said that."

"I understand you're in pain right now, but let me carry it with you. We're a team, Hawke. Don't carry this by yourself."

"I want to carry it by myself." I tossed the gun on the table then sat in the chair beside it. "I'm sick of listening to you talk. My mom just died and all you care about is yourself. You want me to pay attention to you and kiss the ground you walk on. Get over yourself."

She didn't move from her spot on the floor. "No, not at all. I just don't want you to alienate yourself from everyone because you assume you don't deserve our love

E. L. Todd

and support. How many times do I have to tell you that you aren't your father? There're only so many ways I can say it."

I held my hands together and stared at the floor. "He's dead." I was indifferent to the revelation.

"What? How?"

I looked up at her with narrowed eyes. "What do you mean how?" I went over there with a gun. What did she think happened?

"I know you didn't kill him so what happened?"

How did she know that? Did she follow me? It just pissed me off that she knew me so well. "What makes you so certain I didn't put a bullet in his head?"

"Because I know you, Hawke. You wouldn't do that."

I eyed the gun on the table and felt the suspicion cloud over. I snatched it then opened the barrel.

There were no bullets.

"You took them out when I was sleeping." I should have known she would pull a stunt like this.

"I knew you wouldn't need them."

I threw the gun on the floor. "You have a lot of nerve."

"I was protecting you from yourself."

"If you knew I wasn't going to kill him, why did you take the bullets?" I knew I had her there.

"Accidents happen. What if he grabbed the gun and shot you instead?"

I wanted to scream. "Get the hell out of my room. I'm sick of talking to you and looking at you. Just go."

"I'm not leaving." She sat at the edge of the bed. "You aren't alone in this no matter how much you want to be."

Wednesday

"Then I'll leave." I stood up and headed to the door.

"Hawke, what's your problem?" She stood up and rested her arms by her sides. "It's me. Why aren't you coming to me? Why aren't you letting me comfort you? Why are you pushing me away?" Tears bubbled in her eyes.

"Because we both know I don't deserve it. We both know I'm not good enough for you. We both know that this relationship was doomed to fail from the very beginning. We're from different worlds. I'm a violent man with a temper I can't control. Ten years down the road, you're going to be buried six feet under—because of me." I got in her face, ignoring the tears that started to leak down her cheeks. "Let's stop pretending this is going to last forever. We're done—for good."

CHAPTER FIFTEEN

Heartbreak

Francesca

I met up with Axel and Marie in their room.

"How is he?" Marie immediately asked.

Axel was sitting at the edge of the bed when I walked inside. He jumped up and came right at me. "Did you calm him down?"

I looked at Marie. "He's terrible." Then I turned to Axel. "And no."

Marie deflated like a balloon. "He's taking this really hard."

"I get he's struggling but acting like an asshole isn't okay." Axel was turning into the protective older brother I didn't miss.

"He said we're done." My body was numb from our last conversation. He actually bought a gun to murder his own father. I knew he wouldn't do it but I removed the bullets just in case. I couldn't let him suffer for the rest of his life for something he couldn't take back.

Wednesday

"What?" Marie blurted. "He broke up with you?"

"What the hell?" Axel said. "You can't be serious."

I nodded. "I tried to be there for him, but he didn't want it. The harder I push, the more he lashes out."

Marie came to my side and hugged me. "God, this is a nightmare."

Axel started to pace, his arm folded across his chest. "I'm gonna kick his ass."

"Just leave him alone," I said. "He didn't mean it."

"He didn't?" Marie asked.

"He's just upset." I walked away from her and sat at the edge of the bed. "Anytime his family comes up, he pushes me away. He thinks he's just like his father, which he's not. He gets lost all over again."

"I get that," Axel said. "But he can't just dump you every time things get hard."

I hated to remind him of the past but I had to. "Axel, when Dad shot himself, you were out of your mind. You were angry and bitter for a very long time. To this day, you still aren't the way you used to be. I changed too, and it took me a really long time to find myself again. Then when Hawke left me, I took a turn for the worse and tried to OD on painkillers. When tragedy strikes, we all do things we wish we could take back."

Axel dropped his argument because he knew I was right.

"Right now, we just need to be there for Hawke in whatever way he'll allow us to. We'll go to the funeral and be by his side. When he comes out of his funk, we'll know."

"So, you don't think he meant to end things with you?" Axel asked.

"No, of course not." Hawke would never do that to me. I was the only family he had left. He loved me more than life itself. "He just needs some time to get through this. We all grieve differently. The guy just lost his mother, and even though he hated him, he lost his father too."

"Whoa, what?" Marie asked. "When did his father die?"

"Did Hawke kill him?" Axel asked.

I wouldn't tell either one of them about Hawke's darkest moment. "No. He had a heart attack."

"Oh..." Axel rubbed the back of his head. "That's a lot of emotional garbage to take at once."

"No wonder why he snapped," Marie said.

"So, just let Hawke yell if he needs to yell." Even though Hawke said a lot of unforgivable things, I would let it go because I knew what it was like to lose both parents—at the same time. "Let him do whatever he wants to get through this. It's not about us right now. It's about him."

***

The funeral was held in a big white church near the coast. I went there a few times with Yaya on Easter. Hawke couldn't have picked a better place to have the ceremony.

When we walked into the church, he was already there. He was sitting in the front row next to the aisle. A few other people were scattered around in the rows, but it was a relatively small crowd.

Wednesday

"We'll sit back here." Axel grabbed Marie's hand and took her down a row.

I took a deep breath then walked to the front, hoping Hawke would want me beside him. I bought a black dress at the mall along with some heels because I didn't bring extra clothes with me. When I came to his side, he slowly looked up at me.

The brutality wasn't in his eyes anymore. But there wasn't joy either. He stared at me like I was a random person, someone he didn't know and had no interest in knowing. His indifference was worse than any insult.

"May I join you?" I suspected he would say no, maybe even tell me off.

He slid one seat over, allowing me to have the aisle. He didn't look at me anymore, and not once did he speak.

I sat beside him and crossed my legs. Instead of grabbing his hand like I normally would, I sat still. The locket he gave me hung from my throat, and I hoped seeing it would bring him back to me. He was in a thick fog, lost like a hound abandoned on the side of the road during winter's night.

He held the pamphlet in his hand, and it was crinkled from gripping it so tightly. No one else sat in the row beside him, meaning he was the last family member she had.

"I'm here if you need me." I didn't need to say those words, but he needed to hear them.

He stared straight ahead and watched the casket. It was pristine white with gold trimming. Flowers were displayed on top of the casket. It wasn't an open viewing, probably because she was too beat up to show her face.

Everything was of the greatest elegance. Hawke did everything he could to give her a beautiful funeral.

The pastor approached the podium then began the ceremony.

***

When it was Hawke's turn to speak, he walked up to the podium and pulled his speech out of his pocket. His face was emotionless, like the funeral and his mother's passing didn't bother him in the least. He was numb, unable to feel anything whatsoever. He cleared his throat and stared at his speech.

I suspected he would tell everyone the truth of what happened, that his mom wasn't some clumsy woman that didn't know how to take the stairs one at a time. He would tell the world what really happened, that her life was taken away by an abuser. If that were what he wanted to do, I wouldn't advise him otherwise.

"When I was ten years old, I wanted to dress up as a cone head for Halloween." Hawke looked down at his paper as he spoke. "I wanted to be something different than all the other kids, and I wanted to be funny. But we didn't have a lot of money at the time and my family simply couldn't afford it. My dad told me I had to be something else, preferably something I could make out of cardboard. I was upset I didn't get my way but I understood it was a lost battle. I decided not to go trick-or-treating with my friends at all.

"Little did I know, my mom had been working endlessly to make a cone head costume for me. She had a few friends from her arts and crafts class help her out. Together, they made the perfect cone head costume—and it cost her three bucks. The day she gave it to me, I jumped around and screamed. I couldn't believe she did that for me—and spent so much time trying to make it happen. I didn't care that we didn't have a lot of money. All I cared about was having a mom that was willing to give her son anything—not matter how much time it took."

I covered my lips with my fingers because I felt them quiver. My eyes watered at the story, picturing Hawke as a little boy with his friends. The only time I spoke to his mother was that one instance when she found shelter at his apartment. Now I wish I knew her better—that I could have heard these stories from her.

"That was the kind of mom she was," Hawke continued. "She did everything for me, sometimes packing a chocolate pudding in my sack lunch just to surprise me. While I only know her as my mom, I know she was something different to the rest of you. She was a friend, a relative, and so much more. Now that she's gone, my life feels empty, like there's something missing. But I'll try to remember that her spirit lives on in me. In my heart, I can feel her. And I'll always feel her." He folded up the speech then sighed into the microphone. "Thank you." He left the podium then returned to the seat beside me. His face was still stoic, hiding everything deep inside. There was a war raging inside him, but he kept it buried within.

I sniffed before I grabbed his hand, suddenly feeling empty. I'd never know my future mother-in-law as well as I wished I did. It was a shame to lose the opportunity.

Hawke didn't pull his hand away but he didn't reciprocate either. Cold and distant, he let his fingers lay there. It was like he wasn't holding my hand at all—just letting me hold it for him.

***

They placed her casket into the ground, and everyone took handfuls of dirt and sprinkled it on top as they passed. Quiet prayers were whispered under their breaths before they walked away.

People mingled for a few minutes before they left and headed to the wake at the city center. Marie, Axel, and I waited at the gravesite until everyone else was gone. Hawke was still there, standing alone at the grave. His hands were in his pockets and he stared into the hole, seeing the beautiful white casket covered with pieces of moist dirt.

Axel turned to me. "What do we do?"

"You guys can go. I'm going to stay here until he leaves."

Marie gave me a sad look, clearly wishing she could do something more. "Call us if you need us."

"I will."

They left the gravesite without speaking to Hawke, assuming he didn't want to speak to them anyway.

I slowly walked across the grass, making sure the heels of my shoes didn't puncture the soft ground. Hawke didn't look at me or acknowledge me in any way. It was like I wasn't there at all.

I came to his side but refrained from touching him. All I wanted to do was comfort him, to let him cry on my shoulder and release all his pain. I knew he was dying inside, unable to handle all the loss and regret.

I wished I could say the right thing, something to lift his spirits. But there was nothing, no matter how good, that I could say to change this situation.

"They were going to have my father buried on top of my mother." It was the first time he spoke to me since he screamed at me a few days prior. "I said no. I told them to cremate him and sprinkle his ashes on dog shit."

I didn't flinch at his ferocity because I expected it.

"So, she'll be buried alone."

My silence was my only response.

He grabbed a handful of dirt then tossed it on top of the casket. "I'm sorry, Mother." He turned away and left the gravesite, not waiting for me to walk with him. His hands were in his pockets, and he walked with a straight back despite the baggage he carried.

And I watched him go.

CHAPTER SIXTEEN

Agony

Francesca

A week had come and gone, but I didn't hear a word from Hawke.

We were back in the city, ready to return to our lives like nothing happened. The streets were jammed with traffic, and the bakery was just as packed as it usually was. Everything was exactly the same, only it was different.

I'd never seen Hawke this upset. When he screamed at his mom in front of me, he destroyed all of his furniture until there was nothing left. But that was a different kind of anger.

Now he was absolutely silent.

I had to be patient and wait for him to come to me. Eventually, he'd break out of his haze and need me. He'd open up to me and apologize for shutting me out. And I'd forgive him instantly.

But he still hadn't called.

Wednesday

Axel came by the bakery, something he hardly ever did. He came into my kitchen where I was frosting a cake I didn't care much about. "Have you talked to him?"

All of us were worried about him, particularly Axel. "No."

He leaned against the counter and watched me work the spatula. "You think I should give it a try?"

"You can do whatever you want. But when he's ready, he'll come to us."

He rubbed the side of his face, his black wedding ring visible against his fair skin. "I know everyone deals with grief differently but this is...hard to understand."

"Hawke is complicated."

"I'll say."

"He'll come around. He's dealing with a lot right now."

He sighed like he didn't believe me. "Well, since you know him so well, I guess I'll trust your judgment."

"That's always a good idea."

He didn't make a smartass comment, which was rare. "Are you doing okay?"

I shrugged. "I worry about him every second of the day and I miss him. But other than that, I'm fine."

"I know he said a lot of mean things to you..."

"He didn't mean them." Hawke struggled to control his temper, and as a result, he screamed at people. But that was the worst of it. "Have a little more faith, Axel."

"Honestly, I don't know if I could have the same kind of patience if it were Marie."

"You would." I knew he would.

160

He rose to his full height and put his hands in his pockets. "Well, I'll see you around. You can call me if you need anything."

"I already knew that. But thank you."

It looked like he was going to walk out but he remained rooted to the spot. He stared at me like he wanted something else. Then he moved in and gave me a quick hug. "Love you."

My arm moved over his. "Love you too."

***

Another week went by, and I still didn't hear from Hawke. Not only was I worried, but I was terrified he did something stupid—to himself. I knew I should take my own advice and wait for him to come to me but I was getting antsy. Maybe he was too ashamed to reach out to me. Or maybe it was something else entirely.

I arrived at his door but didn't use my key to get inside. While he gave me permission, I didn't think that was the smartest move at the moment. I knocked and waited for him to answer.

He opened the door a minute later, wearing sweats and a t-shirt like he hadn't gone to work. He stared me down without any expression whatsoever. "Yes?"

His coldness was getting old but I somehow remained vigilant. "I was in the neighborhood and wanted to see how things were going."

"They're fine." He started to shut the door.

"Whoa, hold on." I pushed the door back open and let myself inside. "Hawke, I just want to talk."

161

Wednesday

"About what?" He crossed his arms over his chest. Those beautiful blue eyes used to emit a warmth that surrounded me and kept me warm all night long. Now they were icicles, ready to stab me at a moment's notice. "How my mother was murdered? How not a single person showed up to my father's funeral because they knew he was a dick? How I almost killed him but he had a heart attack instead? Which topic did you have in mind?"

It took all my strength not to put him in his place. "I want to talk about you—and if you're okay. That's all."

He leaned against the kitchen island, and near his feet were three boxes. Everything else in the apartment hadn't moved so he couldn't be leaving. But they were oddly out of place. "I'm fine. Now you can go."

I wanted to slap him across the face. "Hawke, stop shutting me out. It's not getting you anywhere."

He grabbed one of the boxes on the floor and set it on the counter. "I gathered all your things. It might take a few trips but you can have Axel help you."

What did he just say?

My eyes looked at the top of the box, and peeking from the folds was the blanket I made him for Christmas.

And I snapped. "Knock it off. I understand you're going through a hard time right now, but breaking up with me isn't the solution. I'm sick of your attitude, your bullshit, and everything else up to this point. You need to knock it off or I'll have to slap some sense into you." I grabbed the box and threw it on the ground. "Don't you dare insult me like that again."

He watched me, and for the first time, he didn't seem so intimidating. He was almost apologetic.

"I'm giving you a freebie. I'm going to pretend this conversation never happened—for your sake." I stormed out of his apartment and slammed the door so hard it almost snapped off the hinges.

***

Another week went by, and I didn't hear from him.

Now I was starting to get scared.

Really scared.

What if he continued this behavior? What if he didn't snap out of his depression? What if he was lost?

I spent all my time in my apartment because I didn't want to do anything else besides lay in bed. There was no drive or motivation in my body anymore. I didn't go for a run after work like I usually did, and I didn't even cook anymore. All I could do was think about Hawke and hope the worst would pass like a bad storm.

When another week passed and I still didn't hear from him, I stopped eating altogether. The anxiety of not knowing what was going to happen was drowning me. My chest ached because my lungs couldn't breathe. My thoughts were suffocating me.

I couldn't even think.

I needed to hold my ground and refuse to speak to him until he spoke to me first, but I couldn't wait it out any longer. I went to his apartment, determined to set him right once and for all.

Wednesday

When I got to his door. I didn't knock. I used my key to unlock the door, but when the key moved inside the lock, it didn't fit right.

He changed the locks.

What a slap in the face.

I banged on his door and stomped my foot anxiously, needing to see his face so I could get everything out. I was angrier than I could digest. My hands shook from the adrenaline. I could handle a lot, but like everyone else, I had my limit.

Hawke opened the door with the same disinterested look on his face.

"Ugh." I shoved him hard in the chest and forced him back inside his apartment. "You changed the locks?"

"I needed to." He was calm, talking to me like he was bored with the conversation before it even began.

I threw my key on the ground. "Because of me?"

"I told you we were done."

This was unbelievable. One little bump in the road demolished our relationship? We couldn't get through this together? "Hawke, we were stupidly in love just last month and now you're telling me we're over?"

"Yes. We've been over."

"Because...?" I couldn't be patient anymore. The smartass girl inside me came out. "Because a tragedy that has nothing to do with either one of us happened? So, if the stock market crashed, we would have broken up too?"

"You know exactly why. Don't play dumb."

164

"I have to play dumb to be at your level." Insulting him wouldn't help, but I was insane at the moment.

"I'm exactly like him—"

"No. You. Aren't." He sounded like a broken record. "Stop saying that. It's not true."

"But it is. I'm not good enough for you, and I'll never be good enough for you."

"You know what? That's actually true."

His eyes narrowed.

"Because you're treating me like shit right now. You're hurting me when I've done nothing but support you through this difficult time. Now you're breaking my heart when I did nothing to deserve it. You're digging your own grave, Hawke. You're sabotaging our relationship for no reason. You think you don't deserve to be happy, so you purposely make yourself suffer."

He crossed his arms over his chest, still hiding his true self behind his mask. "No, I'm not."

"Hawke, have you ever hit me?"

"Yes."

"That incident two years ago doesn't count."

"Yes, it does."

Tears of frustration burned in my eyes. "You're nothing like either of your parents. You're strong, compassionate, and the most loving person I know. Don't let your hate mask that."

He looked out the floor-to-ceiling windows, the Christmas tree still in the corner even though it was

Wednesday

February. "I shouldn't have gotten involved with you again. I was weak and made a rash decision."

"You mean, you loved me and wanted to be with me. That's rash?"

"I knew nothing had changed. I knew I was still a monster. But I was selfish and I did it anyway."

"Hawke, I wish you understood how ridiculous you sound right now."

He kept staring out the window.

"Hawke." I begged him with just the word.

He wouldn't look at me.

"You're being selfish by acting this way. Knock it off."

"I'm not going to change my mind about this." He turned back to me and glanced at the boxes on the ground. "Take your stuff and go."

This couldn't be happening.

"I made sure everything was in there so you don't have to come back."

I hated this. "Have you slept with anyone since we 'broke up?'" I stared him down and hoped he wouldn't give me the wrong answer. If he did...I wasn't sure what I would do.

"The answer doesn't matter."

"It does to me."

He kept his arms across his chest.

"Hawke, you better answer me."

"No."

The answer washed through me in the form of relief.

"But that doesn't mean anything. Please take your stuff and go."

This was the worst nightmare I've ever had. "You told me you wouldn't hurt me again. You promised me, Hawke." Somehow, I stopped the tears falling from my eyes. This man hurt me again, and now I felt stupid for giving him the opportunity.

He closed his eyes like something finally penetrated that stone exterior. "I know..."

"Then don't do this to us."

"I have to."

"No, you don't."

He covered his face with his palms and took a deep breath. Then he slowly pulled his hands down, grief written all over his features. "Don't make this harder on either one of us."

My hands were starting to shake. "I gave you another chance because you promised me."

Now he wouldn't look at me again.

"You begged me to take you back because you loved me, because we would get it right this time. And now you're leaving me over something that isn't even true?" I steadied my voice and filtered out the sorrow. I refused to give him the satisfaction of stabbing me in the heart all over again. If he was really going to do this to me, then he didn't deserve my sadness. I only allowed the anger to get through. "Hawke, when I walk out that door, that's it. I'm never coming back."

He stared at the ground.

Wednesday

"I don't care what you say or what you do. If you ever want me back, I'll never give you another chance. I will move on with someone else and I will forget about you. This isn't a bluff."

His words came out as a whisper. "And that's exactly what you should do."

He was making me do the one thing I didn't want to do, but I didn't have another choice. I eyed the boxes on the ground, comprised of the stuff I left there over the past year. "I'm not taking any of that. If you're ending this like a coward, then toss it out with the garbage—just like you've done with me."

CHAPTER SEVENTEEN

Moving On

Francesca

Instead of being devastated like last time we broke up, I was oddly numb. He'd been treating me like shit for the past months, so I had more time to process this betrayal than the last time.

Vividly, I remembered exactly what happened with our last break up. He left, and I spun out of control. My grades plummeted and I barely scraped by with a C average. I quit my job at The Grind because I couldn't get myself to go to work. Axel covered my bills because I couldn't support myself. I was a ghost around the house, haunting every corner and every room. There was no life in me anymore. My entire purpose for living had disappeared.

And when his absence became too much, I took Marie's bottle of painkillers and decided to end it then and there.

It was the dumbest thing I've ever done.

Wednesday

I woke up in the hospital to my brother crying. Marie too. Without realizing it, I turned suicidal. It was the darkest time of my life, and I was disappointed in myself for losing everything I worked so hard for. I almost left my brother completely alone in the world.

And I never forgave myself for it.

I couldn't go down that path again. I couldn't let Hawke's departure ruin my life. What kind of person would I be if I let the same guy ruin me twice? I would lose all respect for myself.

I wasn't going to spiral out of control again.

No.

Hawke and I were a fairytale. Somehow, I fell more in love with him when we got back together than when we were together for the first time. Perhaps it was because our relationship lasted much longer. To have that taken away was the most painful thing I've ever known.

But I couldn't let it get to me.

He completely destroyed me last time, and I wasn't going to give him that satisfaction again. No guy could treat me like that and expect me to cry over him.

No fucking way.

It didn't matter what Hawke was going through. His treatment of me was completely unacceptable. I wouldn't make excuses for him—not this time. He obviously wasn't man enough to handle a real woman—someone who gave him everything he could ask for.

This time, I held my head high and kept my back straight. This time, I didn't let the weight strike me down. This time, I would survive without a scar.

***

"What?" Marie couldn't process what I said. "I just...what?"

Axel sat beside her, brooding in silence.

"We're done—for good." Surprisingly, it didn't hurt to say those words. I lost all respect for Hawke after he treated me like that, especially after everything I did for him.

"I just...how can that be possible?" Marie was just as worked up over it as I was. She encouraged Hawke to win me back in the first place. I bet she wished she'd just left it alone now.

"He's not the same person anymore." Losing his mom and watching his dad die permanently changed him. The man I fell in love with wouldn't have let me go for any reason—so I could only assume he was dead. And he wasn't coming back. "Maybe one day we can be friends—probably acquaintances—but we're never getting back together."

"I should kill him." Axel massaged his knuckles like they were already sore just from thinking about it.

"No." That wouldn't solve anything. "He's not worth it, Axel. If anything, it's my fault. I gave him another chance when I shouldn't have. I should have turned my back and kept walking. I shouldn't have broken up with Kyle." I shook my head. "It was all a big mistake."

Axel continued to rub his knuckles. "I can't believe this...a few weeks before he was going to—"

171

Marie elbowed him in the stomach. "Get you a dog."

"A dog?" I asked. "Why?"

"You know, as a pet," Marie said, her voice high-pitched. "It seemed like he was going to take your relationship to the next level."

I didn't want a dog until I had a house first. But that was a conversation Hawke and I never had. "Good thing he didn't. I would be stuck with it."

"I just..." Axel shook his head. "I really can't believe this."

It was hard to wrap my head around it—but I had four weeks to prepare for it. "Axel, I don't want you to stop being friends with him. Please don't do that."

"How can I not? He's a fucking asshole." He stared at me in disbelief.

"Because Hawke is in a dark place and he needs someone there for him—you."

He shook his head like that was never happening.

"Axel, what happened between him and I shouldn't affect you. They are completely different relationships."

"But—"

"It doesn't matter," I said. "Besides, I don't care enough for you to stop talking to him. If you act like everything is normal, then he'll realize he didn't get to me. I'm not taking this break up like last time. I'm too good to put up with that bullshit."

Marie sighed in relief. "Really? You're okay?"

"I'll be fine," I answered. "Don't worry about me."

"Because if you aren't, it's okay." Axel looked at me with concern in his eyes. "We were there. We know what the two of you had. It's okay to be devastated. This break up came out of nowhere and no one could prepare for it. If Marie left me like that...I wouldn't be able to go on."

Marie's eyes softened.

"Axel, I'm really okay." Maybe I wasn't okay right that second but I would be—eventually.

They both remained on the couch, staring at me like they expected me to explode in a raging ball of fire. I didn't blame them for not believing me, not when they'd seen me in the hospital after I got my stomach pumped. They had every right to be doubtful. "Don't worry. You'll see."

Wednesday

CHAPTER EIGHTEEN

Drifting

Francesca

I focused on the shop and the annual Manhattan cake-decorating contest. I won twice in the past two years, and I was eager to compete again. A design came to my mind when I was asleep one night, so I worked on perfecting it when I had downtime at work.

I never thought I would be so grateful for the insanely loud noise of the bakery. The sound of people ordering a dozen cookies for a party, the blenders going on and off, and the constant beep of the cash register was soothing. It distracted me from unwanted thoughts.

I got back into shape and started running again, jogging through Central Park after I got off work. I'd never run in a marathon before but I signed up for my first. It was approaching next month, and I was making great progress.

Staying busy kept the sadness away, and whenever Hawke entered my mind, I wouldn't allow the thought to linger. I quickly changed the subject and thought about something else, usually the shop or my new fitness goals.

Not once did I run into Hawke anywhere. I suspected he would come into the bakery after a few weeks of silence. Eventually, he would wake up and realized the grave mistake he made.

But he never did.

In my heart, I wanted that moment to happen. I wanted him to beg me to take him back just so I could tell him off. But I suspected I wouldn't be strong enough to do that.

It was fun to fantasize about it anyway.

Business was always good, but it reached a new level after The New York Times ran an article about it. Since things were going so well, I decided to get a bigger apartment in a nicer area. I moved to the east side and got a nice view of the bay. It was a farther walk to work, but that didn't matter to me.

Axel and Marie constantly checked on me, making sure I didn't have a slip-up. They both made excuses to come by my apartment and spend time with me even though I knew they'd rather be having dinner alone together. On the weekends, they always asked me to tag along with them, not that I needed their pity. I started going out with friends of my own.

But I never started dating.

As much as I wanted to be ready for that, I wasn't. I promised myself to hold my head high and refused to let Hawke's absence weigh me down, but I couldn't force something that wasn't ready to happen. It wouldn't be fair to any of the guys I dated, to be with someone who was hung up on someone else.

But I knew Hawke was sleeping around.

I didn't need to see him to know it was true. He would go back to what he did before, and as ashamed as I was to admit it, it broke my heart. The idea of him being with anyone but me was excruciating. Those thoughts hurt me the most and I did everything I could not to think about them.

It was hard to believe I was so happy just a few months ago. Hawke gave me a beautiful locket and told me we were forever. We made love by the fire and promised ourselves to one another.

And then it was gone.

Did it really happen?

Was that just a dream?

Was I experiencing nostalgia? Did I believe the past was better than it really was? Were we really in love? Were we really soul mates? If we were, how could he do that to me? Was I just a stupid, hopeless romantic?

Now I questioned everything.

Maybe none of it happened.

None of it was real.

It meant nothing.

Wednesday

CHAPTER NINETEEN

Time Heals All Wounds

Francesca

Six months had come and gone, and for the first time in forever, I was happy.

I didn't have to force myself not to think about Hawke. No longer did I stare at my phone and hope for a text message. Now, I didn't bother watching the store window in the hope he might pass by.

I let it go.

It was unclear if what we had was real. It was impossible to know if it ever meant anything to either one of us. Since it didn't matter. I stopped thinking about it.

I held my head high the entire time, and every day, it got easier. Now I didn't have to remind myself to be strong. I just did it on my own, naturally.

After I got off work, I headed to the bar where I was meeting Marie for a drink. I quickly changed into a sundress with a jean jacket so I wouldn't look like the Pillsbury Doughboy when I walked inside.

Wednesday

She had a table in the corner, and when she waved me over, her wedding ring glittered in the light.

"Hey." I gave her a quick hug before I took the seat across from her. "Dude, the cute bartender better bring me a drink ASAP."

"Actually, the bartender is a chick."

"Oh." I glanced at the bar and spotted the brunette. She had an enormous rack. "Well, she is cute."

Marie laughed then pushed her cosmo toward me. "You can start on mine. I'll order another."

"Sounds like a sweet deal—because you're still paying for this one."

She rolled her eyes then got the bartender's attention. She ordered another cosmo for herself then stared at me, a big smile on her lips.

"What?" I asked. "Had a good day?"

"Not particularly." All her teeth were still showing.

"Then...are you high?" I didn't realize Marie was into that.

"No." She tapped my wrist playfully. "It's just nice to see you happy."

My heart skipped a beat at her words, and my previous joy deflated from my body. "I've been happy for a long time now." There was no need to bring up the past. It seemed like a lifetime ago.

"I know. It just makes me happy." She took the drink from the bartender and took a drink. "I'm sorry I brought it up."

I changed the subject. "How's the magazine?"

"Good. These really hot guys modeled for us the other day. I'm not even in the fashion department but I watched anyway."

"Axel must have been jealous."

"Like I'd ever tell him. He's the most jealous guy I've ever been with."

"He's just in love with you," I reminded her. "Before you came along, he didn't care about stuff like that."

"I know. He's still a girl about it though."

I clanked my glass against hers. "You said it, sister."

We both took a deep drink then slammed our glasses on the table.

"How's the shop?" she asked.

"Great. I've been thinking about it for a while and...I think I might open a second one. Maybe in Brooklyn."

"Oh my god." She slammed both hands on the table. "That's so great, Frankie."

"I know."

"Watch out. You're going to be in Forbes soon."

I rolled my eyes. "Yeah, Elton John, Morgan Freeman, Taylor Swift...and then me."

"Hey, it could happen."

"It's fun to dream about."

Marie took another drink and her eyes moved past my shoulder. Instead of looking back at me, her stare was frozen in place. "You'll never guess who's here."

Hawke. It had to be him. I'd managed not to run into him for this long but my luck was bound to run out. "Please

181

tell me it's a pony." Those were so damn cute. "A white, fluffy one."

"Actually, it's Kyle."

"Oh..." I hadn't seen him in forever. We stopped talking after we ran into each other in a bar about a year ago. "Cool."

"He's coming this way." She set her drink down and started to fidget. "Act cool."

"I am cool. You're the one acting like a weirdo."

Kyle reached our table, looking almost the same as before. His brown hair was a little shorter than it used to be, and his body was a little thicker. It seemed like he hit the weights a little harder this past year. He wore a gray t-shirt that showed his nice arms, and black ink marked one of them.

He didn't have that before.

"Long time, no see." He gave me a genuine smile, like seeing my face brought him nothing but joy. His entire face lit up like the Christmas day parade. "Wow, your hair is crazy long."

I felt it in my fingertips. "I know. I've been too busy to get it cut."

He turned to Marie. "You look beautiful as ever. Still with Axel?"

"Yes." She smiled and touched her ring.

He snapped his fingers in disappointment. "Darn." He turned back to me, the same glow in his eyes. "It's just as well. I've got a pretty amazing girlfriend. She runs a yoga studio in Brooklyn."

He had a girlfriend? I knew I shouldn't be surprised. Kyle was a good-looking guy and would find someone eventually. I was happy for him. He deserved to be with someone who appreciated him. "That's awesome. Good for you."

"Thanks," he said. "I'm guessing you and Hawke are married by now?" He chuckled and glanced at my left ring finger.

Marie tensed at his assumption.

I took the lead on this one. "Actually, we broke up. It happened a long time ago."

"Oh..." Kyle clearly didn't know how to take that information. "Uh, I'm sorry."

"It's okay. Like I said, it happened a long time ago. I guess it wasn't meant to be." I couldn't believe how effortlessly I talked about Hawke. It made me happy but also sad at the same time.

Kyle rubbed the back of his neck.

Marie watched him then looked at me, her eyebrow raised.

Kyle drummed his fingers on the table.

What did I say?

"So...you're single?" he asked. "Like, totally available and ready to jump back into the dating world?"

I shrugged. "I guess." Why did he care if he had a girlfriend? He seemed happy with her.

"Well, I have a confession to make," he said. "I don't have a girlfriend. I made that up."

Marie beamed like the morning sun.

Wednesday

"Why would you make that up?" Kyle was always a little quirky but he never made stuff up.

"I just wanted to save face, you know?" He put his hands in his pockets. "I assumed you were happy with Hawke and I guess...I didn't want you to know I still hadn't found someone."

Marie couldn't stop smiling. "I just remembered I have a hair appointment..." She grabbed her purse and slid out of the booth.

"No, you don't." I was calling her out on her shit this time.

"Man, I'm late." Marie kicked it into gear and practically ran out of the bar.

I tried not to be embarrassed that Marie practically pushed me into Kyle's lap.

Kyle eyed the empty seat across from me. "May I join you?"

"Please do. Otherwise, I'm just drinking alone."

He sat down and faced me, his blue eyes beautiful like always. "So, what's been going on with you for the past year?"

"Nothing much." Now that I was face-to-face with him, I was oddly nervous. "I ran my first marathon a few months ago."

"Congratulations. That's awesome."

"And I'm thinking about opening another bakery."

"That's even more awesome. Are you going to call it The Donut Guy?"

I raised an eyebrow. "Why would I call it that?"

"Well, I'm a guy. And I like donuts."

I laughed at the stupid look on his face.

"Hey, I think it's a great idea. It'll attract a whole new demographic."

"Yeah," I said. "Cops."

"And boom. You have yourself a successful business."

I laughed before I took another drink. "Thanks for the suggestion."

"No problem."

I finished my glass and set it on the table.

He eyed it for a few seconds before he looked at me. "Francesca, can I buy you another?"

I held my breath for a moment as I considered the offer, unsure if I wanted to go down this road again. But when I looked into those inviting eyes and warm smile, I knew what my answer was. "Please."

***

"Where do you live now?" Kyle walked beside me down the sidewalk.

"Just a few blocks from the park."

"Ooh…someone upgraded."

I smiled. "I really like it. It's much bigger than my old place. I even have an office now."

"Swanky."

"How's your practice?"

"Same," he answered. "There's nothing too interesting about it."

"I think it's interesting."

"Yeah?" he asked. "Because of all the power, huh?"

Wednesday

"No. I think law is interesting. If I didn't become a baker, I might have considered becoming a lawyer."

He nodded in approval. "I can totally see that. You would be a sexy lawyer—all work and no bullshit."

"Well, thanks."

We entered my building then took the elevator to the top floor.

"Your other place didn't have an elevator," he noted.

"I know. It's so nice." We walked out the open doors then approached my door.

"I can already tell it's nice just by looking at the front door." He stared at the panel surrounding the entrance and the doorbell that glowed in the wall. He leaned against the wall and stared at me, not intending to leave anytime soon.

"Well, thanks for walking me home." I dug my keys out of my purse.

"Sure thing."

I got the door unlocked before I stowed my keys again.

"So...can I ask you out sometime?"

I suspected this was coming. Even though I had all night to think of my answer, I didn't know what to say. "You want to go out with me?"

"Definitely." He stared at me with confidence, his eyes on the prize.

"Even after what I did to you?"

"You didn't do anything, Frankie. You told me what we were from the beginning. I was the one who took it too far."

"Even so..."

"How about this?" He took a step closer to me. "No thinking. Just doing. Have dinner with me tomorrow night. We'll get Italian then some ice cream. It'll be super romantic."

"Super romantic?" I couldn't help but smile at his choice of words.

"Oh yeah." He wiggled his eyebrows just the way he used to, and the memory made my body relax. "We'll have a great time. Maybe we'll have some really good sex afterward." He winked.

"You're being a bit presumptuous, don't you think?" It was hard to say it seriously when I kept smiling.

"I said maybe. You'll have to control yourself if you want to remain PG."

I smacked him playfully on the arm. "You're still full of yourself, huh?"

"Some things never change." His arm hooked around my waist naturally, just as it did a million times before. "So?"

I already liked the way he touched me. And I liked the way we flowed together like water. Our conversation took off naturally, and he already made me laugh a few times. "I would love to have dinner and ice cream."

He smiled.

"And I would love some hot sex too."

Wednesday

CHAPTER TWENTY

Broken

Hawke

My life was complete shit.

It passed slowly, like a bad dream that just wouldn't end. I prayed for the next thing to look forward to—the sweet release of death.

My company was doing better than ever, and I just hired five more guys for the office. My father was gone and I didn't have to deal with his shit anymore. And now that my mother had passed, I didn't have to worry about her dying anymore—because it already happened.

I was angry all the time, at nothing in particular. Weeks passed but that ferocity never diminished. Francesca came into my mind every day, and when I remembered the way I treated her, I hated myself more.

Why don't I just kill myself and be done with it?

Axel met me at our usual bar after work. He was still in his suit just as I was. We never spoke of Francesca or what happened between us. His resentment was still clear in his look sometimes, like he'd never truly forgive me for leaving her a second time.

I didn't blame him.

"How's the money life?" he asked as he slid into the booth.

Meaningless. "Good. What about you?"

He waved down the waitress and ordered a beer. "I like my job and everything but I hate having a boss. They suck."

"They do." I was pretty terrible.

"What are you doing this weekend?"

Something I'd been dreading for a long time. "I have to head back to South Carolina...gather my mom's things and figure out what to do with them." I'd been putting it off as long as possible. I didn't want to be in that house with her ghost. I didn't want to look at the closet I'd been locked up in. The bat that broke my ribs in eighth grade was probably still tucked under the bed.

"Oh..." He fingered the handle of his glass.

"I've put it off too long. It needs to get done."

"Well, if you need any help, let me know."

I appreciated the offer but couldn't subject anyone to that torture. The only person who would offer because they genuinely wanted to be there was Francesca—but I couldn't ask her for anything.

Despite my constant state of ferocity, the softer side of me slowly began to emerge. I thought about Francesca every night before I went to sleep, wondering what she was doing and if she was sleeping alone. Her scent was all over my apartment, even after all this time later. I thought I did the right thing when I let her go, but now I started to question everything.

I assumed I would go back to my old ways once we were done, but I hadn't. I hadn't slept with anyone or even made the attempt. Women made passes at me the second I was available and plenty of offers were on the table.

But I couldn't do it.

The past six months had been nothing but lonely. I spent most of my time alone, and when I was in my apartment, all I did was sulk. I blamed my father for robbing me of everything that ever mattered. First, he took my mother. And then he took my innocence. I couldn't be with the one woman who mattered because I would hurt her.

I was a beast.

When she tried to stop me from killing him, I wanted to shove her as hard as I could. When she exposed her neck to me, I wanted to break it. The violent tendencies overtook me, and it was a miracle I didn't give in to the weakness.

If we were still together, she'd probably be dead by now.

***

I didn't want to pack up my mom's things alone. I was a grown man that was invincible to everything, but I was still intimidated by the four walls I used to be surrounded by. There was one person who could battle the front with me because she wasn't scared of anything.

But I kicked her out of my life for good.

Wednesday

The last conversation we had in my apartment was brutal. I was out of my mind with rage, and I took it out on her. Desperate to push her away, I did whatever was necessary to get her to leave.

Then she did.

Before I left for South Carolina, I walked to her apartment and stood in front of her door. It was stupid for me to go there but I couldn't help it. My legs automatically took me there, and my heart also had a hand in it.

I stared at the wood and released a deep sigh, knowing how this conversation was going to go. We hadn't seen each other in six months. The second I asked for help, she would turn me down—and she should.

I knocked.

Footsteps sounded on the other side, and then the door opened. A man in his late forties stood there. He had a bushy mustache and black beady eyes. "Whatever you're selling, I'm not buying."

"Francesca doesn't live her, by chance?"

"I don't know who you're talking about. But I just moved in a few months ago."

She moved? I had no idea. "I'm sorry to have bothered you." I darted down the hallway with my head bowed. She moved and I didn't even know about that. How did I miss that?

What else in her life had changed?

CHAPTER TWENTY-ONE

First Date

Francesca

He knocked on the door right at seven.

I checked my hair in the mirror one last time before I opened the door. Marie and I went shopping that afternoon, and I got a black dress that pretty much had no back to it. My ass almost hung out like a damn slut. "Hey."

He looked me up and down then whistled. "Day-yum." Both of his hands were behind his back, and when he pulled them forward, he revealed a single red rose. "For my date."

"Awe, thank you." I took the flower and smelled the petals. The scent of summer washed over me like a warm breeze.

Kyle scanned me up and down, his eyes lingering on my legs. "Please tell me that's one of those backless dresses."

I shrugged. "You'll have to wait and see."

He crossed his fingers. "Please...please...please."

Wednesday

I chuckled then grabbed a cup from the cabinet. After filling it with water, I set it on the table and placed the single rose inside.

"Oh yeah." Kyle came behind me and pressed a kiss directly against the back of my neck.

I took an involuntary breath at the touch.

"You have the sexiest back, Francesca. Look at all that definition." His fingers slowly moved up my spine until he reached the area between my shoulder blades.

"Thanks. I can't see my back so I never knew."

"Well, use my words as a mirror." He was affectionate with me right from the beginning, picking up exactly where we left off. Kyle seemed to realize he crossed the line because he stepped back slightly and cleared his throat. "Ready to go?"

I grabbed my purple clutch. "Yeah."

"Good. I'm starving." His arm circled my waist as we walked out together. The touch didn't feel rushed. In fact, it felt just right.

***

Kyle eyed his menu. "Would you judge me if I ordered two lasagnas?"

"Just for yourself?"

"Yeah."

"Actually, if you ate both of them, I'd be impressed."

He closed the menu and set it on the table. "Then you're about to be entertained."

The waiter came over and took our orders before he moved back into the sea of tables. The restaurant glowed by candlelight, and other patrons spoke quietly to each other at their tables.

"This is the first date I've been on since…yeah." I grabbed a roll and tore off a piece with my fingers.

"Then we'll make it memorable." Kyle had the ability to lift my spirits with a simple smile. His happiness was infectious.

"What have you been up to this past year?"

"Romantically?"

I shrugged. "I meant in general, but sure."

"Well, in my journey to find the right girl to have a meaningful relationship with, I hooked up with a looooot of people. Like, I can't even keep count."

"That's a good thing, right?"

"I guess. But every time I told a girl I was looking to settle down, they jumped my bones. I think I invented the best pick-up line ever."

I took a bite of my bread then laughed. "Share the wealth."

"Nah," he said. "When I said those words, I actually meant them. But if other guys start throwing that line out just to get laid, a lot of hearts are going to break. That's not cool."

"No, it's not. So, you didn't like any of them?" New York was full of so many beautiful women. He really didn't have a connection to a single one?

"They were all great. There's nothing to complain about. Some of them were smart, others interesting, and I even met one girl who tried out for the Yankees—true story.

But...that thing you need to really feel something was never there. There were sparks here and there, but nothing that led to a bonfire." He took a drink of his wine. "But don't get me wrong, I had a lot of fun sleeping with all of them."

"I'm sure you did," I said with a chuckle.

"My mom still asks about you."

The comment made my stomach tighten.

"She really liked you. Or she's afraid I'll never bring another girl home and I'll die alone."

"I really liked her too." Kyle had a nice family. They were sweet to me the moment I set foot on their soil. "Is she still seeing that guy? Who owned some hotels in the Caribbean?"

"You remember that?" he asked with a smile. "Yeah, they've been together for a while now. She's really happy— so I'm happy."

"That's awesome."

"He treats her right, and that's all I can ask for."

"You think they'll get married?"

"I hope so. I want my mom to have a companion. I know she's in her fifties, but she's really not that old. She's still got a long life ahead of her."

Kyle could have had a much different opinion about the whole thing. He could have been selfish and said he didn't want his mother being with anyone besides his father. But all he wanted was for her to be happy. "Very true."

"And I had 'the talk' with him."

"The talk?"

"You know, the one where I say I'll murder him if he hurts my momma. I think I scared him a bit."

I smiled. "You're such a momma's boy."

"So? I love my mom. What's wrong with that?"

"Nothing. I think it's really cute."

"Hey." He leaned over the table with his arms resting on the tablecloth. "You know what they say, right? Watch the way a man treats his mom, because he'll treat his lady the same way."

"Wise words."

He leaned back and took another drink of his wine. "So, I'm a safe bet."

"Yeah, but I already knew that." I'd already had a relationship with Kyle and knew he was perfect in every way imaginable. He treated me right and made me happy. When I dragged him through the mud with my Hawke drama, he still stood beside me. I wish I'd never gone back to Hawke and broken Kyle's heart. While that relationship was beautiful for a long time, he burned it to the ground. It was all a waste.

Kyle watched me closely, like he was trying to read my thoughts. "Still think about him sometimes?"

His words pulled me back to the conversation. "Sorry."

"It's okay. I understand. I did that a lot when I was on dates—thought about you."

My eyes softened and my heart ached in a painful way.

Kyle tried to cheer me up with a smile. "More wine?"

Wednesday
***

Kyle walked me to the door then gripped both of my hips. He faced me head on, his lips dangerously close to mine. Instead of kissing me like I expected, he brushed his nose against mine. "Did you enjoy our date?"

"Yeah."

"Am I going to get a second one?"

"More than likely."

He chuckled then squeezed me gently. "Playing hard to get?"

"No. Just keeping you on your toes."

His arms wrapped around my torso, caging me in like a wild animal. He brought me to his chest then kissed me with aggressive slowness. He took his time feeling my lips, trying to memorize them. One hand slowly snaked into my hair, feeling the curled strands with his fingertips. He kissed me the way any woman wanted to be kissed, with desperation and a little lust. "Are we still on for some hot sex?"

"I've had you booked since yesterday."

***

Kyle kissed my shoulder as he spooned me from behind. "That was good."

"I liked it too." When he unzipped my dress, Hawke came into my mind. It was difficult not to compare other lovers to him, not when I held him in such high regard. But I had to let that memory of him die—because he was gone forever. Once I pushed him to the back of my mind and locked him away, I focused on Kyle and nothing else.

E. L. Todd

"You aren't going to kick me out, right?"

"No."

"I like this arrangement. I don't feel like a hot piece of ass anymore." He kissed my shoulder again, his soft lips caressing my skin.

I reached behind me and gave his ass a gentle squeeze. "No. You'll always be a hot piece of ass."

He chuckled into my ear. "I can live with that."

I pulled the sheets to my shoulder then got comfortable for bed.

Kyle was still wrapped around me, his chest pressed against my back. His hard muscles tensed with every breath he took. The skin was warm, like an organic heater.

My phone beeped on the nightstand with a text message from Marie.

I hope you aren't reading this because you're too busy getting laid.

I smiled before I set the phone down again.

Kyle pressed his lips to my ear. "Did I ever tell you how much I like her?"

"Everyone likes her."

"Well, I really like her now."

***

I stood at the stove and prepared the eggs and bacon.

Kyle came out of the room in just his briefs, his hard chest looking delectable. His hair was messy from rolling around in my bed, and his eyes still contained the crumbs of sleep. "What smells so good?"

"Breakfast."

Wednesday

"I'm pretty sure that's you." He came up behind me and wrapped his arms around my waist. Then he took an exaggerated sniff. "See? I knew I was right." He gave me a quick kiss on the neck before he poured himself a cup of coffee.

"Wow. I haven't even showered."

"That's why." He wiggled his eyebrows.

I set the hot pans aside then carried the plate of food to the table. We sat together then ate quietly. I didn't work on the weekends even though it was the busiest time of the week. I only went in to decorate cakes, but there wasn't an order for that Sunday.

Kyle devoured his food. "You can do more than bake cookies."

"Thanks." I pulled out my phone and checked my emails.

Kyle kept staring at me from across the table. "Interesting necklace."

My hand immediately went to the locket around my throat. I hadn't taken it off since the day Hawke gave it to me. Every time I tried, I just couldn't do it. Despite the way he hurt me, I still treasured that memory. The past caused me pain but I couldn't forget about it—not when it was so beautiful. "Uh, thanks."

Kyle continued to eye it but didn't say anything else.

When I didn't give him any details, he probably figured it out on his own.

"You have plans for the day?"

"Just laying around in my pajamas. Axel and Marie might come over. They usually stop by on Sundays." Not that I needed their company anymore. I was in a good place.

"Cool. Do you need someone to lay around with?"

"Sure. I feel less lazy when someone does it with me."

"Oh, we won't be lazy." He gave me a dramatic wink.

"Why do you still do that?"

"Because it's cute."

"Not really."

He reached under the table and gave me a quick tickle. "Whatever. You know it's cute."

"Do not." I slapped his hand away.

"The next time we get it on, I'm going to do it. And you're going to come."

"I really doubt it..."

"Then let's find out." He scooped me out of the chair and carried me back to the bedroom.

I kicked my feet in protest but didn't want to go back to the kitchen anyway. Having sex with a hunky guy, even if he did wink in the middle of it, was better than breakfast—hands down.

Wednesday

CHAPTER TWENTY-TWO

Gossip

Francesca

As soon as lunchtime rolled around on Monday, Marie was in the kitchen at The Muffin Girl. "You never texted me back." She wore a designer dress with cute pumps. She worked for a fashion magazine as an editor but she looked as good as all the models. "Which means you were too busy to text me back."

I just pulled a batch of muffins out of the oven. "You caught me."

She took a seat beside the counter and prepared herself for story time. "From the top."

"Isn't your lunch break only an hour?"

"So what? I'll say I got mugged or something."

I removed each muffin with a set of metal tongs. "Kyle and I had a great time. We went out to dinner and got some ice cream—"

"And had some great sex?" She snatched the muffin I just removed and peeled away the wrapper.

Wednesday

"I don't like to kiss and tell but...yeah."

"Yes!" She fist-pumped the air before she took a bite. "Kyle is a great guy."

"He is."

"I'm so glad you guys hit it off."

"He's exactly the same as he used to be, as am I."

"You're going to see him again?"

"I think so."

She picked off pieces of the muffin and shoved them into her mouth. "He's still amazing in bed?"

"Actually, he's even a little better. Learned some new moves."

"Lucky you." She squeezed my forearm affectionately.

Marie was desperate for me to be happy, and now that I was, she was in the clouds. "Personally, I love Kyle. He's handsome, sweet, smart—and he's got a great body."

"I won't tell Axel you said that."

She rolled her eyes. "He's too sensitive about that kind of stuff. If I even glance at a guy, he sticks out his chest and acts like I'm about to upgrade."

"I think it's cute. He's so into you—even though the honeymoon phase is over."

She stared at the muffin in her fingers, a smile on her lips. "Yeah...you're right."

Once the tray was empty, I poured the new batter inside. "What did you guys do last night?"

"You know, boring married stuff."

I knew she downplayed her happiness with Axel. She started doing that the moment Hawke viciously dumped me.

204

"So, you're going to go out with Kyle again, right?"

"Yeah. We had a great time."

"Perfect." She finished the muffin then wiped her fingers clean. "Well, I should get back to work."

"So, you get your free muffin then take off?"

"I mostly filled up on gossip, but yeah." She blew me a kiss then walked out.

***

"You're super in shape." Kyle jogged beside me through the park.

"Thanks. It took me a long time to build up the endurance."

"Fit chick—I like it."

I kept up his pace as we jogged down the trail through the park. When I told him I was going for a jog, he immediately volunteered to join me. "I didn't think you were the running type—just a bodybuilder."

"No. Cardio is important too. I just don't do as much of it."

After we finished the sixth mile, we slowed to a brisk walk.

"When is your next marathon?"

"I don't know. The last one was pretty brutal."

He chuckled. "I'm sure you did great."

"I definitely didn't win—or was even close."

"Well, I'd be surprised if you did. Unless you're training for the Olympics, that would be difficult."

Wednesday

I placed my hands on my hips as I walked, breathing through the distant cramp in my side. "I used to hate running but now I actually like it."

"What changed?" He wasn't as out of breath as I was.

"I don't know. I guess I just needed some fresh air." Or a distraction so I wouldn't think about the way Hawke broke my heart. Keeping myself busy was the best way to forget about him. With every passing month, it got easier and easier. I didn't think about it at all anymore.

"You want to go to a karaoke bar tonight?"

"What?" I asked with a laugh.

"Yeah, we'll sing some stupid love songs together. It'll be fun."

"You'll have to get me crazy drunk if you want that to happen."

He nudged me in the side. "Deal."

CHAPTER TWENTY-THREE

Haunted

Hawke

I never went to my mother's house as I planned. For some reason, Francesca's relocation jolted me. She changed apartments, and I didn't even know about it. While I hid away and licked my wounds, things had changed. This entire time I thought she was accessible, living her life in the same way.

But she moved.

I still couldn't figure out why it bothered me so much.

Was she supposed to tell me? Did I expect her to?

I had no right to expect anything from her.

I had a particularly good week at work—in terms of revenue. I invested a lot of money into a new bioengineering company, and almost overnight, I quadrupled my clients' money. When they made a gain, I made a gain. Plus, I had some of my own money in there as well.

But that didn't mean much to me.

Wednesday

Tony came into my office at the end of the day. "We're going out to celebrate. You coming?"

I didn't see myself as their boss—per se. I was more of a delegator. If I didn't go out with them, I'd just be sitting at home alone. Like always, I would stare at my window and watch the lights of the city come alive as the sun set. My thoughts would mull over things I couldn't change. My mind would go insane if I didn't focus on something else. "Sure."

***

"A karaoke bar?" I asked in surprise. This wasn't their usual scene. They preferred quiet places where they could drink a scotch and scope out the talent.

"Yeah," Tony said. "This is the place."

"Were you planning on singing?" I asked, amused.

"Hell no," he said. "But the chicks get really drunk just so they can sing on stage. After they make that mistake, they look for another."

"Sounds like you've thought this through."

"Definitely."

We walked inside and headed to a large table in the corner. There was already a couple on stage singing a love duet. They were in my peripheral. When we got to the table, I ordered a beer, deciding to start light.

"I got you, babe." The guy and the girl sang together, their voices in harmony. They didn't sound like professionals but it seemed like they were having fun. The girl laughed into the microphone and kept singing.

That laugh was familiar.

I turned to the stage in curiosity. My eyes weren't ready for what I saw. Francesca held the microphone with both hands and swayed side-to-side with the music. She was looking at her singing partner.

Kyle.

One of the guys said something to me but I couldn't make out his words. Everything blurred together. My vision became distorted and my heart started to ache. The music kept playing in the background, sounding like Satan's song. Heat scorched through my body, making my temperature rise to a painful level.

"I've got you, babe."

Their voices kept playing over the speakers. Kyle watched Francesca with affection in his eyes, loving her with just a simple look.

"I've got you, babe."

Please be a nightmare.

Can I wake up now?

Pain. Agony. Rage.

The song ended—thankfully. And incoherent voices became the background noise.

Kyle grabbed Francesca and did something that made me want to hurl. He dipped her dramatically then kissed her, making the crowd clap and whistle. He pulled her back up and gave her a smile.

Her cheeks were red in embarrassment but she smiled like she enjoyed it.

She smiled.

Wednesday

They hopped off the stage and returned to their table. Sitting with them were Axel and Marie, and they both seemed to be having a good time. Kyle put his arm over the back of her chair then took a drink of his beer. Axel said something that made everyone laugh.

And I died inside.

CHAPTER TWENTY-FOUR

New Beginnings

Francesca

Kyle lay beside me in bed, naked and wrapped up in his sheets. We stayed at his place because it was much fancier than my upgraded apartment. It was big enough for a family and sleek enough for a wealthy man like himself.

"Sleep with me." He wrapped one arm around my waist while he looked me in the eye.

I had to work early in the morning but I didn't want to leave either. "I don't know if I should. I wake up at five."

"That's fine with me."

"When the alarm goes off, it'll wake you up."

"I don't care. I'll fall back asleep after you leave."

"You're sure?"

"Absolutely." He pressed his face into my chest and kissed the valley between my breasts.

"Then I'll stay."

"Good." He pulled away and rested his face close to mine, his eyes still open. After several minutes of silence, he spoke. "There's something I have to ask you. And just know there isn't a wrong answer."

I already knew what it was. "Okay."

"What happened with Hawke? You said he was your soul mate and everything and then...you just break up. That sounds a little crazy to me. How do two people who love each other the way you did just call it quits?"

That wasn't an easy question to answer. "It's complicated..."

"I'm prepared."

I hadn't talked about it in so long that it felt strange to bring it up now. I was picking at an old wound that finally scabbed over. "Hawke has always had a problem controlling his anger. He had a rough childhood and could never really cope with it."

"He hit you?" His eyes immediately smoldered in rage, and his muscles tensed in preparation to take off and hunt him down.

"No. Never."

He calmed down again.

"He had an alcoholic father that beat up both him and his mother. He left the house the moment he turned eighteen but his mother refused to come with him. Years went by, and she would call him every time things got bad. He would protect her, but every time he tried to take her away, she refused to leave. No matter what Hawke's father did to her, she always forgave him.

"Years went by and we met. I fell in love with him immediately but he kept me at a distance. After dancing around for months, he finally told me why we couldn't be together, because he was afraid he was just like his father, violent, scary, and abusive. Of course, he was none of those things.

"We fell in love anyway and we were happy together. But when his father put his mother in the hospital, Hawke flipped out. He left me because he feared he would do the same thing to me—nearly kill me."

Kyle hung on to every word without interrupting me.

"We got back together, as you know. We were happy together for nearly a year. But then his mother died."

Sadness filled his eyes. "Was it his dad?"

I nodded. "When that happened, Hawke was never the same. He fell off the ledge and was engulfed in darkness. He pushed me away and refused to let me in. He erected steel walls around himself, completely closed off. He said a lot of mean things to me. Then he left me without a backward glance."

"Shit..."

"That was six months ago."

"I'm sorry." Despite his feelings for me, he seemed sincere.

"I told him I wouldn't put up with it. If he really walked away from me, I would never take him back—no matter what. He was in a lot of pain but that didn't mean he could throw me around like a toy. But my threats didn't mean anything to him. He still walked out on me."

"Idiot."

I rested my arm on his. "And that's the story."

Wednesday

"So, you guys are really done?"

I nodded.

"If he wanted you back, you wouldn't give him another chance?" He was looking for reassurance that he wasn't going to get trampled on again.

"No."

"So...I have a real chance this time?" His thumb caressed the skin over my ribs, his excitement boiling.

"Yes."

He breathed a sigh of relief, like every worry he ever carried disappeared.

"But...you need to know something."

His thumb stopped moving.

"I can't picture myself ever loving someone the way I loved him, not because we're soul mates or because I'm still in love with him. I just don't think it's possible for me to have two loves like that. If this goes somewhere, maybe one day I'll love you, but it'll never be in that hopelessly romantic way. It'll always be in a duller form, almost a friendly way. I don't want you to get your hopes up and expect something grand and beautiful. If that's not enough for you, I completely understand."

His hand grazed my back then moved into my hair. Instead of being hurt by my words, his eyes shined with greater intensity. He seemed encouraged rather than dismayed. He even seemed hopeful. "Love is love, Francesca. And I know whatever we'll have will be grand and beautiful."

***

214

Kyle walked into The Muffin Girl the second I got off work. "What a coincidence. I was just about to pick up a muffin on my way home."

"On your way home?" I asked. "From where, exactly?" He was wearing jeans and a t-shirt so he obviously didn't work today. "And you clearly didn't just go to the gym." I smiled because I had him cornered.

"For your information, I just had a consultation with a client—freelance stuff."

"Uh-huh."

He tried not to smile. His lips tensed in odds ways, like an unstoppable laugh was about to emerge.

I continued to glare at him.

Finally, he cracked. "Fine, whatever. I didn't come here for the muffins—but the muffin girl."

It would be difficult to hear any man call me that in an affectionate way—not when Hawke was the original person who bestowed it upon me. "At least you admit it."

"Can't a guy just stop by to see his girlfriend?"

"Girlfriend?" I shouldered my purse and closed the gap between us. We stood next to one of the empty tables while the customers remained in line.

He rubbed the back of his neck. "Sorry, I just assumed..."

I wasn't going to hold back anymore. Kyle was a great guy, and I was happy with him before Hawke intervened. Maybe we wouldn't have a fairytale love story but I didn't believe in those anymore. I wasn't even sure if Hawke and I had something worthwhile. Maybe we were never soul mates. It was just a stupid dream for a stupid romantic. "It has a nice ring to it."

He slowly lowered his hand, his charming smile returning. "Yeah?"

"Yeah."

"Awesome. Would my girlfriend like to go for a bite?"

"I have been craving Taco Bell…"

He chuckled. "You're the coolest girlfriend ever." He wrapped his arm around my waist and walked me out.

"Because I like Taco Bell?" I didn't realize that was a good quality.

He kissed me on the cheek. "It's one reason—of many."

***

We lay together on the couch and watched TV. His chest was a perfect cuddling spot. It was a little hard but it was also warm. His hand ran down my naked back and gently massaged the small muscles that flanked my spine.

We were watching *Tangled*, my favorite Disney movie.

"I like the horse," he said. "He's proud—like a soldier."

"I like the chameleon."

He rolled his eyes. "Everyone likes the chameleon."

"He's cute."

He stopped staring at the TV and looked down at me instead.

"What?" My eyes were on the screen but I could feel his stare.

"I hate to bring this up again but...does what happened with Hawke mean you don't want kids and a family?"

I suspected Hawke would haunt my new relationships, but I didn't expect it to happen through my lovers. "I never said that."

"So, you do? You want a husband and kids someday?"

"Absolutely."

"But you said you would never love someone."

"I never said I wouldn't love someone." My feelings were impossible to explain to anyone because they didn't make any sense. "I have the capacity to love. I already love lots of people. I just meant I wouldn't have that Romeo-Juliet thing going on. Having a family is something I really want. I want to help my kids with their bake-off sales, and sports, and homework. I want to be a mom, to love someone special with my whole heart. And I want a husband to share that experience with, a best friend that makes me enjoy life."

"Can you picture me as your husband?"

"I don't know...it's a little soon for that."

"But it's a possibility? You aren't reserving that spot for Hawke?"

"I told you I'm never getting back together with him." I moved off his chest because the conversation became too serious to enjoy the movie.

"I know what you said. But I don't understand why. I agree his reaction to his mother's death wasn't right but...I don't see why you can't forgive him. How is this any different than what he did the first time?"

Wednesday

Just when I thought this was over and in the past, it came back. "It's different because I'm not letting some guy pick me up whenever he feels like it just to drop me off when things get too complicated. I may love him, but I'm not a pushover. A real man doesn't throw in the towel when things get difficult. I won't let anyone treat me like that. I don't care who it is."

He watched me with an unreadable gaze. "So, it's a matter of pride."

"I wouldn't say that. He promised he wouldn't hurt me again. Then he betrayed that promise the next time there was a bump in the road. I gave him plenty of chances and tried to help him, but all he wanted to do was push me away. Now, I'm looking for the right guy to spend my life with, someone who won't hurt me."

"I won't hurt you."

I felt my heart soften. "I know."

"Do you still think he's your soul mate?"

That was a bitter topic. "I don't know what I believe anymore. When we were together, it was beautiful and perfect. But how great could it have been if he left me like that? I'm starting to think I'm just some stupid girl that doesn't know an ass when she sees one."

"I wouldn't say that."

I pulled the blanket over myself to keep my naked body warm.

"I think you loved someone with everything you had. You gave it your all until there was nothing left. And now that you've seen it through, you're certain he wasn't the right one for you. Maybe he was your soul mate, maybe he wasn't. But now you know he wasn't the person you are going to spend your life with. Now you can move on—for good."

"How can I move on if you keep asking about him?" It was a mean jab but I couldn't help it. I finally stopped thinking about Hawke all the time but Kyle wouldn't let the topic die.

"You're right. I should let it go."

I turned my gaze to the TV.

"I guess I just wanted to make sure he's really gone—that I'm not competing with an unbeatable god. I wanted to make sure it's safe to put my heart on the line. I wanted to know that I had a real chance."

I turned back to him, subdued by his words. "You have nothing to worry about."

He stared into my eyes and searched for my certainty. When he found it, he released a deep sigh. "Then I won't bring it up again."

"Thank you." I crawled back on his chest.

"Can I say one last thing?"

"I guess."

"I'm sorry he's caused you so much pain, but I'm really glad he's an idiot that can't see the diamond right in front of his face. Because I can see it. It's flawless and bright, containing more light than all the stars combined. It's rare and remarkable, endlessly beautiful. I will treasure it and take care of it. Not a day will come when it will tarnish or be forgotten. It will always be kept safe—with me."

Wednesday

CHAPTER TWENTY-FIVE

Regret

Hawke

I was sick to my stomach.

Seeing her with someone else, especially Kyle, was brutal. My heart was cloven clean in two and now it didn't work anymore. It was broken to begin with but now it was massacred into pieces. While I was high on my rampage, I wasn't sure what she was doing.

But I didn't expect her to be with him.

Not only was she with him, but she was happy. They were singing songs together in a karaoke bar, stupid love songs you heard at a convenience store. They acted like a couple, like they'd been together for years.

It was like our relationship never happened.

How long had this been going on? Did she go back to him the second we broke up? I hadn't been with anyone else in six months but she was already back together with her ex?

Would she really do that?

Wednesday

Axel never mentioned it, and I couldn't figure out why. A heads up would have been nice. He never said Francesca's name but I assumed it was because there was nothing to say.

I stayed in my apartment and hardly moved. I didn't hit the gym because I was too depressed. Hours passed while I lay on the couch, staring at the ceiling with all the lights off. Sometimes I could hear Francesca's ghost if I was quiet enough. The memory of her life brought me comfort—but it also brought me pain.

***

Axel and I played basketball after work. We usually played one-on-one unless we found other guys to play with. Running up and down the court with a ball in my hand was a lot better than hitting the treadmill.

The treadmill was boring.

He talked about Marie on and off as we played, his favorite subject to discuss.

"Kids anytime soon?"

"God, no." He dribbled the ball then tucked it into his side. "I'm not ready for that. Right now, I'm just enjoying being married. It's weird to think I actually got married. And it's even weirder to think I actually like being married."

"You found the right person. It's not that strange."

"I don't know if Marie is necessarily the right person." He walked to the bench where his water bottle was. "I don't know if I'm the right person for her. I just know I want her more than anyone else."

I stared at him with new eyes, knowing that was the wisest thing he'd ever said.

He sat down and took a drink. When he noticed my stare, he said, "What?"

"Nothing." I took a seat and rested my arms on my knees.

"I want kids someday. The idea of seeing Marie big and round with my baby would be cute."

I understood the sensation. I'd thought about Francesca in the same way. It was hard to believe we'd been broken up for so long. When I took this emotional journey, I never expected it to last this amount of time. "So, Francesca is with Kyle again?" It was stupid to ask Axel about it but I needed to know. I couldn't ask her myself and pry into her life like that. It was none of my business.

He noticeably tensed beside me, abandoning his water bottle. "What?" The threat in his voice was unmistakable.

"I saw the four of you together at karaoke the other night."

He leaned back against the bench and stared at me.

"How long has that been going on?" I stared across the court, careful not to make eye contact with him.

"Why do you give a damn?" Axel hadn't told me off for what I did to Francesca. I suspected he bottled it inside because Francesca asked him to. I lost one parent then tried to murder the other one. I was in some serious shit at the time.

"Why wouldn't I?"

Wednesday

"Because you dumped her and took off—again."

I rubbed my palms together, knowing what was coming.

"You have a lot of fucking nerve, you know that?"

I kept my voice calm so the argument wouldn't escalate. "I was just asking—that's all."

"Why are you asking? Because you don't want to be with her until someone else wants her? You don't want her, but no one else can have her?" He left the bench and rose to his feet, the ball slowly bouncing away and his bottle abandoned on the chair.

"That's not what I said."

"Well, that's what I'm hearing. You really fucked up Francesca the first time and then you ditched her again a second time. All she was trying to do was be there for you but you wouldn't let that happen. You pushed and pushed until she finally turned her back. In case you didn't notice, my sister isn't the type of girl who puts up with an asshole like you. She's much better than that—much better than you."

***

I was beginning to understand the extent of the damage I'd caused.

I chased away the woman I loved.

I turned my best friend against me.

Obviously, Marie wanted nothing to do with me.

If my plan was to get everyone to hate me, I succeeded.

Six months ago, I wasn't in the right state of mind. When I lost so much so quickly, I fell into a dark abyss I couldn't crawl out of. Francesca claimed I wouldn't have shot my father, but I would have. The guilt weighed my shoulders down dangerously, causing so much strain they could snap at any moment.

The fact I had no one to blame but myself made everything worse.

I shoved her things in boxes and demanded she take them with her. I told her I didn't want her anymore and that I would hurt her without any warning. Unforgivable words left my mouth as I tried to get her to stay away from me.

Now I was here—alone.

Axel didn't provide the information I needed. I wanted to know how serious this relationship was with Kyle. Did she immediately call him the second I was gone? How long had they been sleeping together?

Did she still love me?

I should keep my distance and leave her in peace. After what I did, I didn't even deserve a conversation. And if she really was happy with Kyle, the right thing to do was stay out of it. Maybe he fixed all the broken pieces I shattered. Maybe he gave her the normal, healthy relationship that I could never provide. Maybe he never struggled with his anger.

But I couldn't stop thinking about her. Every memory came back to me, more vivid than the previous one. She and I shared so much together. We created so much beauty in just our embraces. What I had was rare and pure.

Wednesday

Then I threw it away—again.

Sorry wouldn't cut it. Another promise would be meaningless. There weren't any tricks left up my sleeve. All I had was love.

Would that be enough?

***

The only time I could speak to her alone was when she got to The Muffin Girl early in the morning. She opened the store for her employees and got to work in her kitchen. I stood a few feet away and watched the distant rays of the sun peek over the skyscrapers. It was a cold morning, cold enough for dew to form on the leaves of the trees.

She walked up the sidewalk with her Beats on, looking cute as hell. I hadn't seen her in so long and never forgot her face, but I was amazed by her beauty—as always.

Her hair was in a high ponytail, slicked back with experienced hands. She wore skinny jeans with distant flour stains on the front, and her black sweater had the bakery logo on it. She was staring at her phone, probably playing a game to pass the time on her walk.

When she arrived at the store, she inserted her key and got the door open. The alarm went off so she immediately jogged to the panel in the back of the store to disarm it.

I slipped inside and locked the door behind me.

The alarm stopped beeping, and her voice trailed to my ears. She was singing quietly under her breath, something from Shakira. Instead of making my presence known, I just listened, missing the sound of her voice.

Her words suddenly died in her throat, like she realized she wasn't the only person in the shop. She couldn't see me and had no way of knowing I was there, but somehow she knew.

She knew it was me.

She didn't reveal herself from the back of the store. It was dead silent, the kind of silence that makes your skin prickle. The lights were on but it suddenly felt dark. My heart ached in my chest, loving the fact she could still sense me after all this time. We were still in tune just as much as before. There was static in the air, a different hum that only the two of us could hear. We operated at a different frequency than everyone else.

Her footsteps slowly thudded against the checkerboard black and white tile as she came from the back of the shop. She walked slowly, taking her time before she reached me. She dragged it out as long as possible, dreading the forthcoming conversation.

Then she appeared.

Her rose gold beats were around her neck and her phone was stuffed into her front pocket. She stared at me with shielded eyes, hiding every thought deep inside herself. Instead of appearing livid by my unwelcomed entrance, she didn't show any kind of emotion at all.

She kept walking toward me, her eyes trained on me like we were about to draw weapons on each other.

Feeing her look at me, acknowledging that we were in the same room together, gave me the oddest sense of satisfaction. It gave me a high that wouldn't die down. The connection that we both recognized long ago was still there. I could feel it in the thump of my heartbeat. It was loud in every breath I took.

She stopped when we were five feet apart. Her eyes locked on mine and she didn't blink. Her stance wasn't hostile but it was clear she didn't want me there. Even five feet was too close for her.

Without saying a single word, she told me how she felt. Last time, she was indifferent to my presence. But now, she despised me. She loathed me for the way I treated her. There was nothing she wanted more than to never see my face again. My actions were unforgivable, and on that day, when she told me she would never give me another chance, she meant every word.

I kept my breathing controlled despite the blow I just received. She tore me into pieces with just a simple look. Somehow, she told me exactly how she felt with her eyes.

And I never felt worse in my entire life.

I made her look at me this way. I was responsible for destroying the most beautiful thing we'd ever shared. My gaze could hardly hold hers any longer. Shame washed over me, and I knew I didn't deserve her. I had no right to walk into her shop that morning.

Then I looked down. My eyes focused on the chain that hung around her neck. It was made of platinum, the same material of the necklace I got her a lifetime ago. The pendant disappeared under her shirt so I couldn't see it. But I suspected it was the very one.

She took a step closer to me, silently threatening me to walk out and never come back.

I took a step back, yielding to her aggression. It was difficult to stand up like a real man after what I did to her. Instead of being strong for her, I was swallowed by my grief and became...a coward.

Worse than anything else was the disappointment. It was written all over her face. She expected so much more from me, stood by me despite the odds, and gave me faith when no one else did.

The undeniable truth hit me square in the chest. She may be the love of my life, but she would never forgive me. Not now. Not ever. I stared at the floor between us, feeling the distant moisture enter my eyes. I'd lost a lot in my life but losing her was something completely different. She was everything to me. Even when I didn't make that clear, she was.

I kept my head bowed and walked out of the shop— knowing I was no longer welcome.

Wednesday

CHAPTER TWENTY-SIX

Carved

Francesca

I expected Hawke to walk back into my life at some point, but I expected it to come a lot sooner than six months. Without saying a word, I knew why he was there. The look in his eyes told me everything I needed to know.

But I refused to listen to a word of it.

I kicked him out of my life and threatened him to stay away from me. I wasn't his anymore, and I didn't owe him a damn thing. His problems were his own, and I was sick of his emotional games.

He meant nothing to me.

I never told Kyle what happened. After he asked me all those questions about Hawke, I thought it was best to keep it quiet. There was nothing to tell anyway. Hawke and I didn't exchange a single word—with our mouths at least.

Hawke wouldn't return to that shop—not after I ripped into him like that with just my eyes. He backed up and bowed his head, knowing he deserved every look I gave him.

Wednesday

He knew he didn't belong there. And like a dog, he tucked his tail between his legs and bowed out of the game.

I tried to forget the whole thing.

***

Axel sat beside Kyle on the couch. They both had beers in their hands and they were enjoying the basketball game.

"Dude, I love the Knicks." Axel was one of the biggest sports geeks I ever knew.

But Kyle was too. "They're awesome. My firm has season tickets but I always forget to go."

"Say what?" Axel almost spilled his beer. "How can you forget?"

Kyle shrugged. "I've got a lot on my plate."

"You hardly go into the office."

Kyle chuckled. "Well, I have a girlfriend so that takes up most of my time." He gave me a dramatic wink before he turned back to Axel. "I golf a lot—getting pretty good, actually. And I still have to do paperwork and all the boring stuff."

"I wish I had your life."

"No, you don't," Kyle said. "I'm dating your sister, remember?"

"Gross." Axel shook his head. "Good point."

Marie's voice came from the kitchen. "Babe, can you give me a hand?"

Axel set his beer down. "Looks like my wife needs me."

Marie came around the corner and looked at me. "Frankie, can you help with the kabobs? I never know how to skewer them."

I smiled triumphantly then walked with her into the kitchen.

"What the hell?" Axel said to Kyle.

"What a burn," Kyle said. "But I can't blame her. Frankie is a very desirable woman."

"Don't make me break this bottle over your head."

I came to Marie's side and tuned out the guys' conversation. "They're funny, aren't they?"

"They get along really well." She set a bowl of different ingredients aside and we skewered everything on wooden sticks. "Axel loves Kyle."

"He does?" I didn't think Axel loved any of the guys I saw.

"Yeah, he really does." Marie concentrated on her fingers and slid the mushrooms and peppers on the stick. "He said he hopes Kyle is the last boyfriend you'll ever have."

I couldn't believe my ears. "Seriously?"

She nodded, a smile on her lips.

I'd always thought Axel wanted me to be with Hawke. But I guess the brutal way we broke up changed everything. "Well, I'm glad you guys like him."

"He's so perfect for you." Marie snuck a bite of chicken.

"I don't know about that...but he is pretty great."

"He's more than great." She grabbed the tray of completed kabobs then carried them into the living room.

Wednesday

I stayed behind and worked on a new batch of sticks.

Axel walked in a moment later and grabbed a beer from the fridge. "I'll try not to take offense to that babe comment. After all, you're the one in here slaving away."

"It's better than listening to you talk."

Axel stood beside me and twisted the cap off his bottle. "Kyle said he'll take me to a Knicks game next week."

"Cool."

He continued to stand there, lingering in an obnoxious way.

"What?"

"I really like him." He blurted that out of thin air. "I just want you to know that."

"Uh, thanks. But I've never cared about your opinion."

"Yes, you do." He argued with me but not in a smartass way. "I wouldn't mind being his brother-in-law, if it ever came to that."

Now this was getting weird. "Axel, I'm glad you like him, but where is this coming from? Kyle and I have been dating for a month. Why is marriage even being mentioned?"

"You're right." He raised both hands like that was supposed to keep me calm. "I shouldn't have said that. I'm sorry."

My brother never apologized for anything, even when he was wrong. "What's up?"

"What do you mean?" He stood awkwardly, like he was trying to be cool but failing at it.

"Why are you being weird?"

"I'm not."

When I looked into his eyes, I finally figured it out. "Don't worry about Hawke. I'm never going back to him. There's nothing he could ever say or do to change my mind."

"So...does that mean you've spoken to him?"

Not technically. "He came by the shop last week. He was there for two minutes then left. He won't bother me again."

He set his beer down and sighed. "I told him off when he asked about Kyle. Apparently, he saw all of us together at karaoke."

Now I actually felt bad for him. Hawke walked into that bar expecting a regular night only to see Kyle and I exchanging kisses and under-the-table touches. But then that pity disappeared. "He'll get over it."

"He only came to talk to you because he realized you moved on. Frankie, he's an ass—"

"I'm not going back to him, not now or ever. But I really don't want you to change your relationship with him because of it. Hawke was in a really dark place when everything happened. The last thing he needs is to lose his best friend."

"Well, he shouldn't have fucked with my sister." Axel slammed his beer down then walked away.

I stared at the pile of sticks for a moment before I got back to work, forgetting the argument the second it was over.

***

Kyle and I went to his place after dinner.

"Axel and I are going to a game next week."

Wednesday

"He told me." I walked into his bedroom and immediately fished for one of his t-shirts out of his drawer.

"He's actually a pretty cool dude."

"He's alright." I tossed it on the bed then began to undress, ready to get to bed. When my bra came off, Kyle blatantly stared at my tits. "He's a good brother, but he annoys me sometimes."

He stared at me without processing a word I said.

I kept my panties on and pulled his shirt on.

"Why are you putting clothes on? I prefer it when you take them off."

I pulled back the covers and got into bed. "I like to tease you."

"Well, consider yourself successful." He got into bed beside me and immediately pulled me underneath him. "You have one smoking body."

"I have small tits, a tummy, and a flat ass."

"Shut the hell up." He lifted my shirt and kissed my stomach. "Baby, you're perfect."

"You're the one who's perfect." I lay back and turned my neck, giving him full access. I liked it when he kissed me there. His tongue felt good on my skin, making my inner thighs ache in longing.

He sucked my bottom lip slowly before he pulled my underwear off. "I've been thinking about this moment all night."

"Even when you were bonding with my brother?"

He moved his face between my legs. "Every. Second."

***

236

I opened the shop then got to work in the back. Around six, the other workers came in, getting started on the pastries and other goodies we offered during breakfast time. I usually listened to my headphones in the morning. It was my alone time when I worked on my craft, designing beautiful cakes that people stuffed in their bellies.

When I felt the tension slide up my back and rest on my neck, I knew he was there. I couldn't explain it in words. Somehow, I just knew. The air was different. The lighting was different. Music blared in my ears but I could swear I heard him. I pulled them off and tossed them on the counter before I turned around.

He stood in jeans and a hoodie, his brown hair a little longer than it used to be. The same devastated look was on his face. Apparently, my brutal rejection wasn't enough for him.

I didn't think he would be stupid enough to come into this bakery again. When he came by last week, I assumed that was the last interaction we would ever have—no matter how silent it was. "I'm very busy, and I don't have time for people who don't matter. Please go."

He didn't leave.

I knew he wouldn't make it easy. "I told you exactly how I felt last week."

"You didn't say anything."

"I didn't need to." I placed one hand on my hip and glared at him. "And that says a whole lot more."

Hawke stood absolutely still but his eyes showed every ounce of emotion. A war was raging inside him, and it'd been going on for some time. But there was something else there as well—a demented surge of hope. "Muffin—"

"Don't. Ever. Call. Me. That." My temper flared up like a volcano. "You do not get to walk in here and talk to me like I'm yours. I'm not yours, and I never will be again."

He put his hands in his pockets and bowed his head.

"Please give me five minutes."

"No. You had all the time you would ever need. I was there, ready to listen and be whatever you needed me to be. You don't get five minutes of my time. Actually, you don't get any of my time." I grabbed the spatula and returned my attention to the cake.

Hawke didn't move. "I've been miserable—"

"Don't care." I hoped my brutality would shut him down and make him leave. I'd given him too many chances to be the man I knew he was capable of being. I'd cut him too much slack. But I was done with that.

"Francesca, listen to me."

"I don't owe you anything."

"I'm not going to make excuses for my behavior. I'm not going to talk my way out of it. All I want is to apologize to you. I need you to understand that I regret what I did. I want you to know I'm suffering."

The rage disappeared when I heard those words. It didn't matter what he did to me or how much he hurt me. I never wanted him to suffer, to feel any unnecessary pain. A part of me would always love him, and that part couldn't handle his grief.

I tossed the spatula in the bowl and faced him head-on. "I'm listening."

His eyes glowed slightly, showing his appreciation. "I'm sorry for everything. I'm sorry for what I said to you all those months ago. I'm sorry for how I treated you. I'm sorry I ruined that beautiful thing we had. And I'm sorry...for breaking your heart."

"You didn't break my heart, Hawke. I didn't mourn for you like last time. I got over it." I turned back to the binder on the counter with the specifications of the decoration. "The moment I walked out of your apartment, I was done. I'd said my goodbye at the door and moved on. We both know the only reason you're here is because I'm with Kyle now."

"No."

"Yes." I gave him a dark glare.

"I've felt this way for the past six months. Nothing has changed."

I wanted to scream. "Whatever. You went back to your old ways the second I was gone, fucking anything that moved and taking supermodels on vacation. The second I start sleeping with someone new, that's when you get a wakeup call." I shook my head in disapproval. "You're the most selfish man I've ever met."

He bowed his head again, his shoulders slumped. "I haven't been with anyone else."

Now I wanted to stab him with my spatula. "Don't insult me."

"I'm not lying. I've never lied to you and I never will." He held my gaze as he said it, the sincerity in his eyes.

Wednesday

"You expect me to believe you've remained celibate for the past six months?"

"Yes."

"I don't believe you for even a second."

"I jerked off a lot but I was never with anyone. The only person I want is you."

"That makes zero sense." I held my hand up, forming a circle with my forefinger and thumb. "Then why haven't I seen you in half a year?"

"Because I know I'm not good enough for you. I don't deserve you. But I want you anyway." He held his breath as he stared at me. "My life has been a meaningless blur. The only thing that keeps me going is our memories. I know there's still something here, underneath your resentment and hatred."

"You're mistaken." I said goodbye to our future the second I left his apartment. "Kyle is a great guy, he treats me right, and he would never hurt me."

"So, you're going to be with someone just because they're safe?" He came closer to the counter, infecting my personal space. "Because they won't hurt you? Francesca, no matter how much people love each other, they will get hurt. It's just the way it is."

"I'm with Kyle for other reasons too."

"You don't love him so those other reasons don't matter."

I slammed the utensil on the counter. "You have no right to make such an assumption."

"Yes, I do. Because you still love me."

I shook my head and looked away. "Whether I love you or not is irrelevant. You walked out on me when I needed you. You broke your promise to me and broke my heart. I'm not a doormat, Hawke. You can't just come and go as you please. I would rather be with someone who respects me than be with you." I gripped the counter as I remained still, needing something to grab onto.

He was quiet for so long I thought the conversation was over. He remained at my side, breathing quietly. "I wish I could take it back."

"But you can't."

"I know. But I want another chance—one more."

"Look, it didn't work the first time or the second time. It sure as hell isn't going to work the third time." There was nothing he could do or say to change my mind. When I made a decision, I stuck to it. I was sticking to my guns now. Letting him walk back into my life like his behavior was acceptable wasn't an option.

"Francesca—"

"No." I kept my voice steady and fell prey to my rage. "The answer is no. I'll always be here for you if you ever need anything else. That's a commitment that will last my lifetime. If there's anything you ever need, I'm always here. But that's it. So, unless there's something you need, it's time to walk away." I couldn't tell the future but I knew what would happen if I went back to Hawke. He would hurt me the way he had before, over and over. While I would always yearn for that burning love we shared, I needed something tamer. I needed a partner I could rely on, someone who wouldn't crash and burn the second things got tough. There was no way to know what would happen with Kyle down the road, but I was more likely to end up with him than Hawke.

Hawke looked across the kitchen as he worked out his next line. He was trying to find a loophole, something to fix the mess he just made.

Hawke hurt me in the past but I knew he wouldn't lie to me. If he said he wasn't with anyone else since we went our separate ways, I believed him. As ashamed as I was to admit it, the revelation made my heart ring like a distant bell. It hurt to picture him with anyone else, and knowing he'd been alone this entire time broke down a lot of my defenses.

But I stayed strong.

CHAPTER TWENTY-SEVEN

Turmoil

Hawke

I was naïve to think I could sweet-talk her into changing her mind. When I said I wasn't with anyone else while we were apart, I thought that might be enough to make her consider giving me another chance. My hands hadn't touched anyone but her since we got back together the second time. Unfortunately, it wasn't enough.

I really hated Kyle.

I hated the fact he was good to her. He was loyal and appreciated her in a way I failed to. He made her laugh and made her smile. Right before my eyes, he was sweeping her off her feet.

And he might get her for the rest of his life.

If I didn't fix this, I was dooming myself to an early grave. Without her in my life, there really was no point in going on. She was still my soul mate, and she would always be my soul mate.

Wednesday

I waited outside Axel's office until he got off work. He walked out in a gray suit with a satchel over his shoulder. We hadn't spoken since the awkward conversation at the courts a week ago.

"Hey, man." I came to his side and acted like everything was normal.

Axel turned his look on me, and his eyes burned with threat. "What?"

"I just wanted to say hi. I saw you as I was passing."

"Well, hi." He turned on his heel and walked in the opposite direction. "And bye."

I bowed my head in sadness before I caught up to him. "Hold on, talk to me."

"What do you want to talk about?" He kept walking, determined to get away from me.

"I didn't mean to piss you off the other day."

"Well, you did."

"I was just asking a simple question. There's no need to get angry."

He stopped walking and turned on me. "You went to Frankie's shop and cornered her. You tried to get her back when you knew she was seeing someone else."

I was afraid she'd told him that. "I just wanted to talk to her."

"You only want her when someone else is interested. I know you're my friend and everything but you're really just an asshole. My sister and I aren't that close, but she's my family. It's one thing to break up and go your separate ways, but to pick her up and drop her again like she's not a human being is despicable. I'm sorry, but I don't want to see you anymore." He started walking again, determined to get away from me.

I felt like he slugged me in the stomach. "What?"

"You heard me. Stay away from both Frankie and I. We don't want your bullshit anymore."

Was my best friend of five years really walking away? I stopped in my tracks and watched him go, realizing I really did just hit rock bottom.

***

I waited outside her bakery until she arrived. She walked up to the doors and pulled her Beats off her head, giving me a venomous glare. "I'm getting really tired of this."

"You said you would be there for me no matter what I needed. I need your help." I wasn't there for her. But I admit, it was nice to look at her beautiful face. Her complexion was clear as a porcelain doll. She made my body ache in longing, wishing we could lay together in bed and never leave again.

"Help with what?" She unlocked the door and walked inside.

I followed. "Axel."

She gave me a sad look that said she already knew everything. "Hold on." She disarmed the alarm and turned on all the lights. She returned then waved me to follow her back into the kitchen. "I've got stuff to do but I can talk at the same time."

I hated the fact she was so unaffected by my presence, but I suspected it was all just an act. If she was still in sync with my emotions, then we were still connected, even if she tried to deny it.

"Did something else happen with Axel?"

"He told me to stay away from both of you."

She tied her apron around her waist then released a deep sigh.

"I understand why he's mad but...I don't want to lose him too."

"You shouldn't." She grabbed the supplies she needed from the cupboard and set them on the counter. "I'll talk to him."

"I don't want you to talk to him. It's not your problem."

"Then what do you suggest I do?"

"Tell me how to fix this. You understand him better than anyone else."

"Honestly...I don't know." She poured the ingredients into a metallic bowl then stirred them with a large whisk. "He was fine with it until...you brought me up."

"How can I not bring you up? Was I supposed to never mention you again?"

"He's protective of me. You know that."

"I do."

"I think you should give him some space and then try talking to him again."

"I don't know..." The longer I waited, the worse it might be.

"Maybe all three of us can talk together."

E. L. Todd

"In the same room?" Anytime with her was time well spent.

"Yeah. We can have a calm conversation between the three of us. He'll see that you and I are fine being in the same room together. When he realizes everything is okay, he'll chill."

The problem was bigger than that. "He knows I still want you. That's the biggest problem."

"Well, stop wanting me." She said it like it was as simple as turning off a light switch.

"You know that's not possible."

She wiped her dirty hands on the front of her apron. "That's how it's gonna be. If you want to be friends with Axel again, you're going to have to let me go. Axel never wants us to be together again. He made that clear."

"Since when did you start caring about what he wants?" I already had to convince Francesca to give me another chance. How would I manage to accomplish that when her only family wasn't on board?

"I care when he's this upset about it."

It was unrealistic for me to expect her to take me back so easily. I took her love for granted, and now, I realized my deadly mistake. The right thing would be to walk away and let her be happy. But I couldn't do that. "When do you want to do this?"

"You guys can come over to my place. I won't tell Axel you're coming."

"You think that's a good idea?"

She shrugged. "It's the only idea."

Wednesday

Even though she wouldn't take me back, she was giving me more than I deserved. "Why are you helping me?"

"You've been a good friend to Axel. Your friendship shouldn't change because of what happened between us."

"I did hurt you."

"Yes, but I'm a big girl. I can take care of myself. Axel doesn't need to get involved. You two need each other."

Now I hated myself even more. If I hadn't slipped away and lost myself, I'd still have her right now. We would be holding each other instead of talking about her brother. She would ask me to come over after work and keep her warm through the night.

But I pissed that all away.

***

I headed to her new apartment and realized it was near my own. She was just a block away, so close but so far away. Instead of moving to this new place, she should have brought her stuff to mine.

What a dream.

Why did I have to sabotage everything we worked so hard for? The second tragedy struck, I snapped. A haze blurred my vision and I didn't wake up until five months later, the wreckage of my stupidity lingering behind. Francesca was no longer in my life, and to make things worse, I was the one who sent her away. I coped with my emotions and licked my wounds, but it took me too long to recover.

Now she was gone.

E. L. Todd

I knocked on the door and waited for her to answer it. Anytime I saw her, a thrill moved through my body. My heart felt a distant jolt that made me feel alive. Even though she was no longer mine, I couldn't fight the feeling that she was.

She opened the door and her eyes didn't light up like they used to. She was never happy to see me. Now it looked like she greeted a friend, one that she didn't like very much. I'd fall for her act if there wasn't one obvious contradiction staring me right in the face.

The locket.

She still wore it. I couldn't see the pendant under her shirt but I knew it was there. She hadn't taken it off since I gave it to her so long ago. She still carried it directly next to her heart, believing in us even if she wouldn't admit it.

"Right on time. Come in." She invited me inside and shut the door behind me.

Axel stood up when he saw me, his hand almost shattering the beer he was holding. "What the hell, Frankie?"

"Sit down and chill." She grabbed a beer from the fridge and handed it to me.

I took it but had no intention of drinking it. I wasn't in the mood.

Francesca sat on the sofa and crossed her legs. She wore a pink sundress that showed her gorgeous legs. They were tan, like she'd been in the sun a lot lately. Nude wedges were on her feet, highlighting her nice calf muscles. Her hair was done in loose curls, like she had plans after our meeting was over. "We're gathered here just to have a conversation. No fighting."

Axel set his beer down. "You better not be giving this asshole another chance." He pointed at me like I was an object, not a person.

"It's really none of your business if I do or not," she said calmly. "It's my life, and I'll do whatever I want. Stop picking my side over a battle that's not being fought. Despite what happened with Hawke and I, we've learned to carry on. There's absolutely no reason why the two of you can't still be friends. Our break up has nothing to do with your relationship."

Axel massaged his knuckles and shook his head in disappointment.

"Hawke and I are never getting back together." Francesca continued on like those words didn't hurt me. "We loved each other very much in the past, and we'll always love each other in the future. But it's clear he and I can never make it work."

I was drowning in sorrow.

"You mean that?" Axel asked in hope.

"Yes," Francesca said. "We're all adults here, not high school drama queens. Instead of making it into a bigger deal than necessary, let's carry on. Your friendship is too important to throw away."

Since Axel was coming around, I didn't object to anything she said. There was no way I was going to roll over and just give up. What we had was too important to let it slip away. But now wasn't the time for that.

Axel sighed then grabbed his beer. "Okay. I can let it go."

Francesca turned to me, her beautiful green eyes vibrant.

I knew she was telling me to say something to Axel. "I'm sorry I screwed things up with Francesca. I was out of my mind at the time, in a dark place that no one will ever truly understand. I said and did things I wish I could take back. Hurting Francesca is my biggest regret. But I understand the consequences of my actions and take responsibility for them."

Axel watched me in silence.

"Your friendship means a lot to me. Whether I'm with Francesca or not, I need you in my life. I hope you'll forgive me and move on."

Francesca turned to Axel and stared him down.

Axel released another sigh. "Yeah, we can be friends again."

It was a success, but I still felt like I lost something more important. "Thanks."

Francesca snapped her fingers. "Now hug. No arguments."

"Dudes don't hug," Axel said.

"But you guys do." She crossed her arms and waited for it to happen.

Axel stood up first then came to my place near the couch.

I rose to my feet then gave him a quick embrace. "We're cool again?"

He clapped me on the back. "Yeah, we're cool again."

It was still a little awkward but I suspected that would go away in time. The tension still hung in the air like a heavy cloud.

"Well, I've got to run. Marie wants me to pick up some stuff for her at the store."

"Awe," Francesca said. "You're going to buy her tampons. That's adorable."

"Who said anything about tampons?" he demanded.

"Why else would you be going to the store for her?" Francesca asked. "Besides, I knew she's on her period. She snapped at me earlier today."

Axel ground his teeth together in embarrassment. "Well, I'll talk to you later." He walked out quickly so neither one of us could say another word.

Francesca left the couch then slowly sauntered to the door, intending to let me out. "Well, I guess I'll see you around."

Even though I didn't want to leave, I walked with her. A white cardigan clung to the steep curve of her back and the swell of her breasts. It was impossible for me not to check her out, not when she was the definition of perfection. "Thanks for helping me out."

"Of course. You know I'm always here." She opened the door and dismissed me with her eyes. I didn't want to walk across the threshold but I didn't have any other choice.

"See you later."

"Bye." She shut the door and locked it. Then her footsteps echoed as she walked away.

I listened to them until silence replaced the sound. Then I left, returning to my miserable existence without her.

Wednesday

CHAPTER TWENTY-EIGHT

Bluegrass

Francesca

"Since when did you get into bluegrass?" I walked beside Kyle with my hand in his. He usually listened to rock or alternative music, and to know he was interested in a completely different sound was a surprise.

"When I heard this band, I really liked them. They're local."

"When did this happen?"

"A few months ago. I was on a date and they came on the stage."

When he talked about the women before me, it didn't bother me at all. Not once did I feel jealous. I wasn't sure why. Whenever Hawke's old lovers were mentioned, it made me uncomfortable. "Cool."

We walked inside to the loud sounds of a banjo and a washboard. They reminded me of Mumford and Sons with their own twist. We got our drinks from the bar then took a seat at a table.

Wednesday

I nodded my head along with the music. "They're pretty good."

"I told you." He rested his arm around my shoulders and leaned in close to me. "I thought you would like them."

I sipped my drink and moved my hand to his thigh.

"I like it when you touch me."

"I always touch you."

"Yeah...but things like that are different."

"How?"

"It's not sexual. It's affectionate."

I didn't understand the difference.

He pressed a kiss to my hairline before he drank his beer. "Axel and I had a good time at the game the other night."

"Yeah?" I forgot about that. "Good game?"

"It was."

"Axel didn't drive you crazy?"

"No, he's a pretty cool dude. I see the similarities between you."

I stuck out my tongue. "Don't insult me."

He took a long drink of his beer before he set it on the table. "So...you've been talking to Hawke?"

Why did Axel have to throw me under the bus? "I'm sure Axel made it sound worse than it really was."

"He's been showing up to your shop to talk about getting back together." Now he wasn't as affectionate. The warmth was absent from his voice. Despite the calmness of his tone, his irritation shined through. "More than once."

I kept my mouth shut because I was in dangerous territory. The fact I didn't tell him this myself made it seem like I had something to hide—even though I didn't. "The only reason I didn't mention it was because it wasn't worth mentioning. I told him there was never any possibility of us getting back together. Whether he believed me or not isn't my problem."

Kyle stared at my profile, watching every expression that formed on my face. "It doesn't sound like he's given up."

"Again, not my problem."

"Well, it's my problem," he snapped. "I don't want some guy wooing my girlfriend every day."

"It's not wooing. It's him trying to justify his behavior. There's not a single excuse that can redeem his behavior. We all fall on hard times. That doesn't mean we can treat people however we want."

Kyle drank from his beer again, downing nearly half of it. "I don't want you to deal with this anymore."

"He doesn't bother me."

"Well, he bothers me."

"Eventually, he'll get the hint and throw in the towel. You have nothing to be worried about, Kyle. I'm not the cheating type."

"I never said you were." His voice turned gentle, like he realized how aggressive he was being. "I'm not worried about that."

"Then what are you worried about? I said I wouldn't get back together with him so you have nothing to stress about."

Wednesday

He dropped his hand from my shoulders then rested it on the table. His fingers played with the coaster on the table, spinning it across the surface. "With all due respect, you said that last time too."

Now I was eating my own words.

"If you want to be with him again, it's okay. But don't waste my time."

"I'm not wasting your time, Kyle."

He searched for assurance in my gaze before he looked away. "Then why did you arrange for Axel and Hawke to work it out? Why did you care?"

"Because Hawke has been a good friend to my brother. Axel needs that in his life. I don't care about what happened between Hawke and I. Axel should have everything he needs regardless of how it affects me."

His eyes drifted to my chest. "Then why do you still wear that, Francesca?" He knew exactly what it was without ever asking me about it. He just knew—somehow.

My hand automatically flew to my locket, the one Hawke gave to me for Christmas. Since that day, I'd never taken it off. The one time I tried to, I chickened out and stopped. It was such a beautiful gift and it was too difficult for me to part with, even after all this time. "Because I like it."

"What do you like about it?" he asked coldly. "That it has the engraving 'we are forever' on the outside? Or because it has a picture of the two of you on the inside?"

My fingers felt the warm metal as humiliation washed over me. It truly was pathetic that I still wore it, still carried

258

a piece of him with me everywhere I went. But then I realized something. "How did you know that?"

"I have eyes."

"No. How did you know what was inside of it?" Axel wouldn't have told him that.

He looked away and rested both elbows on the table. "Lucky guess."

Lucky guess, my ass. "You looked at it when I was sleeping, didn't you?"

He didn't meet my gaze, the guilt written everywhere.

"I can't believe you would go through my stuff like that. Do you look at my phone too?"

"Don't get mad at me. You shouldn't be wearing that."

"I shouldn't be *what*?" I snapped. "When did you start deciding what I should and should not wear?" The fun evening turned to shit really quickly. Our relationship was perfect until Hawke came up. He always sabotaged our time together without even being present.

Kyle remained silent.

"I asked you a question."

"How would you feel if I wore a ring an old girlfriend gave me?" He turned back to me, his face starting to turn red.

"I wouldn't care."

"Oh really?" He gave me an incredulous look.

"Yes, really. I told you I already had my great love. I've never misled you about that. If you can't handle that, maybe we shouldn't see each other anymore."

"Yeah, maybe we shouldn't."

"Then go."

Wednesday

"I will." He left the seat and threw some money on the table.

I held my ground and didn't show him how hurt I was. I crossed my arms over my chest.

"Uh...is this a bad time?" Out of thin air, Axel appeared. And he wasn't alone.

Hawke was standing beside him, holding a beer in his hand. His eyes were locked to mine and he could read all my emotions even though he just walked into the conversation. He picked up on every little detail, knowing I was dying inside.

I didn't look at him because I didn't want to give anything else away.

"Not at all." Kyle hopped back into the seat and pretended everything was fine. "Arguing about money. You know, what couples do." He didn't look at Hawke, acting like he didn't exist.

"Well, can we join you?" Axel asked. "All the tables are full."

This was a terrible idea, but I didn't see any way around it. If Hawke and Axel were to remain friends, I'd have to deal with him from time to time. I could handle that but I wasn't sure if Kyle could.

Kyle saved face and pretended everything was perfectly fine. His arm returned around my shoulders where it was a moment ago, silently claiming me. He grabbed his beer and took a drink, oddly calm.

It was like nothing ever happened.

E. L. Todd

Axel pivoted his body and watched the band on the stage.

Hawke did the same thing, resting his leg on the opposite knee. His eyes weren't on me but I could feel his envelopment anyway. With just his presence, he was comforting me, calming me after the fight I just had.

I didn't like it. I didn't like the fact he could still communicate with me like that. Wordlessly, we still had conversations.

Axel leaned toward him. "I've always wanted to learn the banjo."

"Really?" Hawke asked. "I can't picture it."

"I think Marie would be into it." He wiggled his eyebrows.

"I'm sure she's happy with the man she's got." Hawke crossed his arms over his chest. "Where is she, anyway?"

"Had to work late." The sigh Axel released showed just how sad he was. "Her office is so lucky."

Kyle gripped my shoulder so tightly it was almost uncomfortable.

I couldn't speak to him, not the way I did with Hawke, so I rested my hand on his thigh.

Immediately, he relaxed at the touch, like that was exactly what he needed.

I sipped my wine then clanked it against his glass, trying to get him to loosen up further. "To good music."

He turned my way and smiled slightly. "To good company."

***

261

Wednesday

Kyle left money in the tab then stood up. "We'll leave after I use the restroom."

"Alright."

He pushed through the crowd just to reach the other side.

"Man, now I have to pee." Axel set his empty glass down then followed Kyle on their difficult journey through the throng of people.

Hawke remained behind, his unwavering stared fixed on me.

I tried to find something else to look at until I realized there was nothing. He was the only person in my line of vision. With a gentle sigh, I turned my gaze in his direction.

He wore a gray t-shirt with dark jeans. His body was thick and hard like it'd always been. Every muscle in his body was sculpted and defined. Sometimes, he reminded me of a gladiator.

He stared at me hard, sharing a million thoughts at once. I could feel his pain from watching me with Kyle. It was heavy and suffocating. He was drowning in misery, not jealousy. He had no right to complain or think less of me, but he still ached. "I hope you weren't fighting because of me."

For the oddest reason, I wanted to laugh. "I know you don't mean that."

"Actually, I do."

"Then that doesn't make any sense."

"I want you to be happy. But I also want you for myself. So yes, it is contradictory."

I eyed the bathroom and hoped one of the guys would come back soon.

"I can tell he's threatened by me."

"He has no reason to be." If Hawke kept popping up everywhere like this, it would be really difficult for me to have a relationship...with anyone. "I told him I would never go back to you."

"But you said that last time, didn't you?"

I clenched my jaw in irritation. My past decisions were haunting my current credibility. Neither Hawke nor Kyle believed a word I said. "This is different."

"No, it's not. We still have that same connection. It's never going to go away."

"The connection was never the problem. You know that."

"I know I had a lot of emotional baggage—"

"That was never the problem either. Leaving was. I refuse to be with a man when he doesn't treat me right—regardless of my feelings."

Hawke remained absolutely still. People still carried on conversations around us, and music played in the background. To anyone watching us, it would seem like we were having a conversation about the weather. "When my world came crashing down, I made a lot of stupid decisions. I've never known that kind of hatred. If my father hadn't had that heart attack, I would have murdered him myself—that's how insane I was."

"Stop making excuses."

"But before that, I was everything you deserved. I made you happy and supported you in every way that mattered. I was faithful to you and always true. What we had was a goddamn fairytale. Even after we broke up, I remained faithful to you. My mind snapped but my heart never stopped beating for you. I walked away from us because I was afraid of what I might do to you. I bought a loaded gun and prepared to murder someone. Imagine what might have happened to you."

My heart softened at his words but I tried to remain strong. "Hawke, you were upset with your father—not me. You would never do anything to me. When will that get through your head?"

He took a deep breath.

"I pissed you off, got in your way, and crawled on your back to get you to stay. Did you raise a hand to me?"

He remained silent.

"Did you?"

"No."

"But you keep punishing me for something that didn't even happen. I always get the bad end of the stick. I'm tired of it."

"I don't blame you."

"Then just drop this. Move on with your life and find someone else. You can have any girl you want."

"There's only one that I want." He held my gaze, oblivious to everyone around us.

"Well, she's taken."

His eyes left mine for the first time and moved to the necklace that hung from my throat. I wasn't wearing a t-shirt or a cardigan to cover it up. The small engraving glowed in the dim lighting, reflecting in his eyes. "Is she?"

Wednesday

CHAPTER TWENTY-NINE

On The Town

Hawke

"Dude, I miss my wife." Axel walked down the strip beside me, his hands in the pockets of his jeans. He was kicking a rock as he went, playing a strange game of soccer.

"What's she up to?"

"One of her coworkers got promoted so she went out to celebrate."

"Why doesn't she just take you along?"

"She says I'm too clingy." He rolled his eyes. "Whatever that means."

He probably shoved his tongue down her throat when she was trying to talk to her boss. I could picture it. "Why don't we swing by? You can say hi." I'd been spending a lot of time with Axel lately. The one person I really wanted to be with was unavailable. She was probably with Kyle right that second, doing something I didn't want to think about.

She wore that locket everywhere she went, so I knew I still had a chance—despite what she said. When that locket came off, I'd be in trouble. Until then, I had a reason to keep trying.

There were two brunettes standing together in skin-tight dresses. They spoke quietly to each other, waiting for someone as they stood outside the piano bar. I glanced their way in the hope one of them was Francesca, but when it wasn't, I looked away.

"That one in purple is checking you out."

"Thanks." There was a wad of gum on the pavement so I maneuvered around it.

"You aren't going for it?" Axel stopped kicking his rock and turned his attention on me.

"Nah." Being with another woman might make Francesca jealous enough to come back to me but it wasn't a risk I was willing to take. I'd gone six months without human touch. If that wasn't a declaration of my love for her, I didn't know what was.

"Excuse me?" A feminine voice with a French accent came to my ears.

We both turned to see the woman in the black dress.

Axel immediately held up his left ring finger. "Sorry, sweetheart. But I'm off the market. I've been married for almost a year now."

"Uh...good to know." She dogged him before she turned to me. "Do you have the time?"

"Sure." I pulled back my sleeve and looked at my watch. "It's nine fifteen."

"Is it also time for you to ask for my number?" She held her hands together in front of her ribs, looking thin and curvy at the same time. Her skin was dark like she laid at the pool on a daily basis. She was beautiful.

But she wasn't Francesca.

"You're a very beautiful woman and I'm flattered, but I'm not available."

"Huh?" Axel whispered.

"Take care." I turned away and kept walking.

Axel came to my side until our shoulders were touching. "What the hell was that? You are available."

"No, I'm not."

"Francesca is dating Kyle. You're free to do whatever you want."

"But I don't want to be with anyone else. She's it."

"Dude, she's got to be a Victoria Secret model or something."

"Probably." She fit the bill.

"So, what the hell are you doing? It was so hot when girls would come on to me."

I found it attractive too.

"Is this a stunt to get Francesca back? Because it's not going to work."

"No, it's not an act. I genuinely don't want to be with someone unless it's her." I stuck my hands in my pockets. "I haven't been with anyone since we broke up—except my hand."

"Say what?" He stopped in his tracks. "Six months without sex?"

"Yeah." It wasn't that hard when you were miserable anyway.

"Does she know this?"

"I told her."

He rubbed his temple like this information was too much to handle.

"If Marie left, would you have sex with anyone else?"

"No, but that's different. I married her."

"Well, I was going to marry Francesca. Remember?"

"Yeah…"

"It's the same thing to me."

Axel shook his head before he began walking again. "I'll never understand the two of you, and I'm not going to bother trying. If you love this woman so much, why did you leave her?"

"I didn't leave her," I said quietly. "That was someone else—a man that I'm not proud of. He's the other version of me, the dark and twisted one who's a product of a bad marriage, alcohol abuse, and violence. He comes back from time to time."

"Won't he just come back again later?"

"No." I'd figure out a way to prevent that from happening again. If I found a solution, Francesca might come back to me. "I'll make sure that doesn't happen."

***

Making an appointment to speak with a shrink was a difficult decision. I was a man of few words, and I said even less when it came to a professional stranger. But I didn't know what else to do.

Dr. Katie Goodwin was nothing like I pictured a shrink to be. She was fairly young, not a day over thirty. She had dark brown hair similar to Francesca's and the vigor of someone still in their prime. Knowing we were close in age made it a little easier. The last thing I wanted was an old, judgmental therapist who thought they'd already seen everything.

Katie rested her notepad on her knee with her legs crossed. She watched me carefully, but not in an intrusive way. There was a balance she maintained, getting close to me but never intimate. "Hawke, what did you want to talk about?"

I would never do something like this unless I absolutely had to. Francesca was the only person I could be open with, but she wasn't around anymore. "I...I have a problem."

"What kind of problem?"

"An anger problem."

"Why do you say that?"

I told her about my childhood and everything that happened up to my mother's funeral. My father was cremated but I wasn't sure what happened after that. I never claimed his remains.

Katie didn't have any kind of reaction. She didn't seem horrified or even remotely surprised. She probably heard people confess to wanting to murder their loved ones on a daily basis.

"I left Francesca because I was so livid, frustrated, and...I don't know. I guess I was afraid I might lash out at her and hurt her." If I ever made a scratch on her smooth skin, I'd throw myself off a building.

271

Wednesday

"Have you hurt someone in the past?"

I kept one ankle resting on the opposite knee. "My father. Whenever he came after my mother, I did what I had to do."

"Other than him?"

I shook my head.

"Then why do you think you might hurt Francesca?"

Given someone's full attention was daunting. "I look just like my father, I have his name, and I have his temper. I'm afraid...I'll turn into him."

"Do you want that to happen?"

I shook my head.

"Then don't let it happen."

"When I get angry...it's hard for me to control it."

"Eliminate the things that make you angry."

She made it sound so simple.

"And if they do happen, clear your mind. Think of something calm and soothing...perhaps this woman."

Francesca was soothing. "I want her back but she won't give me another chance, not that I blame her."

"Is she afraid of you?"

"Not physically. But she thinks I'll walk out on her again."

"Will you?"

I shook my head. "No. I never want to do that again. But she doesn't believe me."

"You think coming here will change her mind?"

"Maybe if I can get to the root of the problem, fix my anger, she would reconsider."

She nodded then made a few notes. "You're doing this for love."

"I guess…"

"Then you have nothing to worry about. You're nothing like your father and never will be. These insecurities stem from your thoughts, not real events. The moment you start to believe in yourself, these episodes should disappear."

"You think?"

"Yes." She made a few more notes. "And perhaps you purposely sabotaged your relationship with Francesca out of guilt. You feel responsible for your mother's death, and to compensate for that, you're punishing yourself. You think you deserve this."

"I guess."

"Hawke, what happened to your mother was tragic but you can't blame yourself for it. You gave her every opportunity to leave but she didn't take it. Instead of getting law enforcement involved, she downplayed the abuse. And when she was taken to the hospital the first time, she still forgave him. All of those things were out of your control."

I stared out the window and watched a man in his office in the neighboring building. He sipped his coffee then returned to typing on the keyboard.

"What else could you have done?"

I slowly turned my head back to her. "Dragged her out."

"Against her will? Wouldn't she have just returned home the moment you were gone? That doesn't sound like a plausible solution."

"I could have called the police anyway."

"So she could deny everything when they showed up on her doorstep?"

"I don't know. I could have done something."

"That's what I'm trying to show you, Hawke. There was nothing you could do. You're carrying a weight on your shoulders that shouldn't be there. Once you let it go, you'll be able to breathe easier."

There was one solution she didn't consider. "I could have killed him first."

Katie didn't show outrage like a normal person should. She remained as calm as ever. "So you could spend the rest of your life in jail?"

"I could have made it look like an accident."

"Then you would be carrying that weight."

"I wouldn't have felt guilty about it."

"Not right away," she said. "But eventually, yes. I have a lot of clients, Hawke. Some of them are emotionally unstable, and some of them are considered dangerous. You fall into neither category. You're upset over what happened, but you aren't a killer. That wasn't an option, and we both know it."

CHAPTER THIRTY

Memories

Francesca

It was nearly noon when Kyle walked inside. "What's the genius working on now?"

"Genius?" No one had ever called me that before.

"Yeah." His arms wrapped around me when he gave me a hard kiss on the mouth. "You know, geek. Same thing."

I wiped my thumb across his lips and smeared frosting everywhere.

"Mmm..." He licked it away then pulled my thumb into his mouth. "That's delicious." He sucked my finger dry before he moved another one inside.

This tongue tickled my skin slightly so I pulled my hand away. "You can eat right out of the bowl."

"I'd rather eat off of you." He wiped a spoonful on my neck then licked it off.

The affection felt nice but I was worried an employee would walk in. "Did you come here for a reason?"

"Do I need to have a reason?"

Wednesday

"No. Just don't slow me down." I turned back to the pan and poured the batter inside.

He came behind me and wrapped his arms around my waist. "Have plans this weekend?"

"No. Just sleeping." Kyle and I never revisited the argument we had the previous week. He dropped it the second Hawke appeared and never brought it up again. He must have realized he would have lost the argument anyway.

"Well, would you like to sleep with me?" He pressed his lips against my ear, his lips brushing the shell as he spoke.

"Always."

"How about we do all this sleeping at my beach house?"

"I forgot about that. You still have it?"

"I do. And I want to make love to you all over it."

"What about on the beach? I've never done that before."

"We can give it a try," he said. "But sand will get everywhere. You've been warned."

"We'll just have to shower afterward."

He snapped his fingers. "I like your thinking. So, let's clean up here and get going."

I chuckled. "I still have to finish the workday."

"You're the boss. You do whatever you want."

"Yes, but I'm not a lazy one like you. I have a lot of stuff that needs to get done."

"So serious all the time." He moved his hand to my ass and rubbed it gently. "I'll pick you up later tonight."

"Okay. Be warned, I pack a lot of crap."

He squeezed my ass then kissed me on the cheek. "Yeah, I remember."

***

Kyle unlocked the door then we walked inside. The place was exactly as I remembered it, sleek and nice. The large back window faced the pool and the ocean, the sand just beyond that. Everything was clean because no one was ever there. "Home sweet home."

"I'm surprised you don't just live here."

"Eh. Gets boring after a while. And it's a lot more fun when I have a hot date." He carried the bags inside and set them in the entryway.

"You bring a lot of girls here?"

"Not a lot. Just the ones who are good in the sack." He winked then turned on all the lights.

If I had a beach house, I'd probably shack up with a ton of guys too. "What should we do first?"

"What do you want to do?"

I peeked through the back window. "I think I want to go skinny dipping in that hot tub…"

"That sounds like a great idea." He stripped down to his briefs then walked outside.

"People might see you."

He looked beyond his backyard to the sand and the water. "What people?"

***

We laid in bed for most of the day. We had a quick breakfast of toast before we got under the covers again. We shared a book together then played a game on his iPhone.

Wednesday

With Kyle, we never really did anything but the time still flew by.

His phone rang and his mother's name appeared on the screen.

He answered it immediately. "Yo, Mom. What's up?"

Her voice could he heard through the speaker. "Hey, sweetheart. What are you up to?"

"Nothing much. Just being lazy like always."

"My son is never lazy."

I had to stop myself from chuckling.

"What are you doing? Going shopping?"

"Rick is off on a business meeting so I'm home today." She sighed at the end of her sentence, like being alone in a mansion was torture.

"I'm staying at the beach house this weekend. Want to have dinner?"

The idea of seeing his mom again gave me anxiety. I doubted she wanted to see me.

"Oh, I would love that." Her voice lit up like a Christmas tree. "I love seeing that handsome face of yours."

"You and everyone else on this planet," he said with a chuckle. "I have a sexy lady with me and I'm going to bring her along."

"Really?" Now she sounded even more excited.

I shook my head vigorously, telling him I wasn't going to dinner.

"Yeah." He shrugged then ignored me.

"Who's this girl?"

"Actually, it's Francesca. I'm sure you remember her."

"Oh...yes, I do."

I couldn't tell what that reaction meant. It wasn't clear if she was revolted by the idea or intrigued. If it were me, I'd be pissed if my son was dating a girl that left him in the past.

"How about that Mediterranean place you like?" he said. "That hummus rocks."

"I think that's a great idea. I look forward to seeing both of you."

"Me too."

"Love you, sweetheart."

"Love you too, Mom." He hung up and tossed the phone on the bed.

"What the hell?" I sat up, pissed I was forced into this dinner.

"What?" he asked innocently.

"You really think it's a good idea to have dinner with your mom?"

"Why not?" he asked. "You don't like her?"

"Of course I do. But do you think we're ready for that?"

"I don't see what the big deal is. My mom has already met you, and I hang out with Axel pretty often."

"Doesn't she hate me?"

"Hate you?" he said the words in an awkward way like he'd never spoken them before. "Not at all. Why would you think that?"

"Because we broke up..."

Wednesday

"I told my mom it didn't work out. I didn't give her any details."

"But, she doesn't dislike me for leaving in the first place?"

"Honestly, I don't know what my mother thinks. I don't really pick her brain about it." He propped himself up on one arm. "But I really doubt she feels that way. Of all people, she knows love can be complicated. If you're the only girl I've ever brought around, then she knows there's something special about you. She trusts my judgment."

I couldn't fight the feeling in my chest, the stress that wrecked my entire body. What if this dinner was a complete nightmare? I agreed to a relaxing trip to the beach, not hanging out with his mom.

Kyle saw the uneasiness in my eyes. "I'm sorry. I should have asked you first."

"It's okay."

"You don't have to come if you don't want to. I'll say you aren't feeling well or something."

"No, you don't need to do that. I'll be there."

"Are you sure?"

I nodded. "Yes." Kyle's mother was important to him, and I witnessed their close relationship the first time I was around them both. I wouldn't put a wedge between them.

"I think we'll have a good time."

"Yeah."

"And if we don't...I'll make it up to you." His lips grazed the valley between my breasts.

"Orgasms are the best way to fix any problem."

"They really are."

***

The moment his mother walked in, she hugged Kyle like she hadn't seen him in forever. "My baby." She squeezed him like a teddy bear. "I missed you."

"I missed you too, Mom."

Did they not see each other much?

"Mom, you remember Francesca?" Kyle turned to me, giving me a look of support.

"Of course. I could never forget." The smile on her face seemed genuine, and there wasn't resentment in her eyes. She pulled me into a hug and held me firmly, like she missed me as much as she missed him. "It's great to see you again."

Kyle mouthed to me behind her back. "Told you."

I narrowed my eyes at him.

She pulled away and looked at my outfit. "Your dress is very cute."

"Thank you."

"Here you go, Mom." Kyle pulled out a chair for her.

"Thank you, dear." She sat down then picked up a menu.

Kyle quickly came to my side and pulled out a chair for me as well.

I held back the smartass comment that came to mind and took a seat.

Kyle sat beside me then rested his hand on my thigh under the table. "So, what's new?"

Wednesday

"Nothing much," she said. "I did some landscaping for the house, new flowers and stuff."

"What kind?" I said.

"Hydrangeas." Her blonde hair was shorter than it was last time I saw her. She seemed thinner as well, even though she was already on the slender side. "Some pink and purple ones. I needed some color since the house is fairly plain."

She thought her mansion was plain?

"Gardening is good," Kyle said. "I've never had a knack for it."

"Your sister was so good at it. Her garden felt like a completely different world."

His sister? Kyle had a sister?

"Yeah," Kyle said. "I remember. Her cucumbers were practically the size of melons. I still think she buried dead bodies back there to fertilize them."

Why did they keep talking about her in past tense?

His mother's eyes trailed off, distant with old memories.

Kyle cleared his throat then opened the menu. "I'm getting a fruity drink tonight. Maybe a mai tai."

"That sounds delicious," his mother said. "I'll have one too."

"Talk about peer pressure," I said. "I guess I'm in."

His mother chuckled. "What have you been up to, Francesca?"

282

"I'm thinking of opening another shop. My business has really grown and now the building isn't big enough to hold the customers."

"A good problem to have," she said. "I remember when Kyle's father opened his law firm. It was a small little office in the back of a deli. It was all he could afford at the time. But over the years, his business grew into the law firm it is now."

"That's amazing," I said. "He must have been a great lawyer."

"He was awesome," Kyle said. "The best lawyer I've ever known. He never lost a case."

"Really?" I asked.

"Not once," Kyle said. "He had a perfect record. That's unheard of."

"Wow."

"Yeah," Kyle said proudly. "He was badass."

"He was a great man," his mother said. "Truly. I'm so grateful I have a son that shares his likeness so much."

Kyle looked away, clearly touched by the compliment.

I wanted to ask about his sister but I decided to do it later. Maybe it was too personal to mention in front of his mom. But then again, Kyle would have told me about her if he wanted me to know. Maybe he wasn't ready to talk about it at all. I'd never got into detail about my parents. Kyle just knew they passed away but he didn't know the specifics.

Kyle looked at the menu I was holding. "Baby, what are you getting?"

Wednesday

He called me baby right in front of his mom but I didn't react. "I don't know. What do you recommend?"

"I always get the chicken kabobs," he said. "Mom gets the vegetable panini."

"Hmm...chicken sounds pretty good."

"You'll like anything you order here," he said. "This place is awesome. Dad and I used to come here all the time."

I closed the menu and set it down. "Then it sounds like I made a good choice."

"You did." He kissed my hairline and squeezed my thigh at the same time. Then he turned his gaze out the window and looked to the sea.

When I looked up, his mother was staring at me. She had a wide smile on her lips, and she looked happier than I'd ever seen her.

***

"Told you. You were being paranoid over nothing." Kyle headed into the bedroom and stripped his clothes off, like he couldn't wait to get back into bed.

"I guess." I grabbed a t-shirt from one of his drawers and changed before I got into bed beside him.

"My mom doesn't dislike people. She just doesn't think that way."

"Everyone thinks that way—whether you want to admit it or not."

"Well, whatever," he said. "We had a great time like I thought we would." He spooned me from behind and wrapped his thick arm around my waist. The bedroom window was cracked so we could hear the ocean waves.

E. L. Todd

The subject of his sister never left my mind. It wasn't like me to be nosey but I was curious as to what happened to her. It was clear she was no longer on this side of the living. "Can I ask you something personal?"

"You can ask whatever you damn well please."

"It's about your sister…"

"Oh…that." He tightened his arm around me. "That's a very sad story. My mom will never get over that."

"What happened…if you don't mind me asking?"

"I don't," he said. "I never mentioned it before because it's hard to swallow."

I prepared myself for the worst.

She was living in the city like I was, getting her Ph.D. in sociology. She was always ambitious from a young age. She was walking home one night when…some guy grabbed her. He raped her and beat her to death." Kyle said it without a single sign of emotion. "My father and I took the case and didn't stop working until the guy was behind bars and Kylee had some justice. This happened five years ago."

My hand moved over his and I squeezed it. Agony like I'd never known washed through me. It was such a tragedy that shouldn't have happened at all. Kyle's entire family had to suffer because of inexplicable violence. "I'm so sorry."

"I know." His lips rested near my ears. "Mom's never recovered from it. Dad was worse. And I…I'll never be the same."

Now I understood why he was strictly interested in sexual assault cases. Those were the only ones that got him into court. When it came to anything else, he didn't seem to care.

"Then Dad passed away and that was even worse on Mom. As a result, she and I became a lot closer. I try to see her as much as I can and make sure she doesn't feel alone. That's why I was so relieved when she started seeing Rick, who's a great guy. She needs a companion to make life enjoyable."

"She's still so sweet..."

"Yeah. There were a few years when she shut down altogether. I try to forget about those."

"I'm so sorry, Kyle." If I lost Axel, I'd be a wreck. He and I spent more time arguing than anything else, but I couldn't picture my life without him. And if he had a violent death, that would only make it worse.

"It's okay. Kylee wouldn't want us to grieve over her death forever. She'd want us to move on and be happy. So, I try to do that as much as possible. Mom follows my lead, but she can only do that so much. The reason she's so excited about you is for grandchildren. I'm her only hope now."

"That's a lot of pressure."

"I'll have them someday—because I want them."

I ran my fingers along his forearms, soothing him the only way I could.

He kissed my neck then pulled up my shirt slightly, exposing my ass in my panties.

No matter what kind of mood Kyle was in, he always had to get some before he went to sleep. I looked over my shoulder and watched him stare down at me. His hand pulled down my panties before he positioned himself up against me. "But tonight I want to practice."

Wednesday

CHAPTER THIRTY-ONE

Back In Time

Hawke

My sessions with the therapist were surprisingly helpful. I bared the complete, honest truth to an objective person, and the feedback I received gave me a surge of hope. If I could fix myself, then Francesca might give me another chance.

Kyle was a serious problem but I didn't know how to remove him. He obviously made Francesca happy and was stupidly in love with her. It was written all over his face anytime he was in her presence.

But she still wore my locket.

She'd never taken it off since I gave it to her, so she can lie to herself and me about her real feelings, but I knew what that really meant. She still hadn't let me go—and she never would.

I had a chance.

Francesca erected her walls and wouldn't let me in, committing to Kyle and completely shutting me out. I knew

Wednesday

she really wanted to make it work with him because he was a safe haven to her. Without any emotional problems, he was a safe bet. He'd give her the life she wanted.

But I was her soul mate.

The only way I could spend time with her was if I asked for help. Otherwise, she would ask me to leave and she'd return to ignoring me. I didn't want to abuse her generosity so I found something I truly needed help with.

I walked into her bakery just before lunchtime and pushed through the crowd of customers. The employees knew exactly who I was from my frequent visits so they never asked any questions as I walked directly into the back of the shop.

She was in her cake kitchen, working on a four-tier cake with zoo animals on top.

I watched her work the frosting with her styling aid, smoothing out the creamy sugar to perfection. Her small hands were perfect for intricate detail. Her eyes were focused on the task at hand, and the love she had for her work was written all over her face.

Francesca dipped the utensil in a cup of water before she moved her focus to a different part of the cake. A spot of frosting was on her right cheek, and a few strands of hair came loose from her ponytail. The sight made me miss her more than ever. If this was a year in the past, she would turn to me with bright eyes and visibly melt at my presence. Her arms would wrap around me and she'd give me a kiss that could floor any man.

But now all I'd get was a stare and an interrogation.

290

I slowly approached her and tried not to startle her. "That's cute."

She flinched slightly when she recognized my voice. She pulled her utensil away from the frosting and looked at me. "This couple went to the zoo on their first date." Her voice contained enough indifference to make me weak.

"Very nice." I put my hands in the pockets of my suit. The last time we spoke, I called her out on the locket around her throat. How could she ever truly belong to Kyle when my claim hung around her neck every day? Even after that conversation, she hadn't taken it off.

She still loved me.

"Is there something I can help you with?" She wiped the frosting off the metal with warm water.

I did my best to ignore her coldness. "I was hoping we could talk when you have a chance."

The irritated sigh she released was loud enough for the entire bakery to hear. "I'm tired of talking, Hawke. I just want silence from now on. Unless you have something important to say, something that has nothing to do with us, then just don't."

"I do have something important to say. And no, it doesn't have anything to do with us."

She set her utensil down then crossed her arms over her apron. It had The Muffin Girl logo on the front. "Why do I not believe you?"

I wanted to kiss the frosting off her cheek. I wanted to kiss the frosting off her entire body. "I need to gather my mother's things and figure out what to do with the house. I was supposed to do it months ago but I haven't gotten around to it."

Her hostility immediately waned.

"I don't want to walk into the place again. I don't want to look through her things and try to decide what to keep and what to throw away. Axel offered to come with me but...he's not the right person for the job." I silently asked her without saying the words. There was only one person I wanted by my side.

Francesca could hide her thoughts from everyone but me. Her eyes formed an indistinct sheen when she was emotional. It was invisible to anyone's naked eye beside my own. When her eyes shifted, she was trying to make a decision. And when she hugged her waist, she was plagued with indecision. My abilities hadn't developed with time. They were innate, present since the moment we met.

And she had the same abilities toward me.

"I want to help you but I don't think I should."

"Why not?"

"Kyle won't be happy with the thought of me spending time with you—not that I blame him."

"Since when did you let a guy dictate what you do and don't do?" She sure as hell never listened to me.

"It's not about dictating."

"If you don't want to go, you don't have to. I'd only want you there if you wanted to be there. And if you don't...that's fine." I took a step back to the door then turned around. I knew Francesca wanted to be there for me—no matter what. When I was in pain, so was she. It didn't matter what happened between us. She would always be there.

"Wait."

I stopped and felt gratitude wash through me. I slowly turned around, my hands still in my pockets.

"I'll go with you."

Triumph didn't blare in my heart. There was no victory when there was no battle to begin with. I'd always known what her answer would be. "Tomorrow?"

"Sure."

***

I parked at the curb and waited for her to come downstairs. I was in my Jaguar, my fancy car that I never used. It sat in the parking garage most of the time. Only when I had a meeting with a new client did I drive it.

She came downstairs with her bag over her shoulder. She wore denim shorts and a pink razorback top. Her hair was in a long braid over one shoulder, and brown sandals were on her feet.

I wanted to grab her and never let go.

She tossed her things in the trunk before she got into the passenger seat. I didn't bother trying to help her with anything because I knew she wouldn't like it. She shut the door then buckled her safety belt. "Hi." She looked out the front window or her passenger window, never looking directly at me.

"Hi." My eyes immediately went to the locket around her neck. It was a beacon of hope for me, a sign that our everlasting love still burned hot like the sun itself.

Wednesday

Her eyes turned to my center console and she looked at all the gadgets. Then she looked out the window again.

"Are you ready to go?"

"That's why I'm sitting here buckled in."

I ignored the resentful jab and took off. She hated the fact she was manipulated into spending time with me, but she hated the fact it was her own decision even more. Despite her free will, there were certain things out of her control.

I was one of them.

I turned on the radio so there was something to listen to besides the building tension.

She looked out the passenger window, watching the skyscrapers slowly disappear until we left the city.

"How are the plans coming along for the second business?" Talking about The Muffin Girl was always a safe bet with her. It was a passion that never caused her any discomfort.

"Honestly, I haven't done much work. There's a space available in Brooklyn and I think I might take it."

"Why Brooklyn?"

"Because it's not Manhattan and it's close."

"Why not open another one here?"

"In the same city?" she asked. "The Muffin Girl may be popular but it's not a Taco Bell."

My lips lifted into an automatic smile. "Manhattan is a huge place. If you put one on the opposite corner of the city, it'll attract a whole new world of people. And it's still close by so you can walk to it."

"I don't know..."

"The people who live near The Muffin Girl aren't going to walk all the way to the other one. Plus, there's a whole new district of offices and business. That's a crowd of workers that will need a lighter-than-air pastry at lunchtime."

"You really believe that?"

"Yes." My business was completely different than hers but I had experience. "And I have a ton of clients over there. I can have our meetings at the second shop to introduce them to it. By word of mouth, they'll tell everyone else how amazing it is. Then you have a new whole stream of revenue."

"Opening a business in the food industry is hard. You make it sound like it's a walk in the park."

"Actually, you're the one who made it look like a piece of cake—no pun intended. You opened that shop and people just started pouring in. The day you opened you were packed."

She slowly turned my way, looking at me for the first time. "How do you know that?"

Even though we weren't together, I always watched her from a safe distance. "I was there." I stood across the street at the coffee shop and watched her cut the ribbon with Marie and Axel. Then I watched her small business become a powerhouse success.

"I don't remember that."

"I was across the street."

She kept staring at me, questioning me.

Wednesday

"You were wearing a Muffin Girl apron with those dark jeans that have a hole in the crotch. The ribbon was yellow, and you cut it with a pair of pink scissors that looked like they belonged to an enormous Barbie." If there was any doubt I was lying, it was now gone.

"Why were you there?"

"I always watched you even if you couldn't see me. I wasn't keeping tabs on you. I just wanted to know you were happy, that I made the right decision when I walked away from us."

She turned her gaze back to the window.

It was tense all over again.

"Did you have a good weekend?"

"It was okay," she answered. "Yours?"

Every day of my life without her was a living hell. "It was fine." I assumed she spent every weekend with Kyle, and I didn't care for the details. But I had to ask her something to keep the conversation going since we had a long drive.

"How's work?"

"Good. The past few months have been unusually good."

"Why?"

"Stocks have been doing well." I didn't want to go into more detail because it became complicated and boring really fast. "The Muffin Girl?"

"I can never keep up with that place."

"Then why are you opening a second one?"

"Since the business has been doing well, I have money sitting aside. I thought I would invest it in something else."

"That's a good idea. But how do you expect to be in two places at once?" Francesca was superwoman and could do anything, but she couldn't do the impossible.

"I'll have to hire a manager for the other place. I'll probably pick my best worker from the shop and have them transfer over."

"Have anyone in mind?"

"A few people, actually. I'm really lucky that I have some incredible people working for me. The college kids that work in the evenings give the place a fun atmosphere, and my morning workers are like worker bees. They operate well together."

"You're lucky."

"I pay them twice the minimum wage."

"Really?" For selling muffins and cakes?

"Yeah. When my workers are happy, productivity really increases. And that happiness and loyalty infects the air and gives it a good atmosphere. I think that has a lot to do with my success."

"I don't know. I think it might be the delicious muffins."

Finally, a smile spread across her face. "I think that has something to do with it. But your service should be as good as your product."

"Where did you learn all of this?"

"I got my degree in business. Or did you forget?"

I never forgot a single thing about her. "Money well spent."

"I think so."

Wednesday

I kept my eyes on the road but desperately wanted to look at her instead. My hand rested on the gearshift but I wanted to move it to her thigh. When we started talking, everything felt the way it used to. Our conversations flowed like water, and the ever-present chemistry sparked.

If I noticed it, so did she. Maybe if it looked her in the face long enough she would stop ignoring it. Her heart would cave, and she would forgive me for the way I hurt her.

And I could have one more shot of getting this right.

***

We stopped in front of the house.

I stared at it, remembering my childhood home. The last time I was there, I had a loaded pistol and was ready to blow my father's brain out of his skull. The place had an eerie look to it, like it was a haunted house more than a home.

Francesca patiently waited for me to get out of the car. She sat in absolute silence and gave me all the time I needed to make a move. Like always, she was in tune with my feelings. She knew I was battling demons from the past, the ghosts that haunted me every day.

I walked into that house when I was ready to murder someone, but now that my purpose was to dig through all my mom's possessions, I wasn't as determined. The visit would just bring back painful memories, the kind I'd spent my life suppressing.

I sat there for an entire hour, waiting for my hand to grab the door handle. I stared at the covered windows and out-of-control lawn. The grass was tall with weeds and the bushes were untrimmed. My father's truck was still in the driveway, as was my mother's car.

Francesca remained absolutely still.

I cleared my throat then opened the door. "I'm ready."

Francesca followed my lead and walked with me into the house. She stood close to me but never touched me.

The musty smell of time hit both of us right in the face. The air was old and heavy, like it hadn't been circulated since the last time I was there.

It was exactly as I last saw it, except my father's body was gone. The place still contained the atmosphere of despair. Sorrow hung in the air, impregnated from years of emotional and physical abuse. Just the smell reminded me of my evenings locked in the closet. Just the sight made me think of the bat colliding against my ribs. The memories washed through me, reminding me of the resentment I felt toward the other kids at school. They all had perfect families and perfect lives they went home to every day. I went home to this.

Francesca came to my side but still didn't touch me, to my disappointment. She stared at the living room, seeing the old furniture that was breaking at the seams. Old glasses of beer and brandy were scattered across the tabletops. The rug contained old stains of brandy.

"This is it...home sweet home."

***

I went through my mother's drawers and found a lot of junk. She had cheap jewelry, packs of playing cards, and tons of painkillers. Nothing was worth keeping so I tossed it into the big plastic bag beside me.

Francesca went through a different dresser. Using her own discretion as she searched through years of garbage.

I didn't bother touching anything that belonged to my father. Whether it was worth something or not, I was going to throw it away. Even if he had a million dollars stashed somewhere, I wouldn't want it.

After I finished cleaning out her nightstand, I peeked under the bed to see if anything worthwhile was underneath. Mom would place storage boxes underneath, full of things she would forget about until she opened them again. Instead of seeing boxes, I only saw a wooden bat.

I recognized it from my childhood. It was the very one my father used to beat me into submission. There were scuff marks around the edges from striking the wall as he chased me down. They looked like teeth marks.

I pulled it out then gripped it by the base. The bat was thirty years old and time had weathered it immensely. My fingers felt the wood and remembered exactly how it felt against my bare skin. I gripped the base so tightly it chafed my skin.

Francesca stopped her search and watched me, understanding the significance of the bat without asking. She watched me with sad eyes, knowing I was combating a past that would never go away.

In that moment, I wanted to demolish the house with the weapon. I wanted to scream and break everything in my path. The raw rage burned inside me painfully, desperate to release like a building volcano.

But I calmed myself. I remembered what my therapist said. I had to control my emotions and let them go in a positive way. If I didn't control my anger, I could never be with the woman I loved.

I rose to my feet, the bat at my side.

Francesca watched me, waiting for me to start my rampage.

But instead of doing that, I walked out.

"Hawke." Francesca chased after me, afraid of what I might do. "Breaking down the house isn't going to change anything. You're just going to make it more difficult to clean up."

I ignored her and kept walking. I made it to the back door then walked across the grass of the backyard.

Francesca stayed close on my heels. "Hawke, I know this is hard but it's in the past."

I placed the bat on an old tree stump that had been there since I could remember. My father cut it down because it endangered a power line. But he never removed the stump from the ground.

There was an axe in the toolshed I snatched it before I came back.

Francesca fell silent and watched me.

I pulled the axe far over the back of my head and aimed. Then I slammed the axe down as hard as I could, breaking the bat cleanly in two. The two pieces broke off and soared in opposite directions, landing in the grass a few feet away. The blade of the axe was embedded deep into the wood. It was so far in I doubt I could pull it out.

I breathed hard and stared at the broken pieces. Now that my father was gone, he couldn't hurt me anymore. My mother was in a better place. And the weapon he used to torture me was gone. Now I could start over and hope for a new beginning.

Francesca slowly came to my side, her eyes trained on my face.

I looked at her for the first time and saw the tears in her eyes. They were coated with distinct moisture, and all the pain she felt was apparent in every feature. She felt what I felt, intense pain coupled with relief.

She moved to my body and rested her forehead against my chest. Her arms circled my waist, and she remained there, giving me the greatest comfort I'd felt in a long time.

My arms wrapped around her shoulders, and I rested my forehead on the top of her head, inhaling her beautiful scent. She was right next to my heart, listening to it beat loudly just for her. The pain thudded deep in my chest, and I felt it travel to my eyes. I wanted to break down, but I held it back. Feeling her in my arms like this was exactly what I needed. When our souls were close to one another, the pain seemed to stop.

She gave me exactly what I needed.

***

Francesca unfolded a piece of paper she found in the drawer. She scanned through a few lines before she turned to me. "Hawke."

"What?" I tossed a box of shoes in the donation bag.

"I think you should look at this." She swallowed the lump in her throat before she handed it over. "I found it in an envelope addressed to you."

I took it with a shaky hand and began reading.

Hawke,

It's one of those nights when I question why I'm here. I know I should go, but I fear my escape will lead to my death regardless. Now that you've moved away, I know I'm on my own.

But I'm so happy.

This may be my last night on earth, and if it is, there are things I want to say just in case I never get to say them in person.

I owe you an apology. I had a child and brought him into a world that he never should have experienced. When I had you, I should have taken you and ran away as far as I could. We've both been through so much, but you never should have known that kind of pain. I'm sorry I didn't protect you from it. I'm sorry for everything.

Knowing you're in New York and starting your own life away from this is exactly what I wanted. You're so smart, successful, and talented. I have no idea what I did to have such an amazing son, but somehow I was blessed.

Wednesday

If I don't make it to see how your life turns out, I want you to know how proud I am of you. You're the greatest son I ever could have asked for. I hope you see the world for the beautiful place it truly is. I hope you fall in love with a woman that will make you understand the true meaning of happiness. And when you have your own children someday, I hope you give them the childhood I never could give to you.

You will be all right, Hawke. I'm sure of that. I know I've told you how similar you are to your father, but that's only in appearance. He doesn't have your strength, your good heart, or your integrity. You're nothing like him. I'm sorry I ever made the comparison.

I love you so much, son. I hope this note finds its way to you just in case I can't.

Love always,

Mom.

A picture came with the note. Mom and I sat at a bench in the park. I had a bag of bread in my hands while ducks gathered around us. It was a warm spring day, and it was just the two of us. I remembered it despite how young I was.

I sat on the ground and leaned against the bed, still holding the letter and the picture in my hands. My mind couldn't process what I just read so I read through the words again, trying to wrap my brain around it.

Francesca sat beside me, her knees pulled to her chest.

After I read it three times, I folded it up, the picture tucked inside.

Francesca said nothing, giving me the floor.

I always knew my mom loved me even though she never rescued me from my insufferable existence. She wasn't strong, not like Francesca. She didn't have the strength to leave because she didn't know how to make it happen. But I never judged her for that.

She wanted me to move to New York and start a new life. She wanted me to get away from this hellhole and find my own happiness. She knew she wouldn't survive that night, but she stayed anyway.

But how could I have prevented that?

And her final words hit me in a dark place.

You're nothing like him.

The words kept ringing in my brain like a distant bell.

You're nothing like him.

Hope surged through my chest.

You're nothing like him.

Wednesday

CHAPTER THIRTY-TWO

On The Other Side

Francesca

Now I understood why Hawke needed me on this trip. No one could take all of that alone.

We walked into the hotel and approached my room. Hawke booked separate rooms for us, but they were right next door to each other. He'd been quiet ever since he read that letter. Not once did he speak but I understood exactly what he was thinking.

But I was surprised by his reaction.

Not once did he rip something apart or flip a table over. He took everything calmly and defused his anger in an appropriate way. Instead of destroying the house where his mother was killed, he went outside and destroyed the weapon that caused so much misery.

He stopped at my door and put his hands in the pockets of his jeans. "Thanks for coming with me. I wouldn't have been able to do that without you."

Wednesday

"I'm glad I came with you." Together or apart, I loved him. When he was in pain, so was I. I wanted to be there for him always, no matter what happened between us. He could always count on me, and I could always count on him. We may not be lovers anymore, but our destiny was still tangled together regardless. "Will you be okay?"

"Tonight?" he whispered. "I probably won't get any sleep. But I never do."

I didn't sleep well alone either. Even with Kyle, it wasn't the best. "I'm next door if you need me."

He nodded. "I know." He turned away and headed to his door.

"Hawke?"

He turned back around.

"You handled everything so well today..." I didn't ask the question because I didn't know how to word it. No matter how it came out, it sounded insulting.

He came back to me, closing the gap between us. No one else was on the floor but he and I. "I've been seeing a therapist."

I hid my shocked expression as much as possible. That didn't sound like something Hawke would do, talk to a stranger about his troubles. He hardly talked to me about it. "Really?"

He nodded. "I think it's helping. I'm learning that I'm a different person than my father was. All I have to do is remain focused, and I'll never go down that path. And the letter my mom left...gives me the kind of encouragement I've needed for a long time."

Whenever his mother said how similar he and his father were, it always ripped me apart inside. Hawke didn't care about anyone's opinion, but he always cared about hers. She poisoned his mind unintentionally, making him fear he was a monster in the same way his father was. "I'm glad."

"I'm going in the right direction now. Even though my mom is gone, I don't feel as much anger anymore. And I'm learning not to shut people out every time I get upset. I'm going to fix myself—for you."

My fingertips and toes tingled in an inexplicable way. My body automatically reacted to those words, feeling a surge of hope that shouldn't be there. I tried to keep my heart locked up tightly in its cage but he picked the lock loose. I kept the door shut but I feared it wouldn't stay that way forever.

"You don't trust me anymore and I completely understand why. But if I show you that I'm different, that I've changed, I hope you can trust me again. This time, I won't hurt you. This time is the last time."

My entire body ached for his but I kept myself under control. "Hawke, I'm with Kyle—"

"I know. But all three of us know it's not going to last forever. It doesn't compare to what you and I have. He may be the safe choice, but I can also be the safe choice. I'm getting better and I'm becoming the man you want. I will give you everything you want—you'll see."

***

I called Kyle before I went to bed.

Wednesday

"Hey." He wasn't happy that I went away with Hawke, and it was clear in his tone alone.

"Hi."

"Going to bed?"

"Yeah. It was a long day."

"I bet."

I ignored the jab. "Hawke found a lot of old stuff at the house—including a letter from his mom."

Kyle wasn't a hateful person. He pitied anyone who deserved it, probably because he lost someone too. "What did it say?"

"That she loved him and wanted him to be happy. And that he's nothing like his father."

"Did that make him feel better?"

"It did." It was the faith he should have gotten a long time ago.

"Maybe that will give him some closure."

"I think it has." Destroying the bat also helped but I wouldn't mention that to Kyle.

"So...has he been wooing you the entire time?"

I never lied and I wasn't going to start now. "Not really. He's made a few comments here and there, but for the most part, he's been pretty quiet. He's going through a lot right now."

"I can always join you."

"I'm sorry, Kyle. It can only be me."

He sighed in the phone, showing all his irritation without actually saying anything.

"You have nothing to worry about."

To my surprise, he laughed. "I have nothing to worry about? You still claim this guy is your soul mate. It doesn't matter how great I am or how well I treat you. I can never compete with that."

His frustration was understandable. "But you don't have to compete with that. I told you that's not what I'm looking for. I'm looking for a friend I can spend my life with. Someone I can have kids with. You fit the bill, Kyle."

"I fit the bill because you'll never love anyone else besides him." His voice was full of defeat.

His sadness hurt, but I didn't let it swallow me up. "I didn't mean to mislead you, Kyle. I told you what this was."

"I know."

"I hope you didn't expect me to change my mind."

"I think you could...if he wasn't around."

"Maybe. But it would take a very long time."

"Well, I have nothing else to do." He sighed into the phone again, his irritation seeping through the line.

Maybe this wouldn't work with Kyle under the circumstances. Perhaps I needed to find a guy who lacked any capacity to love, a relationship of convenience. "I don't think this is working anymore."

Kyle's voice came out louder through the phone. "That's not what I want."

"But I think it might be for the best. I don't want to hurt you, Kyle. I care about you too much."

"You aren't hurting me. I just hate the fact he won't disappear. It's like he purposely haunts you."

"Whether he's here or not, he'll always haunt me."

Wednesday

Kyle breathed into the phone. "So, you still haven't changed your mind about him? You'll never take him back."

After our conversation in the hall, my confidence was shaken. Hawke did something I never expected. He fixed the root of his problem so he could be free of his demons. Without them, he could be the man I'd always wanted. But I still couldn't forget the way he left me again for six months. If I went back to him, I'd feel like a dog crawling back to its owner after it'd been kicked. My pride, sense of self-worth, and stubbornness wouldn't allow that to happen. "No. I won't take him back."

Kyle fell silent.

"I'm not going to cheat on you. I have too much respect for you."

When he spoke, his voice was full of affection. The jealousy and disappointment vanished into thin air. "I know, baby. If you haven't taken him back after this long, I guess you never will."

He was coming around and returning to his former self. Kyle was never possessive or jealous, but Hawke made him say and do strange things. He still didn't realize he was the winner. He was the winner by default—but the winner nonetheless.

***

Hawke searched the closet in the hallway and tossed all the garbage he found. There were old paper receipts, stuffed animals, and random junk. When he uncovered his mother's clothes and jewelry, he boxed it up so he could drop it off at The Salvation Army.

E. L. Todd

"What are you going to do with the house?" I organized the dishes in the kitchen and wrapped them in bubble wrap.

"Sell it."

"Are you going to fix it up?"

"Probably. No one would buy this piece of shit as is." He removed a few binders and flipped through them.

Getting rid of the place was the best decision. I couldn't picture Hawke ever living there or even renting it out. He should put it behind him and move on. "After a new coat of paint and new carpet, the place will look brand new."

"I don't know about that." He flipped through the plastic sleeves of the photo album then stopped. His eyes were trained on something and he didn't blink.

I suspected he uncovered more family pictures. I set the plates in the box before I joined him on the floor. "Whatcha got there?"

"Old pictures." He looked through them slowly then flipped the page. Every picture was either of him as a little boy or of him and his mom. His dad was never in any of the photographs.

"You were so cute."

"Thanks." He turned the page and kept looking. The pictures showed his life from when he was born until he turned six or seven. After that, the pictures ended. That could only mean one thing.

"Your mother loved you so much." Despite what happened, I could tell she cared for her son. It was a shame

313

she wasn't strong enough to leave when she had the chance. Both she and Hawke could have had a much different life.

"Yeah...I can tell."

I rubbed his back gently, trying to comfort him.

He shut the binder and shoved it into the trash bag.

"Whoa, what are you doing?"

"I don't want it. Looking at it causes me too much heartache." He searched through the pile and discarded more junk.

I stared at the binder and watch it disappear under the rubble. It was such a waste to throw it away and I couldn't part with it. I pulled it out then held it to my chest. "Do you mind if I keep it then?"

The look he gave me spoke volumes. He was moved by the gesture but heartbroken at the same time. The two of us were connected in such a strong way and nothing would ever change.

But I think that revelation hurt him more.

***

All the garbage was tossed in a dumpster, and all the valuable things were left on the driveway to be picked up by The Salvation Army. The house was left empty, nothing but floorboards and walls.

When Hawke walked out of there, he seemed relieved the job had been completed. It took all weekend to do it, but together we managed to get it done. The only photo album we found was mine to keep.

I carried it under my arm as we walked down the hall to our hotel rooms. Hawke didn't want it for many reasons, all of which I could understand. But I couldn't part with such a treasure. The photos of Hawke as a little boy were something worth keeping.

He stopped in front of my door and faced me, a whirlwind of emotions etched on his face. He glanced down at the photo album before he looked at me again. "Thanks for doing this with me. I'm glad it's done."

"It's no problem." I didn't mind helping him in any way possible. I wanted the best for him, in any capacity. If I ever needed him for anything, he would be there. "I wanted to be here."

He stared into my eyes with his arms by his sides.

I held the binder to my chest, protecting my heart.

"Did you do the same thing with Axel?"

"And Yaya." I remembered that day clearly. We had to go through all of their things and figure out what to do with them. Some things were kept but most of it was thrown away. We sold the house and saved the money for college.

"Then you understand what I'm feeling."

"I do." The only difference was our childhoods. Mine was happy, with two parents who loved me more than themselves. I never felt unsafe in my own home. Of all the places I wanted to be, home was number one. But Hawke hated his past. I think in many ways it made it worse. "Will you be okay for the night?" If he wasn't, there wasn't much I could do. I couldn't sleep with him.

"I'll be fine." He didn't turn for the door. His eyes were still trained on me, saying the things his lips hadn't. His damaged heart was deep in his eyes. Being back in that home where both of his parents died took a toll on him. And his soul was broken from losing me because of it. He was at the lowest point in his life, having nothing to live for.

Like always, I ached for him. When he left the first time, I was desolated in the same way. The rising and setting of the sun meant nothing to me. Every day was just a painful blur. Without him in my life, I didn't know how to live anymore.

No matter what either one of us did, we were constantly pulled back to each other. Together or apart, we couldn't escape. Our lives traveled on the same line, and while there were breaks in its continuity, it never faltered on its course.

His eyes burned for my touch, needing me to comfort him in a way only I could accomplish. After everything we'd been through, my soul was still tightly wrapped around his. They formed a tangled mess that couldn't be pulled apart. I felt weak, my defenses coming down.

Hawke closed the gap between us and cupped my face with both of his hands. His fingers dug into my hair slightly and they felt warm to the touch. The second his hands were on me, I felt lighter than air. His embrace brought a type of comfort that couldn't be duplicated by anything else.

My hands slid over his, and I gripped his wrists, feeling his distant pulse. I knew he wasn't going to kiss me. Hawke wouldn't do that, put me in a situation that would compromise my integrity and virtue. But he couldn't stop himself from doing—whatever it was.

He pressed his forehead to mine and stood there, our bodies locked together in an intimate embrace. He breathed deeply, treasuring the quiet moment outside the hotel room. A kiss wasn't shared but all of his emotions spread through me like an incoming tide. We touched everywhere, infecting my most intimate place.

My breathing hitched as I felt the tremors. His gentle breaths fell on my face, just the way they used to when we made love. His nose rubbed against mine, just the way it used to before he said goodbye. Every thought and emotion he had was transferred into me. Wordless communication erupted and we just existed together, blocking the rest of the world and focusing on us.

Lovers or friends, it didn't make a difference. The words we used to say to each other were as real as ever. They'd never faltered in their truth, only their context.

We are forever.

***

I dreaded seeing Kyle because I didn't want to tell him what happened. Just the previous day, I told him he had nothing to worry about, but then a few hours later, Hawke and I had a moment neither one of us could resist.

Kyle came into the bakery just as I got off work. We usually spent every weekend together, and since I was gone for the past few days, I knew he was eager to see me. "There's my lady." He wrapped his arms around me and dropped me into a dramatic dip. He kissed me hard on the mouth before he pulled me back up.

"Wow. That was quite an entrance."

Wednesday

"That's what the ladies tell me." He eyed the muffins I just finished and snatched one. "Sometimes I'm not sure if I come in here to see you or to get free food."

"Well, Marie will be the first one to admit it's for the free food."

He chuckled. "Since she was honest about it, I guess I can be as well."

The mention of honesty brought the guilt.

"So, you're coming over, right? I didn't get much sleep this weekend."

Neither did I. "Kyle, I need to tell you something."

He stopped chewing in mid-bite and looked devastated. He watched me with pained eyes before he forced himself to swallow the piece in his mouth. "I'm not sure if I want to hear it."

"I'm not sure if I want to tell it."

He set the half eaten muffin on the counter top. "You slept with him?" He didn't look me in the eye as he asked the question. He didn't even seem mad if my answer was yes. It was like he expected it.

"No."

"So, you kissed him?"

"No."

He raised an eyebrow. "You got back together?"

"No."

"Frankie, I'm out of guesses."

"He walked me to my door to say good night and...we had a moment. He pressed his forehead to mine as he cupped my face and we stood there for a long time... I'm sorry."

Instead of being upset, Kyle looked confused. "I don't understand. What happened?"

"What I just explained."

"But...what's the big deal about that?"

"It was just...intimate. We were standing there close together with our eyes closed. It was a vulnerable experience."

"But there was no kissing, touching, or sex?"

"Yeah."

He shrugged. "It doesn't sound like anything happened, Frankie."

But something did happen. "You can cheat on someone without touching another person. I felt a lot of emotions toward him and he felt them toward me. It was...meaningful."

"Well, I already knew you had feelings for him so this isn't coming out of left field."

"Really? You aren't mad?"

"No." He grabbed the muffin again and continued to eat it. "I thought you were going to say something much worse."

No matter how much Hawke wanted me, he wouldn't make a move, at least not a physical one. I wouldn't cheat or lie to Kyle, and he wouldn't manipulate me into doing it either.

He finished the muffin and tossed the wrapper in the trash. "So, let's go. I got reservations at that new restaurant."

"How did you manage that?"

Wednesday

"Pulled a few strings. And pack your bag. You're staying with me all week."

CHAPTER THIRTY-THREE

Goodbye

Francesca

Marie ignored her menu and looked at me. "Something happened with Hawke, didn't it?"

Marie could read me almost as well as Hawke sometimes. "Yeah." I kept eyeing the plate of fried mozzarella sticks. I shouldn't order them because they were all fat and carbs, but I really didn't care at the moment. "It's one of those days when you really want some fried cheese."

"Then that's what we'll get." She snatched my menu away and looked at the waiter. "Two orders of the fried mozzarella sticks. Stat."

I'd never seen Marie order anything besides grilled chicken or a salad after she got engaged. They'd been married for a while now but she still stuck to her diet religiously.

"Spill it."

I told her everything about the trip and concluded with the embrace on the doorstep.

Wednesday

Marie didn't seem the least bit surprised. "I don't know what you want me to say. That sounds about right for you two."

"He just confused me..."

"How so?"

"It seems like he's changed—for the better. He's been working on himself so he won't have this problem again. He won't leave me again."

Marie wasn't Hawke's biggest fan to begin with but she quickly became his worst fan. "Hawke is a boy in a man's body. He clearly has commitment issues and he always will. No, you deserve someone better than that, someone who isn't going to drop you the second things get difficult. I'm all about second chances, but you've already given him his. Since it's been so long since it happened, it's easy to downplay and forget about it. But don't forget what that man did to you. You tried to be there for him, and he turned his back on you. That guy has officially struck out."

When Marie spun it like that, I couldn't help but agree with her. "What if it was Axel?"

"Axel would never pull that crap on me."

"I know. But what if he did?"

"I'd move on and never look back." She said it with such conviction there was no room for doubt. "We all have our hard times, and some days are more difficult than others, but that doesn't give him the right to treat you like that. No, we'd be done."

I took a long drink of my cocktail and waited for the haze of the alcohol to kick in.

"Just stick with Kyle. I know you really like him."

"I do like him."

"You need to get rid of Hawke—permanently. Stop seeing him, stop talking to him—completely cut him out. Then pursue Kyle with everything you've got. Kyle will be a great husband and father. Hawke...he'll just screw you over down the road."

I wasn't sure if I agreed with that last part, but I agreed with everything else. "It's hard for me to be around Hawke and not feel all those emotions."

"And I don't blame you. That's natural. Don't feel bad about it."

"But Kyle deserves better than that."

She nodded in agreement.

"I told him I'll never love him, and I've never misled him about my feelings for him or Hawke, but I feel like I'm still doing something wrong."

"Then cut out Hawke."

"It's not that simple," I said. "He's the one who comes around, remember?"

"I distinctly remember you agreeing to spend the weekend with him."

"But that's—"

"It doesn't matter. No more, Frankie." She was being a hardass on me, but it was for a good reason.

"You're right."

"Damn right I am. You were doing great before he came back into the picture. The second he's gone, you'll be back to normal. Everyone can move on and be happy."

Wednesday

The idea of removing Hawke from my life was difficult and painful. Any time we went our separate ways, he was the one who made the decision. Now I was the one walking away—for good.

"But I have no idea how you're going to tell him to back off. He clearly does whatever he wants."

My fingers moved to the necklace around my throat. I fingered it gently, feeling the engraving under my fingertips. The day he gave this to me is one I'll never forget. I'd always cherish it. "I have an idea."

***

I placed the photo album inside the box with the other sentimental things Hawke had given me over the years. I stared inside and looked at the collection of things that represented our relationship. The only thing missing was my Muffin Girl baking pan, but that was on display at the bakery.

There was only one thing left to place inside.

I pulled my hair over one shoulder and unclasped the necklace for the first time. The weight was removed from my neck, but it felt like a new one had replaced it. I examined the locket in my palm and stared at the small engraving across the surface. Saying goodbye was much harder than I thought. How did Hawke do this so many times?

I opened it and stared at the picture of us inside. I was looking back in time, to when we first fell in love. Both of us were scared of where the relationship might lead, and we had every right to be scared.

Because we both got hurt.

E. L. Todd

I closed the locket then placed it on top of the photo album. It looked lifeless sitting there, no longer resting against my warm skin. Now it was just a piece of metal, a keepsake I wouldn't look at until I moved again.

I took a deep breath so the tears wouldn't emerge, and I placed the lid on top. When everything was hidden from view, I didn't feel any better. I just said goodbye to the love of my life.

And nothing would ever make me feel better about that.

***

It was only a matter of time before Hawke made his move. He would stop by and see me eventually, or he would run into me on purpose when I was out with Marie.

I just opened the bakery one morning when he paid me a visit. When I walked into the shop, I knew he was there. I could hear his heavy footfalls on the tile. The slowness of his pace told me exactly who it was.

He came to the back where my private kitchen was and stared at me.

I purposely wore a V-neck shirt so my chest would be visible. My back was to him when he walked in, so I took my time before I turned around. I didn't want to see the look on his face, to see the hope drain from his eyes permanently. He would be devastated, far more devastated than I was when I packed everything up.

"Hey." He stayed behind me and didn't approach the counter.

Wednesday

"Hi." I set the whisk aside then wiped my dirty hands on my apron. Now was the moment of truth and there was no looking back. I closed my eyes briefly before I turned around.

His eyes immediately went to my eyes, as they always did. He searched for solace there, finding comfort in the window to the same soul he possessed. Slowly, his eyes moved down, taking in the sight of my nose then my lips. When his eyes trailed further, he noticed the bare skin of my throat. The necklace was gone, removed by my own hands. He watched the area for several heartbeats before he swallowed the lump in his throat. The shock was quickly followed by devastation. Sorrow and misery came swiftly after that.

Hawke didn't look me in the eye again. When his eyes left my neck, he looked at the ground. He didn't react overtly. To anyone else, he would simply look lost, like he walked into the wrong kitchen on accident. But to me, I saw everything.

He turned away and slowly walked out, his shoulders not as broad and powerful as they once were. He carried a new weight that pushed them down, making his entire frame bend in a heartbreaking way.

It was the weight of defeat.

CHAPTER THIRTY-FOUR

The Sad Truth

Hawke

"You're sure you want to sell this place?" Maggie, my realtor examined my empty apartment, mesmerized by the floor-to-ceiling windows and the pristine hardwood floors.

"Yes." I already sold my furniture and everything else I had.

Maggie clearly thought I was out of my mind. "It's just...a place like this is hard to come across. And you got it at such a good price."

"I don't care."

"You'll definitely make a nice profit on it."

"Don't care about that either."

Maggie gave up, realizing I wouldn't change my mind. "I'll take care of it. I can sell this place within a week."

"Great." I grabbed my final bag and walked out. "Thanks."

***

Wednesday

I bought a townhouse that was really close to my office. It was just a block away, and it had a garage for my car as well as a small backyard. I needed a change of scenery, something that didn't contain a hint of Francesca.

Now I shouldn't run into her anywhere. I didn't pass her bakery on the way to work, and I didn't use the same gym, grocery store, or dry cleaning service. Her new apartment was dangerously close to my old one.

I could honestly say I never wanted to see her again.

She made her choice, silently destroying any hope I held for us. Whether she loved me or not, my past mistakes were too grave to be forgiven. I'd hurt her too much, and even though I'd changed, it wasn't enough for her.

I couldn't take back what I did.

She wanted to be with Kyle, to marry him someday and have his children. When enough time passed, she would think of me less and less. And maybe one day, she'd forget about me entirely.

But I would never forget about her.

**

Axel asked me to hang out a few times but I always made an excuse.

Dude, one of my buddies from work got in at the Rainbow Room? You in?

Sorry, man. I already have plans. It was cold to brush him off this way but I didn't have any other choice.

You've ditched me for the past two weeks. What's going on?

Nothing. Just been busy.

328

Axel didn't text me again, probably because he was mad. Hopefully, he would be pissed enough to never text me again.

***

A few days later, Axel called me.

I let it go to voicemail with no intention of ever listening to it.

But he called again.

What did he want?

I ignored the call.

What the hell? His message blew up my screen. *I just went by your apartment and it's for sale? Dude, what's going on?*

Now I knew couldn't keep ignoring him forever. Instead of being angry like a normal person, he didn't quit. I called him.

Axel answered before it even rang. "What the hell happened?"

"I bought a bigger place."

"When?" he shrieked.

"A few weeks ago."

"And you didn't think you should tell me?"

"Everything happened so fast..." I leaned back into my couch and stared at the blank TV.

"Where do you live now?"

"I have a townhouse by my office."

"Cool," he said. "I'll swing by."

"Uh...hold on."

"What? Is there something wrong?"

329

Wednesday

"Axel, this isn't easy for me to say…" He'd been a good friend to me for a long time. I was his best man on the most important day of his life. I would miss him. Actually, I already did miss him. "I don't think we can see each other anymore."

"What do you mean? You're breaking up with me?"

"I guess…"

"But why? What did I do?"

"It has nothing to do with you. It's Francesca…"

"I'm not following."

"She doesn't want me in her life anymore and I have to respect what she wants. I want to stay out of her way as much as possible. I can't do that if I hang out with you all the time."

Axel was dead silent.

"Axel?"

"How is that fair? You and my sister break up so I lose my friend?"

"It's not like I want this."

"Why can't we be friends? You and I will just make sure we don't go anywhere near Francesca. We did it for years when we first came to New York. We can do it again."

"I don't know…"

"Look, I'm not losing you because of Francesca. That's the stupidest thing I've ever heard."

"It's what she wants."

"Whatever," he said. "I've never listened to her and I'm not going to start now."

It actually moved me that he wanted to be in my life so much. There was a time when he wanted nothing to do with me.

"You sound so sad."

The comment made me flinch because I didn't share emotional sentences with other dudes. I only spoke to Francesca that way. "I've been better."

"What happened, exactly?"

"I tried to get her back and I fixed myself...but she wants to be with Kyle."

"Oh..."

"Even though she loves me and not him, she would still rather be with him—because he doesn't hurt her. I understand her perspective, but I'm not the same guy anymore."

Axel remained silent.

"So, I moved to a new place and sold all my things. I'll never be able to move on if her ghost walks my halls. I need a fresh start if I'm ever going to get through this."

"I'll never understand the two of you."

"It's okay. You aren't the only one."

"I'm sorry it didn't work out. I know you've hurt her in the past and everything but...I can tell you really love her."

If only Francesca had the same realization. "Thanks."

"I wish there was something I could do to make you feel better."

Nothing would ever make me feel better. I lost the love of my life, and I was the only person to blame. If I just controlled my rage, I'd still have her in my life. I would have asked her to marry me by now. But I pissed it all away with my stupidity. "Want to come over and watch the game?"

His smile came through the phone. "Will there be free food and beer?"

"Always."

"Then I'll be there."

CHAPTER THIRTY-FIVE

Fresh Start

Francesca

Kyle had been working a lot because he took on a new case. He didn't appear in the courtroom very often, spending most of his time doing whatever he wanted, but when a case really interested him, he took it.

I didn't see him as much as I wanted to but I understood his passion. His line of work helped people and I respected that. All I did was make people fat. Since I had a lot of free time, I pursued my second shop.

Hawke was one of the smartest businessmen I knew. He understood it like no one else even though his business was making money off of other people. He'd met the richest of the rich and knew their secrets.

Since he recommended I stay in Manhattan, I took his advice. I found a vacated corner store. There weren't as many windows as I would like and the inside was a little smaller than my current shop, but that wasn't a bad thing.

Wednesday

"The rent will be cheaper," Axel said. "That'll be nice. And you don't need a huge second location."

"Yeah, you're probably right." I walked around and examined the counter and the kitchen. The place used to be a diner and it had a vintage feel to it. If I took it, I'd have to completely remodel the place.

"I thought you wanted to open one in Brooklyn."

"I think it'll do better here. Besides, it's easier for me to get to."

Axel touched the counters and examined the kitchen appliances. "Will you have to start from scratch?"

"Yeah..."

"That's going to be expensive."

"It will." But it would be worth it in the end. People loved The Muffin Girl so much because it was unique, unlike any other bakery in Manhattan. "This place will look completely different by the time I'm done with it."

"So, you're going to take it?"

"Yeah."

***

I tried to forget about the way Hawke and I said goodbye. Those words weren't actually said, but they were implied. The second he realized my locket was gone, he knew there was no hope. I made my choice—to be with Kyle.

The following weeks after that were difficult. All I could think about was comforting him, but I knew any contact would just make it worse. I had to steer clear of him in order for this to work.

But I missed him.

In my heart, I knew he changed. For the first time in his life, he focused on himself and addressed the true problem underneath the skin. He took a path of self-discovery and realized he wasn't the fiend he always feared he would be. While that was important, it didn't change what happened in the past. He hurt me too many times and I couldn't just look the other way.

I couldn't.

I was going over my business plan when Kyle called me.

"Hey," I said when I answered.

"Baby, I have some incredible news."

"You're taking me out to dinner? Coming over to spend time with me? Giving me some lovin'?"

He chuckled. "I know I've neglected you lately but now I'm free as a bird."

"Did you win the trial?"

"Hell yeah, I did."

"Awe, congratulations."

"It was a slam dunk. I put that fucker behind bars for life. I tried for the death sentence but was rejected. But I'll take what I got."

Now I understood why Kyle only took cases involving sexual assault. After what happened to his sister, he wanted to stop it from happening to anyone else. "I'm so proud of you."

"Thanks. I worked really hard on this case. I hardly got any sleep."

"Then come over. I'll give you a massage."

"Ooh...with oil?"

"Sure."

"What if I can't afford to pay you? Will I have to do something else?"

I laughed into the phone. "This isn't a bad porno scenario."

"Oh, come on. I think it'd be hot."

"How about you just come here and we'll have sex? Right to the point."

"Not too sexy but whatever," he said. "I haven't gotten laid in a week."

"That makes two of us."

"Well, I'll be there soon."

"K."

***

Kyle unbuttoned the jacket of his suit and tossed it on a chair.

I hardly ever saw him in a suit because he never worked. It looked great on him, fitting his broad shoulders nicely. Whenever we went out together, he always wore jeans and a t-shirt.

He removed everything, stripping down to his boxers. "I'm so glad to take off this stuffy suit. I've been wearing one every single day this week."

"I love my work uniform."

"I'd wear that any day." When his clothes were kicked aside, he wrapped his arms around me then leaned into me. "I've missed you."

"I've missed you too."

He gave me a slow kiss, one that wasn't rushed. He took his time even though we hadn't been together in a while. "How about I take you out to dinner after sex? I don't think I can sit through an entire meal and not picture you naked."

"That works for me."

He unbuttoned my jeans and pulled them down to my ankles. He took a knee and slowly helped me out of them, my hands gripping his shoulders for balance. He kissed my thighs until he reached the apex of my thigh. His lips pressed a wet kiss on the lace of my panties before his hands pulled them down.

I gripped his shoulders tighter and felt his lips moved to the same spot, kissing the sensitive skin. Kyle was a great lover and pleased his partner as much as himself.

He rose to his feet then gripped my shirt. Slowly, he pulled it over my head and tossed it on the ground. His hands moved to the clasp of my bra, and with experienced fingers, he unclasped it immediately. It slowly slipped off my shoulders until it hit the ground.

He looked at my naked body, appreciating it like he always did. When his eyes took in my tits, he stopped and stared at the hollow of my throat. The skin was bare and unblemished. The locket was gone and he immediately noticed it was absent. His eyes traveled to mine, his thoughts easier to read than a book. "You're mine."

***

Weeks turned into months. The height of summer had changed to the end, just before fall arrived. Around the

corner were the holidays, looming over our heads. I couldn't forget how I spent my last Christmas, and I knew the next one would be completely different.

Kyle and I allowed our relationship to grow, and now that the locket was gone, Kyle had mellowed out. Hawke didn't make an appearance like I suspected, and Kyle was even more happy about that.

It was just he and I.

We were together every day after work, and on the weekends, we went bike riding or hiking. Sometimes, we went to ball games or bowling. I met a few of his friends and even came to his office to meet the rest of his staff. Everything was great.

But I couldn't stop thinking about Hawke.

He wasn't in my mind all the time, but he did cross my thoughts from time to time. I hoped he was doing well and hadn't reverted back to his dark ways. I hoped he would find a nice girl that could make him happy the way Kyle made me happy. After the pain we both experienced, we deserved to experience joy.

Axel and Marie had dinner with us at a fondue place. The four of us went out often and always had a good time. It was hard to believe Hawke used to be the fourth member of our group. He disappeared off the face of the earth. Axel never mentioned him and neither did I.

"Baby, let's get the cheddar cheese." Axel eyed his menu.

"Sure," Marie said. "I don't care what kind. I'll eat that shit so quick."

Kyle had his arm around my shoulders, where he usually rested it. "What are you thinking?"

"How about the spicy pepper jack?"

"I think that's an excellent idea." He grabbed both menus and placed them at the end of the table.

"What's new with you guys?" I asked. It was a stupid question since we talked to them all the time.

"Nothing much," Axel said. "The stock market has been good."

"Cool," I said.

"Gwyneth Paltrow came into the office the other day," Marie said. "She's going to be on the front cover in the fall."

"Really?" I asked in surprise. "Did you meet her?"

"No," Marie said with a sigh. "But I saw her from, like, five feet away. She's way skinnier is person than in pictures, if you can believe it. I hardly eat and I'm still not that skinny."

"Then maybe you should eat," Axel jabbed.

"Not now," she said without looking at him. "Kyle, what's up with you?"

"I've spent most of my time with Francesca. When she's at work, I go golfing with my buddies." He took a drink of his beer.

"You have the best life ever," Axel said.

Kyle chuckled. "I'm waiting for a case I really want. I don't like to take them unless I'm invested."

"That's good for the client," Marie said. "They have the best lawyer possible."

"Thanks," Kyle said. "Actually, I have other news."

"What?" I had no idea what he was talking about.

Wednesday

Kyle pulled a brochure out of his pocket. "How about a trip to Bermuda? Just you and I."

"Bermuda?" I couldn't quiet the gasp that escaped my throat. "I don't even know where that is."

He chuckled. "It's near the Caribbean. Very tropical."

"Oh my god." I snatched the brochure out of his hands. "That sounds like so much fun."

"You're on board then?"

"Hell yes." I flipped through the pages and liked it more and more.

"When can you get time off of work?" he asked.

"Uh…" It was difficult for me to take off whenever I wanted because I didn't have anyone to cover for me. "Maybe in a month."

"A month?" he asked sadly. "That's forever away."

"I know," I said. "But I can't just leave without preparing for it."

"Alright. I'll wait…for you." He wiggled his eyebrows then kissed me on the cheek. "It'll be fun."

"I'm so jealous," Marie said. "Axel and I haven't been anywhere since our honeymoon."

"Because you're a workaholic," Axel argued.

"You're a workaholic too," she countered.

"Not like you," he said. "I'd love to take you somewhere tropical. You know, where you can wear a thong bathing suit."

Marie laughed. "You would flip if I wore something like that in public."

"Not when we're on vacation." Axel took a drink of his beer.

Marie shook her head as she looked at me. "I'm going to go to the bathroom and wash my hands before we eat."

"I'll go with you." I set the brochure on the table then slid out of the booth.

Kyle gave me a playful smack on the ass before I walked away. "Hurry."

I rolled my eyes then walked with Marie to the bathroom. I actually had to pee so I went inside a stall and did my business. Marie stood in front of the mirror and touched up her make up.

"He's so obsessed with me working," Marie said. "He wants me to quit and be a housewife."

I flushed the toilet then left the stall. "Really?" I got to the sink then washed my hands. "I didn't realize he cared so much."

"He's been pressuring me for a year. He says he makes enough money that I don't need to work."

"Is that true?"

"Well, it is." She cleaned up the smudged eyeliner around her eyes. "But I like my job. I don't want to quit."

"Then don't." I patted my hands dry with the paper towel. "Do what you want, Marie."

"I know... I just know we want to have kids soon."

"Really?" I couldn't keep the hope out of my voice. The idea of being an aunt sent me to the moon.

"Yeah, and I don't know how I'm going to do both," she said with a sigh. "I'm afraid Axel might get his way."

Wednesday

"Well, you don't need to decide right this second. Think about it."

"I guess." She washed her hands and looked at me in the mirror. "Bermuda, huh? You two will have so much fun."

"We'll have a blast." The only other time I'd been on vacation was with Hawke. I tried not to think about it because it wasn't fair to Kyle. Hawke was such an important person in my life even though I didn't see him anymore, but I couldn't keep thinking about him. I had to try to forget him. Kyle deserved that.

"I'm jealous," Marie said. "You guys will have a great time. You need a vacation anyway. You work more than all three of us combined."

I was ashamed to admit that. "I know. But I love it…"

"I'm not judging you, girl." She squeezed me affectionately on the shoulder before she walked to the door. "Now let's go eat a big ass pot of cheese."

CHAPTER THIRTY-SIX

Bad Day

Hawke

Someone started banging on my front door. "Dude, open the door right now. I need to talk to you ASAP." Axel kept knocking, using both knuckles against the wood.

I was sitting on the couch drinking a beer, which is how I spent most of my free time. "I'm coming. Chill out."

"No, this is important. Hurry the hell up."

Marie must be pregnant. I can't think of any other reason for the urgency. I got the door open then headed back to the couch. "Axel, you'll be a great dad. Just calm down." It was hard for me to get excited about anything anymore. I had the perfect life but threw it away.

"What?" Axel asked. "I'll be a great dad?"

"Isn't Marie pregnant? Is that what's so important?"

"No, not that I know of. But that would be pretty cool..." His mind started to drift away. "We've been talking about having kids soon. I'd love to have a little girl that looks just like her."

Wednesday

I was glad Axel was happy, but his joy only reminded me of the woman I lost. "Good for you." I held the cold beer in my fingers, gripping it for dear life.

Axel snapped out of it. "No, that's not what I came here to tell you." He plopped down on the couch beside me.

"What's up?"

He was desperate to get inside my house, but now that he was there, he was hesitant. "I...I know I should stay out of this and just leave it alone but something tells me you need to hear this."

It was about Francesca.

Was she getting married?

Was she pregnant?

I didn't want to know.

"I remember what you guys had and...I can't believe both of you are going to let it fade away."

"It's been two months since I've spoken to her, Axel. It has faded away."

"No, it hasn't. You still love her and she still loves you."

"Love isn't enough." Not this time.

"Well..." He fidgeted with his hands nervously. "We were out to dinner last night and the girls went to the restroom. That's when Kyle cornered me and...asked my permission to propose to Francesca."

I bowed my head and felt like someone shot me in the stomach. Just when I thought I was numb, more pain emerged from deep below. I hated picturing her with him, knowing she should be with me. Anytime I imagined her in her mother's wedding dress, she was marrying me—not anyone else. The loss was traumatizing.

Axel stared at me, like he expected me to say something.

"Good for her..."

"What?" Axel blurted. "That's your response?"

"What do you want me to say? I thought you liked Kyle. Why are you telling me this?"

"I do like Kyle. He's a really cool guy and he treats Francesca like a damn princess. I have nothing but respect for him. But...I know she doesn't love him. She's fond of him, of course. But she doesn't look at him the way I look at Marie. I want my sister to be happy, not to settle."

I stared at my beer and felt my heart slow to a dangerous pace. "What do you want me to do? She chose him. She made it perfectly clear what she wants."

"Because she's scared of getting hurt again. Convince her that won't happen."

"You think I haven't tried?" I asked sarcastically. "I did everything I possibly could. Nothing worked."

Axel sighed and ran his fingers through his hair.

"I've learned to let it go. You need to do the same."

"It's just..." His fingers kept moving through his hair.

"Kyle is a great guy. Francesca will be happy." And I'll be miserable until the day I die.

Axel dropped his hand. "I know this is a weird thing to say, but if my mom were here, she would tell Francesca to be with you."

Wednesday

Of all the things I expected him to say, that wasn't one of them. I turned his way, unsure if he really said those words.

"I know my mom never met you. But I just know my mom would tell her to forgive you, to be with the man she really loves, not the one who's safe. My mom was a hopeless romantic and saw the good in people when no one else could. But she was always right about everything. I'm sure she would like Kyle too but...she would want you to marry Francesca. You have the kind of love my mom would have wanted for Francesca. She's not here anymore, so I have to say this girly, mushy crap."

"Why don't you say this to Francesca?"

"It's too late now. It'll be totally random and out of the blue."

"Then why should I say something?"

"Because it'll never be random or out of the blue when it comes from you." He gripped his knees like he didn't know what else to do. "Come on, you have to do something."

I picked at the label on my beer, unsure what I could possibly do to win her back.

"Hawke, you were going to propose to her. Maybe you can do that now."

"That won't work." If anything, that would just piss her off.

"You are going to do something, right?"

"I don't know..."

"Kyle is taking her to Bermuda in a month. That's where he's going to do it. So, you have a month to figure it out."

I would need a lifetime to convince her.

"And if she says yes to Kyle, then that's it." His voice carried the devastation he felt. "I know her. If she commits to something, she won't change her mind about it even if she's unhappy. If you wait too long, you'll lose your chance for good. This is your last window."

I set the beer on the coffee table then rubbed my temple.

"Think."

"Axel, it's not that easy. I said and did everything I possibly could to get her back. The only way I'll make this work is if I march into the bakery and kiss her hard on the mouth. The second we touched, she'll cave. I would take her right there on the counter in her kitchen. Kyle would leave her and she would be mine."

Despite the awkward topic, Axel didn't say anything. "Then why don't you do that?"

"I respect her too much."

"Now isn't the time for respect."

"I would never force her to betray someone else, even if it is Kyle. She would loathe herself forever. I don't want her to carry that. She values her integrity."

Axel sighed in irritation. "Then you better think of something else."

I was out of ammunition. I did everything I could to win her back, but nothing was good enough. I broke her trust and I couldn't repair it. It was too late. All I had left was the ring I bought her and the journal I'd been keeping for three years. Those were the only things that remained.

I went into my bedroom and pulled out the journal and the ring. When I came back to the couch, I pulled out my pocketknife and flipped to the last entry.

"What are you doing?"

"My last attempt." There were fifty blank pages in the back, and I cut a small square through all the pages. Then I placed the engagement ring inside.

Axel watched me.

I grabbed a pen, and despite Axel staring at me, I wrote my final words of love. This was all I had left, and I wasn't sure if it would be enough. If she read my journal, she would know, together or apart, I loved her every day since I met her. I shut the journal then handed it to Axel. "Give that to her."

"What is it?" He felt the black leather covering.

"My journal."

"And why are you giving it to her?"

Francesca would understand—and only Francesca. "Just give it to her."

CHAPTER THIRTY-SEVEN

An Unexpected Gift

Francesca

I just finished vacuuming when there was a knock on the door. I knew it wasn't Kyle because he was having dinner with his mom in The Hamptons. It might be Marie but she usually texted me before she came by.

After looking through the peephole, I opened the door to Axel. "What's up?" My hair was in a ponytail and I wore sweatpants. I expected Axel to make a joke about my appearance, but he didn't.

"Is Kyle here?"

"No. He's visiting his mother." I wrapped up the cord then pushed the vacuum into the closet. "What's up?" Axel wouldn't drop by unless he needed to talk to me. And the only thing he liked to talk about was Marie.

He held a black journal in his hand. It looked old and crinkled, like it'd been opened and closed every day for several years. Even though Axel was holding it, I knew it didn't belong to him. "Hawke wanted me to give this to you." He held it out for me to take.

The mention of his name made me freeze. No one mentioned him in months, and I tried not to think about him as much as possible. Hearing his name felt like someone branded me with a hot iron. It was unexpected and painfully jolting.

Axel continued to hold it out.

"Why?"

"Just read it."

I still didn't take it.

"Francesca." Axel's voice came out gentle, something that hardly ever happened. "He wanted me to give this to you so please take it."

I gave him my journal on our first Christmas and now he was giving me his. No good could come of this. But my body still wanted it. My heart did too. "What else did he say?"

"Nothing."

"He just asked you to give this to me?"

He nodded.

I slowly grabbed the black journal and felt it in my fingers. It was thick and the leather was warm. I could feel the grooves from where his massive fingers had gripped it so tightly. His scent was embedded into the leather, permanently.

Axel returned to the door. "Good night." He shut the door behind him, and his footsteps slowly faded away.

I held the journal without opening it. It was Pandora's box. Terrible things would come out once it was opened and it could never be closed again. But my fingers felt hot touching it, containing entries of Hawke's innermost thoughts and feelings. My fingers ached to open it. My heart wouldn't stop slamming into my chest. I could hardly breathe.

***

I got into bed and turned on the bedside lamp. The journal sat in my lap, waiting to be opened. I grazed the spine with my fingers before I finally opened to the first page.

March 3rd

New York City is everything I pictured it to be. There's congested traffic, hookers on the bad side of town, and Times Square is the biggest tourist trap in the world. It's full of opportunities and possibilities.

But I've never felt so alone.

I only need one person in my life to feel complete, and she is back home waiting for me. Walking out of that door was the hardest thing I've ever had to do. I'm not even sure how I did it.

But I did the right thing.

I hurt the woman I love. Maybe it was an accident. Maybe I thought she was someone else. But it didn't change my actions. I was a monster. Something snapped inside me, and I turned into a different person.

I turned into my father.

I'll never be happy again, but I did the right thing by her. She'll find someone better than me someday. She'll get married and have kids. One day, she'll stop thinking about me altogether.

And she'll be happy.

The short entry was enough to make my eyes water. I was looking into the past, seeing Hawke's thoughts when I wasn't with him. I could hear his voice in my head.

He wrote an entry every single day. Some were short and others were long. The only things he mentioned were his loneliness, work, and me. Women were never mentioned in his thoughts, probably because he didn't care enough about them to mention them.

Every entry was similar to the one before it. He made the right decision leaving me behind despite the pain it caused both of us. He did what was necessary to protect me from his uncontrollable anger.

And he never stopped thinking about me.

June 15th

There are nights like this when I want to get in my car and drive back to South Carolina. I know she's graduating today, walking across the stage and getting the diploma that she worked so hard for. I should be there to tell her how proud I am.

But I can't.

I worked late at the office tonight just so I had something to do. There was never a distraction strong enough to make me stop thinking about her. Sometimes I wonder if she's moved on and started seeing someone, but every time I do, want to stab myself in the arm just so I won't think about it. She isn't mine anymore, but anytime I picture her with someone else, I want to kill myself.

Why do I have to be this way?

I have everything anyone could ever want. My business is a success, I have a nice apartment, and I have good friends.

But everything is meaningless without her.

I was just a shadow before she came into my life. My existence was just one long blur that blended into the darkness. I was miserable and empty. When she walked into my life, she carried the brightest torch I've ever seen. She lit up my life and brought warmth. My life was nothing but sunshine and rainbows. When she left, I thought it would return to the way it was before.

But it was much worse.

Without her love, I'm frozen. Without her smile, I'm dead. Without her touch, I'm numb.

I'm nothing.

Every entry was worse than the last. Hawke's life was a constant of depression. Some days were better than others, but as the days passed, nothing changed. He was stuck in a constant state of sorrow.

September 9th

She's here.

Wednesday

She moved to the city and leased the building where she will open her bakery.

I'm so proud of her.

I knew she would make it. There was never a doubt in my mind she would be successful. Her baking isn't her only talent. Her smile and persona will also make big sales. People will walk in just to see her because she lights up their lives the way she lit up mine.

I want to see her. Now that she is close by, I'm losing my strength. My body yearns for hers. It doesn't matter how many women I sleep with. All I can think about is her. Every touch is dull. There is no passion, no fire—nothing. I just go through the motions because I don't know what else to do.

Will I always feel this way?

A year has come and gone, but it feels like we just broke up yesterday. I still remember exactly how her kiss felt against my mouth. I remember the way her body felt when she slept on my chest every night. I remember everything vividly and with so much detail that it haunts me.

She will always haunt me.

October 15th

Francesca cut the yellow ribbon to The Muffin Girl today.

I was there.

I sat in the coffee shop across the street and watched from a safe distance. I haven't seen her in so long, and having the luxury of just looking at her was a gift. Her hair is longer than it used to be, reaching past her chest. When she pulled it back, the slender curves of her face were hypnotic. She is thinner than she was before, but I have a feeling she didn't do it on purpose.

And she looks happy.

When Axel hugged her and whispered something in her ear, her face lit up. She stared at her bakery with pride written on her face. In that moment, I knew she was thinking about her parents and how happy they would be.

And I knew she was thinking about me.

I stayed in the coffee shop and watched her all day. When she was inside the bakery, I could see her dart back and forth, serving her customers and laughing with her coworkers. The place was packed with people on her very first day.

The Muffin Girl.

The next year had similar entries. Hawke spent most of his time alone, thinking about me and wondering what I was doing. Axel came up from time to time as did Marie, but my name was never mentioned at the same time.

He started to talk about his work more, growing his investment company and moving to a bigger office. He hired more employees and bought a new car. His life centered around work and nothing else. He seemed to be throwing himself into it, giving it everything he had.

I knew it was just a distraction.

I got to the next year and found the entry I was interested in reading.

Wednesday

September 8th

Axel asked me to be his best man, and of course I said yes. It is an honor. Axel has grown so much since he met Marie. Their relationship was rocky in the beginning but I've seen the progression of lust to love.

The fact he asked me told me Francesca doesn't mind seeing me, since she is Marie's maid of honor. I'm not sure if that is a good thing or a bad thing. Maybe she's moved on and doesn't think about me anymore. Maybe I was just a mistake that she's pushed to the back of her mind.

Or maybe she is just as nervous as I am.

I should want to avoid her but I don't. Actually, I want to see her. I want to look at her face and see her staring back at me. I've been watching her from a distance for the past year, but she never knew I was there.

Now she will.

September 16th

I saw Francesca tonight.

She wore a tight black dress and looked absolutely perfect. She cut her hair and curled it for the evening, looking like one of my dreams. When I spoke to her, she didn't seem affected by my presence at all. It was like our break up never happened.

And she hates me.

It is clear she wants nothing to do with me. She didn't even want to talk to me but humored me just to be polite. I could sense the hostility around her, heavy like a cloud. I broke her heart and she will never forget it.

I hated myself all over again.

October 10th

Francesca screamed at me and said she wanted nothing to do with me. Friendship is off the table and she doesn't owe me a damn thing.

Which is completely true.

She is still angry over the way I left, and I can't blame her.

No one could.

The worst part was her indifference. She isn't in love with me anymore, not the way I am in love with her. I didn't think it was possible for her feelings to ever disappear but they have.

Isn't that a good thing? Isn't this what I wanted?

No, it's not what I want.

October 20th

Francesca has a boyfriend.

His name is Kyle.

And I hate him.

I don't know him at all, but I know I don't like him. I don't like anyone that's shared her bed. The raging jealousy

Wednesday

is going to kill me, and I can't stop it. All I feel is heartbreak. It is like I walked out on her again, but this time, she is the one who left.

I have no one to blame but myself. I had her forever. She would have married me if I asked her. All I had to do was stay and control myself.

But I fucked it up.

Now she is with him.

And I am alone.

Hearing his point of view during our separation gave me a new perspective. When we were apart, I didn't think about him. I locked him away and never opened that door. I moved on with my life and refused to let the past bring me down.

But he was thinking of me the entire time.

I read his entries during the wedding planning. Anytime he was near me, he wanted me. It was difficult to keep his hands to himself but he somehow managed. He talked about his sorrow from our conversation in Central Park, when he asked me to take him back but I refused.

That was one of the hardest entries to read.

Then I came to the time when we got back together. His entries were the shortest during this period.

July 5th

Francesca isn't just a visitor in my bed. She is a resident. She hogs the blankets all the time and snores

358

randomly throughout the night, but she is the perfect bedtime companion. Sometimes, I don't sleep at all because I just watch her.

Right now. she's tucked into my side, exhausted from making love all afternoon. Her hands are always on me in some way, and I love that feeling.

I never thought I could be happy again, but here I am. Happy.

July 31st

Making love with her is completely different than all the sex I've had with random women. It is about our spirits more than our bodies. When I am with her, I always look her in the eye. We are connected in that way, reacting to each other in sensual ways. I give myself to her completely, enjoying her body and her soul at the same time.

I love the way she looks at me. Her eyes light up in desire, but she also stares at me like I am her entire world. The love she gives me is paramount, especially when we are in bed together. An asteroid could hit the earth but neither one of us would notice.

I could do that all day every day with her. Time stands still and it is just she and I. She heals my soul with every touch and every embrace. When her legs are wrapped around my waist, I fall deep into her, never wanting to come up for air.

I want to do this for the rest of my life—with her.

Wednesday

When I looked at the clock, I realized it was four in the morning. I'd spent all night reading his entries, getting absorbed in his past. I felt like I was reading his mind, seeing the thoughts I never had access to.

I had to work in an hour so I placed the journal in my nightstand and went to sleep, intent on finishing his journal at my next opportunity.

CHAPTER THIRTY-EIGHT

Passing Time

Hawke

A week had come and gone but I didn't hear a word from Francesca.

Did she read it?

Or did she stuff it into her nightstand to be forgotten?

Or even worse, did she throw it away?

If she read it, I expected her to be done with it by now. My hope was disappearing with every passing day, fearing the inevitable defeat. I lost the final battle and lost the war.

I lost her.

***

"Has she spoken to you?" Axel sat across from me in the bar. As soon as he got there, he slid into the booth, not bothering to order a beer.

"No."

"But it's been a week."

"I told you, Axel. She doesn't care."

"Maybe I should say something to her…"

Wednesday

"Don't bother." I didn't touch my beer because I was already drunk. I'd been drunk a lot lately. "What happened when you gave it to her? Exactly?"

"I told her it was from you. She didn't take it at first but she did eventually. I didn't have to force it on her."

"Did she say she would read it?"

"Actually, she didn't say anything at all."

My last try blew up in my face. "Then that's that. She'll marry him and live happily ever after. And I'll die alone."

"You don't know that. Maybe she's reading it. That sucker was thick. It'll take her some time to get through it."

"I don't know…"

"Let's not throw in the towel just yet. There's still some hope."

Not from where I could see.

CHAPTER THIRTY-NINE

Reading

Francesca

Kyle spent the night every day that week so I couldn't look at Hawke's journal. I felt like I was doing something wrong by reading it at all but I couldn't stop myself. His recount of the past was too interesting for me to ignore. I felt like I was with him, even in a different time than the present one.

Kyle and I grew closer together in the past few months, and he was definitely happier now that Hawke had disappeared. He never asked about him or even mentioned his name. It was like he didn't think about him at all.

I was getting used to a future with Kyle until this journal fell into my hands. Reading about his experience when we weren't together was heartbreaking. Even though I was mad at him at the time, I still pitied him. His internal struggle with his own demons was constantly the focal point of his existence. He wanted me, but his need to protect me was stronger.

Wednesday

His recount of our time together was beautiful, and he saw the relationship in the same way I did. It wasn't a typical relationship that every lover experienced. What we had was different—supernatural.

***

We woke up Saturday morning and made breakfast in the kitchen.

Kyle ate everything on his plate, acting like he hadn't eaten in years.

"What do you want to do today?" I sat beside him at the table and drank my coffee.

"Actually, I have plans today." He said it in a dreadful way.

"What are you doing?"

"Axel and I are going to a Yankees game."

It made me happy that he got along with my brother so well. I said Axel's opinion didn't matter, but it did. "Cool."

"I like hanging out with him and everything, but I'd rather stay here with you—naked."

"Well, I'll be here when you get back."

"Will you be naked?" He wiggled his eyebrows.

"There's a good chance I will be."

"Ooh...then I hope those innings go by quickly." He cleaned his plate and set it on the sink. "I should get home so I can shower and get ready."

"Okay."

He leaned down and kissed me on the forehead. "I'll see you later, baby."

"Okay. Have fun."

"I will." He gave me a quick peck on the neck before he walked out.

The second the front door shut, my eyes moved to my bedroom. The door was open and I could see the foot of the bed. My nightstand was beside it, and the journal was in the top drawer.

I stared at it for a few seconds, unable to stow away my urge. My breakfast sat in front of me, untouched. I suddenly lost my appetite and didn't need a steaming cup of coffee.

I needed to read that journal.

***

January 5th

When Francesca put on her locket, she never took it off. When we make love, I feel it rub against my chest, feeling the tiny engraving I placed in the metal. I love seeing her wear it, even if it is tucked underneath her shirt at work.

She is mine.

This Christmas was even better than the previous one. She made me a blanket from all my old t-shirts, things that she kept and took to New York. It was a token of her love. It survived the years we were apart.

She and I said we were soul mates long ago, and they weren't just romantic words. I really meant them and so did she. We've only been together again for six months, but I don't need more time to understand how I feel.

I want to marry her.

I want to spend my life with her.

Wednesday

When she introduced me as her boyfriend to Logan, it didn't feel right. I am much more than some boyfriend. But she couldn't introduce me as more than that. I am the love of her life, her one and only.

I want to be her husband.

I want to join together and be a single being with her.

So I went with Axel and Marie and designed a custom ring. It took me a long time to figure out exactly what I wanted to get her, but when I found it, I knew. I can picture her wearing it every single day for the rest of her life. In six weeks, the ring will be ready and I'll finally ask her what I should have asked years ago.

To marry me.

My hands shook as I held the journal. "Oh my god..." I couldn't breathe because my body was so tense. I felt lightheaded and dizzy. My heart was about to give out from all the blood that rushed there.

He was going to propose to me.

He had the ring.

Why didn't he?

I kept reading, needing to know that answer.

***

There was a two-week gap in his entries. He didn't write anything at all, and I knew why.

His mother passed away and he took off to South Carolina, leaving his journal behind. Even if he had it, I doubt he would have taken the time to write in it. He was delirious with rage, not himself at all. If you called him Hawke, he probably wouldn't have responded to his own name.

The first entry was after he ended our relationship.

February 5th

Sometimes I picture my father dying—over and over again. Like the coward that he truly was, he panicked at the sight of the gun and went into cardiac arrest. He couldn't handle a moment of fear while Mom and I went through it every single day of our lives.

And he couldn't handle a single moment.

Pathetic.

I'm glad that piece of shit is dead. My only regret is not killing him myself.

Francesca claims I wouldn't have done it, but what does she know? She doesn't get it. All she thinks about is rainbows and unicorns all day long. Her misplaced optimism irritates me.

She irritates me.

I had to get rid of her. I held that gun in my hand and thought it was loaded. I really would have murdered him if I had the chance. She couldn't be with someone like that, someone this maniacal. We are from different worlds and she needs someone better than me.

I am trash.

I am an orphan from a broken home. I have serious anger issues. My emotional development is seriously stunted. I am insufferable, rude, and just an ass.

Wednesday

She should be with someone better.

She threatened to never take me back if I wanted her. That was the best threat I ever heard. Now I can't get her back even if I wanted to. She will make sure of it.

That's how it should be.

For the next few months, his anger burned off the pages. He always talked about his parents, even if he said the same thing. The ink was pressed hard into the paper like he was gripping it too lightly. I could feel the anger just from touching the page.

He mentioned me every time but he never said he missed me. All he said was we shouldn't be together. I would end up with someone else and have lots of children. And he would remain a bitter man.

With every page, I realized just how far he fell. He was stuck in a vortex where no one could reach him. He had a breakdown in every sense of the word. Hawke had died and this other man replaced him.

No wonder why I couldn't talk any sense into him.

He never mentioned Axel, work, or women. All he talked about was his mother and how she died. He went into vivid detail about it, picturing exactly how it happened.

A few months later, his entries started to change.

April 9th

I had a dream about her last night.

She stood in front of me in a white dress. I've never seen her mother's gown but somehow I knew it was hers. Her hair was pulled back, revealing her perfect features. Her green eyes glowed just for me.

She came down the aisle toward me, her hand hooked on Axel's arm. And when she arrived, she had to restrain herself from jumping in my arms. Like nothing happened, she stared at me like I was her prince.

She loved me.

My alarm clock shattered the dream, killing me with the loss. I wanted to hold on to that moment as long as possible, to feel her heavenly glow.

But she was gone.

I didn't go into work because I couldn't get out of bed. The weight of my grief hit me all at once and I realized exactly what I lost. I hurt the one family member I had left. I sent her away and didn't know how much time had passed.

And I cried.

I felt the pages with my fingertips and tried to steady myself. Every entry was more heart wrenching than the previous one. He suffered so much, and what was worse, he was his own tormentor. He could never escape the inflictions he caused to himself.

He wouldn't allow himself to be happy.

It took him four months to wake up from his nightmare, and by that time, I was already a whole new person. Hawke came back to me, entering his own body and returning to this plane, but it was too late.

June 4th

I went to her shop, unsure what would happen when I got there. I needed to talk to her, but I had no idea what I would say. The way I treated her was unacceptable. She tried to stand beside me and help me, but I viciously pushed her away.

Why should she forgive me?

The second I was in her shop, she knew I was there. The fact she was still in sync with my mind gave me hope that we could find our way back to each other. But the moment I looked at her face, I knew that wasn't possible.

She will never forgive me.

She hates me.

And she wants nothing to do with me.

Neither one of us spoke but we didn't need to. I bowed my head in shame and walked out, knowing I deserved her rejection.

I read through the pages until I found the day he realized my locket was gone. I wasn't sure if I wanted to read this but I couldn't stop myself.

August 6th

I walked into her shop with the intention of never leaving. I was going to fix us, get her back where she belonged. Kyle deserved her, but I wanted her more. But when I looked at her, I realized I was too late.

The locket was gone.

She no longer carried a torch for me. She no longer held a vigil in her heart. She removed the necklace and probably threw it away, removing my final hold on her. Now she belonged to Kyle exclusively.

I was out of time.

My mouth stopped working because my body shut down. I lost a gamble I couldn't afford to lose. My heart slowed to a dangerous pace and almost stopped working altogether. My lungs forgot how to breathe. My world came crashing down around me, the painful defeat hitting me hard.

I was too late.

I couldn't take it back.

I lost.

I went home and stood in the entryway, staring at all the furniture she and I lay on. Her ghost was still in this apartment, and until now, it comforted me. But now it just haunted me.

She doesn't want to see me anymore, so I have to move. I'll sell this place even if I lose my investment and find somewhere else to live, a place where I won't cross paths with her again.

She doesn't want me in her life anymore.

And I don't blame her.

The final few entries are short, shortest of them all.

Wednesday

August 15th

What do I do now?

Can I just go back to what my life was like before? Sleep around and focus on work? Can I really go back to a meaningless life after I experienced the greatest love anyone has ever known?

Francesca is with Kyle now. They will be happy together, and one day, they will both forget about me.

And I'll forget about myself too.

August 22nd

Does she still think about me?

August 29th

I still miss her.

September 12th

Will this pain ever stop?

I read every entry, feeling my eyes burn, until I got to the last page.

Francesca,

You should be with Kyle. He's loyal and honest, and he'll give you the life you want. He'll be a great husband and father. You'll know nothing but joy, and I want that for you.

But I want you more.

I really dragged both of us through the mud and ruined something so damn perfect no one would believe it if I told them. I let you down.

I broke you.

I'm sorry for everything I've done. There's no justification or excuse I can make for my stupidity. It's ridiculous that I'm even asking you to be with me again. I know I don't deserve another chance.

But please give it to me anyway.

I've done a lot of soul-searching and have been meeting with a therapist for a long time now. My past is where it belongs, and my anger has faded away. I've made my peace with the way things are. I've learned to let everything go, including my guilt.

Now I just need you.

I can be exactly what you need now. I'll repair all the damage I've caused. I'll be everything and anything you want me to be.

Please.

If you say no, I swear I'll never bother you again and I'll leave you in peace. You shouldn't have to deal with me anymore, not when you've moved on with someone you care about.

So, don't say no.

Muffin, marry me.

Wednesday

I stilled at that final sentence, unsure if I really read it. The words stared back at me from the page, bold and unmistakable. My bottom lip trembled and my eyes couldn't contain all the moisture that had built up.

I turned the page, and realized there were no entries left. The final pages had been mutilated with a square hole. Inside sat a platinum ring.

"Oh my god..."

I stared at it for several heartbeats, unsure if it was real. Then I grabbed it with my fingers and examined it under the light of my bedside lamp. The platinum ring was similar to the locket he gave me. There were three cuts in the top of the ring, making three stripes. There were no diamonds like a typical engagement ring. When I turned it over, I saw the engraving in each bar.

We.

Are.

Forever.

I closed my fingers around the ring and felt the tears fall. The metal felt warm in my hand, like it belonged on my finger. My heart broke in half for all the pain he went through. I thought my heartache was worse, but I quickly realized how wrong I was.

I opened my palm and stared at the ring for a long time, falling in love with its perfection. I never told Hawke what kind of ring I wanted but this was exactly it. I wanted something I could wear to work without fear of tarnishing it. And flashy things never caught my notice.

It was perfect.

I stared at for several moments before I placed it on my ring finger. The second it was there, a jolt ran up my arm. It fit comfortably, the perfect size to keep it snug. My heart skipped a beat because it felt right.

It felt absolutely right.

The front door opened and Kyle walked inside. "Man, that was a long game."

I panicked and looked at the time, unsure how he could be back so early. It was ten in the evening and I realized I'd been reading Hawke's journal all day.

All day.

Kyle came into the bedroom and stopped when he saw the look on my face. "Everything alright?"

I closed Hawke's journal and felt the leather under my fingers. The inevitable was staring at me right in the face. My lips didn't want to move because the words they contained would inflict pain.

But I knew I had to do it.

"Kyle, we need to talk..."

Wednesday

CHAPTER FORTY

Wednesday

Hawke

I sat on the couch and drank a beer. The TV was off and most of the lights were out. Stuck in a dark repose, I kept thinking about Francesca. I wondered what she was doing.

Was the journal forgotten?

If my journal didn't bring her back to me, nothing would. That was my last hope, and if that didn't work, I would have to force myself to let her go. Even though she was with Kyle, I still considered her to be mine.

But she wasn't.

The future before me was terrifying. The idea of living the rest of my life without her actually scared me.

Horrified me.

And I wasn't scared of anything.

I knew I would be alone all my life, and when I died, I'd still be alone. How could I ever love someone else when my heart belonged to her—now and forever? How could I ever move on without thinking about her?

Wednesday

I didn't want to go on.

It was getting late but I didn't go to bed. Sleep was a luxury I'd forgotten about. Without Francesca beside me, it was impossible to fall into my dreams. All I could do was lie awake and think about the woman I threw away.

Regret.

Anguish.

Desolation.

There were nights like this when I wanted to end it all.

A knock sounded on my door.

I was frozen in place, hearing the unmistakable sound echo in my apartment. It was nearly midnight and no one would just stop by at this hour, not even Axel.

My heart kicked into overdrive with the possibility. I slowly rose to my feet, my breathing unable to be controlled. I allowed my soul to relax, to feel the vibration around me.

Francesca.

She was behind the door. I was sure of it.

But what if I was wrong? What if I opened it and came face-to-face with anyone else?

It had to be her.

I walked to the door and stopped in front of it, afraid to look in the peephole. The disappointment would kill me. If it weren't her, I'd die all over again. I grabbed the door handle and gripped it tightly, fearful of what waited on the other side.

Francesca.

I took a deep breath, the kind that hurt, and then I opened the door.

On the other side stood the woman of my dreams. Her green eyes were coated with heavy moisture, and they were bright like the summer grass. Her hair was pulled over one shoulder and she gripped my black journal to her chest. Her bottom lip trembled slightly.

I held my breath, hoping this wasn't a dream. If it was, I never wanted to wake up. I wanted to stare at her forever and enjoy this moment as long as I could.

She gripped the journal tighter, clinging to it for dear life.

And that's when I noticed the ring.

It was on her left finger.

She was wearing it.

My lungs automatically took a breath because I'd stopped breathing. Unwillingly, moisture moved into my eyes. Tears started to form deep inside. Everything hurt.

The tears pooled into droplets and fell from the corners of her eyes. "Yes."

My hands started to shake. I could feel every heartbeat and smell the scent of her perfume. This was real. It had to be. I wouldn't go on if it weren't.

"Yes."

Now that she was right in front of me, I didn't know what to do. I'd always hoped this would happen, but I never expected it to. She was just within reach, and she was giving me an answer I'd dreamed of hearing.

Wednesday

"I'll marry you." More tears fell down her cheeks and her bottom lip quivered.

So much emotion was hitting me at once and my body could hardly take it. My own tears formed in my eyes but didn't fall. But they were growing in size, their weight enough to form a drop.

I finally snapped out of the shock and cupped her cheeks with my hands. I placed my forehead against hers and breathed with her, feeling my body come back to life. All the pain faded away, and I was being put back together, every passing second fixing something that was once broken. Our souls wrapped around each other, anchoring together permanently. Once they clicked, I heard it ring in my mind. My thumbs wiped away the tears streaked across her cheeks.

Her hands moved to my chest, the journal still held in one. Her free hand moved over my heart, feeling it beat through the skin. She continued to cry quietly, the emotion overpowering her. Francesca hardly ever cried, and I knew this instance was a good one.

I tilted her chin up and kissed the tears that continued to fall down her face. My lips felt her soft skin and trembled slightly at the touch. I'd never felt so much joy and pain at the same time. My body could hardly process what just happened. I'd wanted this for so long and now it was finally happening.

I couldn't believe it.

I continued to hold Francesca because I never wanted to pull away. She was finally mine, wearing the ring I bought for her so long ago. She was an emotional mess in my arms, and my heart was just as wrecked.

But we were slowly putting each other back together. Our souls healed each other, and when we were combined like this, we were stronger. I held her on my doorstep and kept kissing her falling tears while she felt my heartbeat, waiting for it to return to normal.

We were getting our forever.

And it was starting now.

Wednesday

CHAPTER FORTY-ONE

Bells

Francesca

Hawke lay beside me in his bed, his fingers interlocked with mine. His thumb brushed across the engagement ring, reminding him that it was real. His eyes never left mine, like he feared I would fly away without any notice.

I didn't work the next day. Actually, I didn't even show up.

He didn't either.

We lay in bed together and held each other. We didn't make love because our souls did that for us. All we wanted was to be together. His eyes drank me in like he was parched and his hands were always on me, feeling my soft skin.

I constantly felt his heart, needing to know it was still beating strongly. That vibration used to lull me to sleep every night. Now it was back, and I realized just how much I missed it.

Wednesday

We hadn't spoken since yesterday on the doorstep. I told him I would marry him and we hadn't said anything since. The only conversation we had was with our eyes.

"What changed your mind?" Hawke brought my hand to his lips and kissed my ring.

"Everything in your journal."

He placed my hand on top of his heart and rested his hand there. "When I was going to propose, I was going to give you that journal with the ring inside—because you gave me your journal."

"It was beautiful..."

"This is the last time," he whispered. "I'm here forever. I'm not going to go anywhere ever again."

I didn't have any doubt. "I know."

The softness in his eyes showed me how much that meant to him.

"We are forever."

"And ever." He pressed a kiss to my forehead and rested his face close to mine on the pillow.

I didn't want to leave his place because it felt so right. I didn't care about my apartment anymore. I never wanted to sleep in a bed other than his. All I wanted was to be there—all the time.

"Do you still want to get married in a field?" he whispered.

"Yes." I'd always wanted something small and quiet. Marie's wedding was beautiful, but a big party wasn't my style.

"Are you busy tomorrow?"

"What?" The meaning in his words was unmistakable.

"I want to marry you now. You've been my other half all my life, even before I met you. I don't want to wait any longer. I want to be husband and wife, to live together and spend every day together. I want forever. What do you say?"

It was rushed, spontaneous, and exciting. "Okay."

He smiled for the first time. "Then we should get to work."

***

Marie was sitting at her desk when I walked into her office. "Hey, girl. You want to get lunch?" She finished making a note on her iPad before she looked up at me.

"Actually, no." I sat in the chair facing her. "I want to ask you something."

"What's up?"

"Will you be my maid of honor?"

Her eyes almost popped out of her head. "Whoa, what?" She jumped out of her seat. "Oh my god, Kyle proposed to you? This is so great—"

"Hawke did. And I said yes."

She froze in place, taking in my declaration with a shocked expression. It took her several minutes to compose herself, to wrap her head around what I said. She stopped liking Hawke when he left me again, and her good opinion of him never returned. I figured she would try to talk me out of it, pushing for Kyle.

But she didn't.

Wednesday

"Frankie, I would be honored." She came around the desk and hugged me hard. "I'm so happy for you. I know Hawke...is the one."

"He is."

"You two will be just as happy as Axel and I."

"I hope so." I pulled away and couldn't wipe the smile off my face.

"So, we'll get to planning this weekend. I still have my wedding binder—"

"We're getting married tomorrow."

"What?" she blurted.

"We're doing it in a field outside the city, just family."

She put her hands on her hips as she tried to take this in. "That's quick." She glanced at my stomach.

"No baby, Marie. But we want to start our lives together."

She eyed her watch on her wrist. "I think I can take off early today. We've got a lot of shit to do."

***

I called Axel on the way to Yaya's. "Hey, Axel—"

"Hawke already told me." The smile in his voice told me his feelings about it. "Congratulations."

"Yeah?" His approval meant a lot to me, although I would never admit it.

"Yeah. I know that guy loves you despite his stupidity."

"He does."

"I'm sure he'll get it right this time. He gave me his permission to kick his ass if I need to."

I couldn't picture anyone kicking Hawke's ass so it made me chuckle.

"But I doubt it'll come to that."

"It won't." I kept the emotion out of my voice before I spoke again. "Will you give me away?"

There was a long pause over the phone. Axel didn't say anything, obviously keeping the tears out of his voice just the way I was. "Francesca...I would be honored."

***

When I told Yaya the news, she didn't seem the least bit surprised.

"'Bout time."

"What?" I grabbed the box from the closet and pulled it out.

"Kyle was a fine young man but he's not Hawke. We all know that."

I was glad Yaya was on board. Despite what Hawke did, everyone seemed to forgive him quicker than I did. "Thanks, Yaya." I pulled apart the tissue paper until I saw my mother's wedding dress. It was laid out perfectly, ready for me to use the day I needed it. It was more perfect than I remember.

"It'll be a little loose on you," Yaya said. "But I can take care of that."

I gathered the dress in my hands and felt the material. I knew if Mom were there she would be happy. She would love Hawke just as much as I did. "Thank you, Yaya."

"You're going to be the most beautiful bride ever."

"Thanks..." Yaya would say that no matter what.

Wednesday

"No, really." She patted me on the shoulder. "Even more beautiful than your mother on her day."

***

Outside the city, we found a meadow with freshly mowed grass. There were yellow dandelions in the field, and the world was alive with the approach of spring. It was a cloudless day and the sun was warm on our skin.

I stood behind the wardrobe changer even though my gown was already fastened. Hawke was just a few feet away with everyone else. We gathered our family, Axel, Marie, Yaya, and Logan. That was all we needed.

Axel stood with me, wearing his suit and tie. "You look beautiful, sis."

"Yeah?" I hadn't even stepped out and I wanted to cry.

"Yeah." He stared at my dress and kept a smile on his face, hiding his true emotion.

"How's Hawke doing?"

"He's the most excited guy I've ever seen."

I gripped the bouquet of fresh flowers that Marie picked from the field. It was a mixture of grass and dandelions.

"Are you sure you want to do this?"

A question like that would normally suffocate me in doubt, especially after everything we'd been through. But all I felt was certainly. "Yes."

He extended his arm to me. "Then let's go."

I hooked my arm through his and allowed him to guide me past the divider. There was no music other than the buzzing bees and the chirping birds. A slight breeze was on the wind, smelling of spring. Our feet crunched against the grass as we walked. I wore flats instead of heels because I knew it would be difficult to maneuver.

Everyone was just a few feet away, and when I looked up, I saw Hawke.

He stared at me intently, not a trace of a smile on his lips. He took a deep breath like the sight of my approach pained him with happiness. His eyes coated over, as if he feared his moment would never come to pass.

His eyes never left mine as he watched me come near. It was quiet enough to hear his breathing, which matched the rapid rate of my own. My long dress trailed behind me, slithering over the grass in an elegant way.

Axel walked me to Hawke and stopped before he handed me over. "Mom and Dad would be so proud of you, Francesca."

My eyes never left Hawke's. "They would be proud of both of us."

Axel hugged me tightly, something that only happened once in a great while.

I hugged him back, thankful I had such an amazing brother.

He took my hand and placed it in Hawke's. "I know you'll be good to one another."

Hawke's fingers immediately clamped around my hand, telling me he would never let me go for as long as we lived. He pulled me toward him gently, looking into my eyes like he never wanted to blink.

Wednesday

The pastor gave us a moment to stare at each other before he began the ceremony. "Today, we're gathered here to witness the holy matrimony of Theodore Taylor and Francesca Gibbons..."

I tuned out everything he said because I was infatuated with Hawke's appearance. Without saying a word, I could feel every emotion running through his body. Gratitude was the most prominent emotion, because I was giving him another chance to be my forever. He loved me, I was certain of that. He told me every day just by looking at me.

I'd never loved another man in my entire life, and I never wanted to. Hawke was it, the only person I could fall so deeply for. My children would have his eyes and his good heart. And when our lives ended, we would still be together, drifting on the wind as bare souls. Never again would we be alone—we would always have each other.

"Hawke, do you take Francesca to be your lawfully wedded wife, in sickness and in health, till death parts you?"

Hawke interlocked our fingers, gripping them with a gentle pressure. "I do—for eternity." He slipped the ring on my finger, returning it to the place where it would remain forever.

"Francesca, do you take Hawke to be your lawfully wedded husband, in sickness and in health, till death parts you?"

Nothing would ever part us again, not life or death. When the world ended and there was nothing left but rock and ash, we would still go on. He and I were connected in a spiritual way, in a godly way. Forever wasn't long enough for the two of us. We would watch the world change, the universe expand indefinitely, and we would be forever tangled together as it happened—as two naked souls. "I do—for eternity."

Wednesday

EPILOGUE

Hawke

"Daddy, you walk too slow." Suzie pulled me forward as hard as she could, determined to get to the bakery as quickly as possible. Her pink dress was brand-new but once she got her hands on a pastry, it would be ruined.

"Sweetheart, I can't walk any faster." I held Hannah in one arm, knowing she was getting too big to be carried around anymore. The day Suzie became too old was a sad one for me. It only reminded me that my kids were getting bigger and older, and one day, they would leave and venture out on their own—my two little princesses.

"Come on." She got to the bakery and yanked it open. "I want to see Mommy."

I chuckled and walked in behind her, immediately combining with the loud crowd anxiously waiting for their muffins and pastries.

Suzie pushed past people and headed into the back kitchen, knowing exactly where to go.

Wednesday

I followed behind her, keeping a close eye on her just in case she knocked into someone. "Suzie, slow down."

Suzie ignored me, like always.

We got to the back where Francesca was working. An apron was tied around her waist, and she had flour smeared across both of her cheeks. It seemed like she was the victim of a flour explosion. But she still looked cute—like always.

"Mommy!" Suzie ran into her and hugged her around the waist. "Happy birthday!"

Francesca was startled by Suzie's sudden appearance, but when she realized who it was, her face lit up in joy. "Awe. Thank you, sweetheart." She kneeled down and hugged her hard, her happiness obvious in the curve of her lips. "What a nice surprise."

"I got you something." Suzie pulled a small box from her pocket.

"What's this?" Francesca took it.

"Open it!"

Francesca opened the lid, and inside was a necklace the girls and I made for her. Three stone pendants were decorated with watercolors. Each one of us made one before we placed it on the chain. It wasn't very pretty but I knew she would love it.

"We each made one," Suzie explained. "Do you like it?"

Francesca's eyes immediately watered. "Oh baby, I love it—so much." She felt the necklace in her hand before she put it on, placing it over the locket she always wore. "It's perfect." Francesca hugged Suzie again.

"I made it too!" Hannah kicked her feet because she wanted me to put her down.

I set her on the ground and watched her move into Francesca next.

Francesca hugged both of our daughters at the same time. "Thank you, Hannah. You guys did a great job."

"Happy birthday, Mommy." Hannah touched the necklace like she expected the paint to be wet.

"It's the best birthday ever." Francesca released both of them and stared at them affectionately.

"It's not even over yet," Suzie said. "We still have the party tonight."

"Party?" Francesca asked.

"Suzie." It was supposed to be a surprise dinner, but of course, my kids were too excited to keep it in.

Suzie bowed her head in shame. "Sorry..."

Francesca chuckled. "It's okay. Now I have something else to look forward to."

Hannah climbed on the chair so she could see what was on the counter. "Ooh...jungle cookies."

"Let me see." Suzie approached the table and looked at the dough and cookie cutters. "Let's make some so Mommy can take a break."

"Good idea." Hannah grabbed a cookie cutter of an elephant and shoved it into the dough.

Francesca knew they were going to make a mess but she let them be. She rose to her feet and looked at me, and like always, she stared at me like she couldn't be more in love. Her eyes lit up in a special way—something only I got to witness. She strode toward me slowly, clearly wanting to touch me in a way that wasn't appropriate in front of our two daughters.

I wanted to kiss her so hard her lips would be sore for a week. "I'm sorry Suzie ruined the surprise."

"I don't care. My birthday is already amazing." She felt the necklace hanging from her throat.

My hands moved around her waist, and I held her close to me. My forehead moved to hers, and my entire body felt hot with fire. I loved my daughters, but sometimes I wished they weren't always around. I missed making love to Francesca in the back of the store. I'd taken her on that counter too many times to count. "I have a gift for you. But I'll give it to you later."

"Birthday sex?" she whispered.

"Well, yes. But something else as well."

"Ooh…lucky me."

I cupped her face and gave her a kiss. I wanted to keep it short, but the second my mouth was on hers, I didn't want to pull away. My lips wanted to remain glued to hers forever, making love to her mouth.

Francesca dug her fingers into my forearms, the heat burning inside her like it did with me. She breathed into my mouth, her desire bubbling like a pot of boiling water.

I found the strength to pull away before it became anything but PG. Our daughters weren't paying attention to us, but it was still inappropriate. "We're having dinner with Axel and Marie when you get off work."

"Awe. That sounds like fun."

I pulled her harder into me so she could feel my hard-on. "Then you'll be mine when we get home."

"This is turning into the best birthday ever."

"I'm glad you think so." I kissed the corner of her mouth before I pulled away. I was losing my willpower. My wife drove me crazy. I made love to her every morning and every night, but it wasn't enough. "We'll pick you up later."

"Okay. I can't wait." She gave me a dark look, one that told me she wanted another kiss.

I didn't trust myself at this point, so I walked around her. "I'll see you then. Love you."

"Love you too."

***

Jason and Calvin, Marie and Axel's twins, played together at the end of the table with Suzie and Hannah. They had a bucket of soldiers and a dinosaur set that kept them busy. It was difficult for us to go to a nice restaurant when our kids were so young—and loud.

I kept my arm over Francesca's chair, my fingers grazing the bare skin of her shoulder.

"Having a good birthday?" Marie asked.

"Oh, it's been the best." Francesca touched the necklace the girls and I created. The house was turned in to a huge mess, and it took me two hours to clean it up. "I have the best family." Her hand moved to my thigh.

"I'm surprised you worked," Axel said.

"I had to," Francesca said. "We had too many orders going out. That place just gets busier and busier."

Wednesday

"That sounds like a good thing—and a bad thing," Marie said.

"I thought that other shop would slow things down," Francesca said. "But it's been the opposite."

"Mo' money, mo' problems, right?" Axel said.

Marie rolled her eyes. "Don't try to talk like a gangster."

"You know you like it, shorty." He kissed her hairline.

I turned to Francesca. "Can I give you my gift now? Before one of their famous fights erupts?"

"Please." She turned to me with anxious eyes.

"Okay. It's not physical."

"That's even better." She couldn't sit still with her excitement.

"Axel and Marie are taking the girls tonight and the rest of the weekend. You and I are leaving on a trip tomorrow morning."

"Oh my god, where are we going?" Francesca loved traveling. It was one of her favorite things to do.

"We're going to the Maldives," I said. "The Four Seasons."

"Really?" She shrieked too loudly then covered her mouth. "Whoops."

I loved making her happy. It made my day. "It'll be a nice getaway for us." Lots of sex without the kids. "Happy birthday."

She hugged me tightly then kissed me everywhere on my face. "Thank you. Thank you. I absolutely love it."

"You're welcome, Muffin." I gave her a kiss on the mouth, feeling that constant spark between us.

"Have fun babysitting while I'm on vacation." She stuck her tongue out at Marie and Axel.

"Brat," Axel said. "We'll turn your kids against you when you come back."

"I don't care," Francesca said. "I'll deal with that after our trip." She hooked her arm through mine and leaned her head on my shoulder. A satisfied sigh escaped her lips. "I'm so lucky I married you."

My heart floated like a cloud.

***

We parked the car in the garage of our Connecticut home in the suburbs. We had a big backyard where the girls could play, and it was quiet. Our neighbors kept to themselves, and we hardly noticed they were there.

The two-story house had gray trimming with blue shutters. It was exactly the house Francesca wanted, and when I saw it for sale, I had to buy it. I didn't think I could leave the city, but once we moved in, I realized it was perfect for our family.

The second we were inside, we were all over each other.

I kissed her hard on the mouth then scooped her up, her legs hooked around my waist. I walked up the stairs. I avoided Suzie's toys littered everywhere and made it into the bedroom. I didn't bother turning on the lights because we were just going to get down to business anyway.

Wednesday

I stripped her clothes off and watched her yank mine off violently. When we were both naked, we lay on the bed together, our bodies tangled. She ran her hands up my hard chest and wrapped her legs around my waist, wanting me inside her as soon as possible. Her eyes were lit up in flames, and her lips were slightly parted in desire.

I looked at her for a moment, trying to remember a time when this woman wasn't mine. It was so long ago that I could barely remember it. She was an innate part of me now, the better half of my soul.

And I loved her so damn much.

I slowly moved inside her, listening to her breathing change as she took more of me. There was nothing I loved more than making love to her. It was when I felt most alive, most connected to her. Raising two girls took up a lot of our time, as did work. We treasured our alone time together, the mornings and evenings when we made love and didn't even speak to each other. It was when our souls wrapped around one another, locking in place and never fraying.

"Hawke…" She wrapped her arms around my neck and dug her fingers into my hair. She locked her eyes with mine, rocking with me on the mattress. "I love you."

I pressed my forehead to hers and continued to move slowly, feeling every touch and sensation. Sometimes we fought and sometimes we didn't see each other much for a few days. Our marriage wasn't always perfect, and times got rough. But our love never changed. It always stayed the same, prevailing through everything—no matter what. And it would always be that way. "I love you too."

I hoped you enjoyed reading WEDNESDAY as much as I enjoyed writing it. It would mean the world to me if you could leave a short review. It's the best kind of support you can give an author. Thank you so much.

What exactly happened between Marie and Axel? How and when did they fall in love? And how did Marie turn Axel into the most committed man on the planet? Find out in the next installment of the series THURSDAY.

Wednesday

E. L. Todd

Want To Stalk Me?

Subscribe to my newsletter for updates on new releases, giveaways, and for my comical monthly newsletter. You'll get all the dirt you need to know. Sign up today.
www.eltoddbooks.com

Facebook:
https://www.facebook.com/ELTodd42

Twitter:
@E_L_Todd

Now you have no reason not to stalk me. You better get on that.

EL'S ELITES

I know I'm lucky enough to have super fans, you know, the kind that would dive off a cliff for you. They have my back through and through. They love my books and they love spreading the word. Their biggest goal is to see me on the New York Times bestsellers list and they'll stop at nothing to make it happen. While it's a lot of work, it's also a lot of fun. What better way to make friendships than to connect with people who love the same thing you do?

Are you one of these super fans?

If so, send a request to join the Facebook group. It's closed so you'll have a hard time finding it without the link. Here it is:

https://www.facebook.com/groups/1192326920784373/

Hope to see you there, ELITE!

Made in the USA
Middletown, DE
12 December 2016